I0682413

Joe Wilson and His Mates by Henry Lawson

Henry Archibald Hertzberg Lawson was born on the 17th June 1867 in a town on the Grenfell goldfields of New South Wales, Australia.

As a youth an ear infection had left him partially deaf and by fourteen he had lost his hearing completely.

He immersed himself in books to make up for the difficulties of a classroom education but later failed to gain entry to a University.

His first published poem was 'A Song of the Republic' in The Bulletin on 1st October 1887. This was quickly followed by other poems with one recognising him as "a youth whose poetic genius here speaks eloquently for itself."

In 1892, The Bulletin engaged him for an inland trip where he could write articles about the harsh realities of life in drought-stricken New South Wales. This resulted in his contributions to the Bulletin Debate and became the experience for a number of his stories in subsequent years. For Lawson this was an eye-opening period. His grim view of the outback was far removed from the romantic idyll of contemporary poetry and literature.

In 1896, Lawson married Bertha Bredt, Jr. but the marriage ended in June 1903. They had two children.

Despite this Lawson was finding his way in the literary world and achieving recognition. His most successful prose collection 'While the Billy Boils', was published in 1896. In it he virtually reinvented Australian realism.

His writing style of short, sharp sentences with honed and sparse descriptions created a personal writing style that defined Australians: dryly laconic, passionately egalitarian and deeply humane.

Sadly, for Lawson despite his growing recognition and fame he became withdrawn and unable to take part in the usual routines of life. His struggles with alcohol and mental health issues continued to drain him. His once prolific literary output began to decline. At times he was destitute mainly due, despite good sales and an enthusiastic audience, to ruinous publishing deals he had entered into.

Henry Archibald Hertzberg Lawson died, of cerebral hemorrhage, in Abbotsford, Sydney on 2nd September 1922.

Index of Contents

The Author's Farewell to the Bushmen

Some carry their swags in the Great North-West
Where the bravest battle and die,
And a few have gone to their last long rest,
And a few have said "Good-bye!"
The coast grows dim, and it may be long
Ere the Gums again I see;
So I put my soul in a farewell song
To the chaps who barracked for me.

Their days are hard at the best of times,
And their dreams are dreams of care—
God bless them all for their big soft hearts,
And the brave, brave grins they wear!
God keep me straight as a man can go,
And true as a man may be!
For the sake of the hearts that were always so,
Of the men who had faith in me!

And a ship-side word I would say, you chaps
Of the blood of the Don't-give-in!
The world will call it a boast, perhaps—
But I'll win, if a man can win!
And not for gold nor the world's applause—
Though ways to the end they be—
I'll win, if a man might win, because
Of the men who believed in me.

Part I

Joe Wilson's Courtship

There are many times in this world when a healthy boy is happy. When he is put into knickerbockers, for instance, and 'comes a man to-day,' as my little Jim used to say. When they're cooking something at home that he likes. When the 'sandy-blight' or measles breaks out amongst the children, or the teacher or his wife falls dangerously ill—or dies, it doesn't matter which—'and there ain't no school.' When a boy is naked and in his natural state for a warm climate like Australia, with three or four of his schoolmates, under the shade of the creek-oaks in the bend where there's a good clear pool with a sandy bottom. When his father buys him a gun, and he starts out after kangaroos or 'possums. When he gets a horse, saddle, and bridle, of his own. When he has his arm in splints or a stitch in his head—he's proud then, the proudest boy in the district.

I wasn't a healthy-minded, average boy: I reckon I was born for a poet by mistake, and grew up to be a Bushman, and didn't know what was the matter with me—or the world—but that's got nothing to do with it.

There are times when a man is happy. When he finds out that the girl loves him. When he's just married. When he's a lawful father for the first time, and everything is going on all right: some men make fools of themselves then—I know I did. I'm happy to-night because I'm out of debt and can see clear ahead, and because I haven't been easy for a long time.

But I think that the happiest time in a man's life is when he's courting a girl and finds out for sure that she loves him and hasn't a thought for any one else. Make the most of your courting days, you young chaps, and keep them clean, for they're about the only days when there's a chance of poetry and beauty coming into this life. Make the best of them and you'll never regret it the longest day you live. They're the days that the wife will look back to, anyway, in the brightest of times as well as in the blackest, and there shouldn't be anything in those days that might hurt her when she looks back. Make the most of your courting days, you young chaps, for they will never come again.

A married man knows all about it—after a while: he sees the woman world through the eyes of his wife; he knows what an extra moment's pressure of the hand means, and, if he has had a hard life, and is inclined to be cynical, the knowledge does him no good. It leads him into awful messes sometimes, for a married man, if he's inclined that way, has three times the chance with a woman that a single man has— because the married man knows. He is privileged; he can guess pretty closely what a woman means when she says something else; he knows just how far he can go; he can go farther in five minutes towards coming to the point with a woman than an innocent young man dares go in three weeks. Above all, the married man is more decided with women; he takes them and things for granted. In short he is— well, he is a married man. And, when he knows all this, how much better or happier is he for it? Mark Twain says that he lost all the beauty of the river when he saw it with a pilot's eye,—and there you have it.

But it's all new to a young chap, provided he hasn't been a young blackguard. It's all wonderful, new, and strange to him. He's a different man. He finds that he never knew anything about women. He sees none of woman's little ways and tricks in his girl. He is in heaven one day and down near the other place the next; and that's the sort of thing that makes life interesting. He takes his new world for granted. And, when she says she'll be his wife—!

Make the most of your courting days, you young chaps, for they've got a lot of influence on your married life afterwards—a lot more than you'd think. Make the best of them, for they'll never come any more, unless we do our courting over again in another world. If we do, I'll make the most of mine.

But, looking back, I didn't do so badly after all. I never told you about the days I courted Mary. The more I look back the more I come to think that I made the most of them, and if I had no more to regret in married life than I have in my courting days, I wouldn't walk to and fro in the room, or up and down the yard in the dark sometimes, or lie awake some nights thinking…. Ah well!

I was between twenty-one and thirty then: birthdays had never been any use to me, and I'd left off counting them. You don't take much stock in birthdays in the Bush. I'd knocked about the country for a few years, shearing and fencing and droving a little, and wasting my life without getting anything for it. I drank now and then, and made a fool of myself. I was reckoned 'wild'; but I only drank because I felt less sensitive, and the world seemed a lot saner and better and kinder when I had a few drinks: I loved my fellow-man then and felt nearer to him. It's better to be thought 'wild' than to be considered eccentric or ratty. Now, my old mate, Jack Barnes, drank—as far as I could see—first because he'd inherited the gambling habit from his father along with his father's luck: he'd the habit of being cheated and losing very bad, and when he lost he drank. Till drink got a hold on him. Jack was sentimental too, but in a different way. I was sentimental about other people—more fool I!—whereas Jack was sentimental about himself. Before he was married, and when he was recovering from a spree, he'd write rhymes about 'Only a boy, drunk by the roadside', and that sort of thing; and he'd call 'em poetry, and talk about signing them and sending them to the 'Town and Country Journal'. But he generally tore them up when he got better. The Bush is breeding a race of poets, and I don't know what the country will come to in the end.

Well. It was after Jack and I had been out shearing at Beenaway shed in the Big Scrubs. Jack was living in the little farming town of Solong, and I was hanging round. Black, the squatter, wanted some fencing done and a new stable built, or buggy and harness-house, at his place at Haviland, a few miles out of Solong. Jack and I were good Bush carpenters, so we took the job to keep us going till something else turned up. 'Better than doing nothing,' said Jack.

'There's a nice little girl in service at Black's,' he said. 'She's more like an adopted daughter, in fact, than a servant. She's a real good little girl, and good-looking into the bargain. I hear that young Black is sweet on her, but they say she won't have anything to do with him. I know a lot of chaps that have tried for her, but they've never had any luck. She's a regular little dumpling, and I like dumplings. They call her 'Possum. You ought to try a bear up in that direction, Joe.'

I was always shy with women—except perhaps some that I should have fought shy of; but Jack wasn't—he was afraid of no woman, good, bad, or indifferent. I haven't time to explain why, but somehow, whenever a girl took any notice of me I took it for granted that she was only playing with me, and felt nasty about it. I made one or two mistakes, but—ah well!

'My wife knows little 'Possum,' said Jack. 'I'll get her to ask her out to our place and let you know.'

I reckoned that he wouldn't get me there then, and made a note to be on the watch for tricks. I had a hopeless little love-story behind me, of course. I suppose most married men can look back to their lost love; few marry the first flame. Many a married man looks back and thinks it was damned lucky that he didn't get the girl he couldn't have. Jack had been my successful rival, only he didn't know it—I don't think his wife knew it either. I used to think her the prettiest and sweetest little girl in the district.

But Jack was mighty keen on fixing me up with the little girl at Haviland. He seemed to take it for granted that I was going to fall in love with her at first sight. He took too many things for granted as far as I was concerned, and got me into awful tangles sometimes.

'You let me alone, and I'll fix you up, Joe,' he said, as we rode up to the station. 'I'll make it all right with the girl. You're rather a good-looking chap. You've got the sort of eyes that take with girls, only you don't know it; you haven't got the go. If I had your eyes along with my other attractions, I'd be in trouble on account of a woman about once a-week.'

'For God's sake shut up, Jack,' I said.

Do you remember the first glimpse you got of your wife? Perhaps not in England, where so many couples grow up together from childhood; but it's different in Australia, where you may hail from two thousand miles away from where your wife was born, and yet she may be a countrywoman of yours, and a countrywoman in ideas and politics too. I remember the first glimpse I got of Mary.

It was a two-storey brick house with wide balconies and verandahs all round, and a double row of pines down to the front gate. Parallel at the back was an old slab-and-shingle place, one room deep and about eight rooms long, with a row of skillions at the back: the place was used for kitchen, laundry, servants' rooms, &c. This was the old homestead before the new house was built. There was a wide, old-fashioned, brick-floored verandah in front, with an open end; there was ivy climbing up the verandah post on one side and a baby-rose on the other, and a grape-vine near the chimney. We rode up to the end of the verandah, and Jack called to see if there was any one at home, and Mary came trotting out; so it was in the frame of vines that I first saw her.

More than once since then I've had a fancy to wonder whether the rose-bush killed the grape-vine or the ivy smothered 'em both in the end. I used to have a vague idea of riding that way some day to see. You do get strange fancies at odd times.

Jack asked her if the boss was in. He did all the talking. I saw a little girl, rather plump, with a complexion like a New England or Blue Mountain girl, or a girl from Tasmania or from Gippsland in Victoria. Red and white girls were very scarce in the Solong district. She had the biggest and brightest eyes I'd seen round there, dark hazel eyes, as I found out afterwards, and bright as a 'possum's. No wonder they called her "Possum". I forgot at once that Mrs Jack Barnes was the prettiest girl in the district. I felt a sort of comfortable satisfaction in the fact that I was on horseback: most Bushmen look better on horseback. It was a black filly, a fresh young thing, and she seemed as shy of girls as I was myself. I noticed Mary glanced in my direction once or twice to see if she knew me; but, when she looked, the filly took all my attention. Mary trotted in to tell old Black he was wanted, and after Jack had seen him, and arranged to start work next day, we started back to Solong.

I expected Jack to ask me what I thought of Mary—but he didn't. He squinted at me sideways once or twice and didn't say anything for a long time, and then he started talking of other things. I began to feel wild at him. He seemed so damnably satisfied with the way things were going. He seemed to reckon that I was a gone case now; but, as he didn't say so, I had no way of getting at him. I felt sure he'd go home and tell his wife that Joe Wilson was properly gone on little 'Possum at Haviland. That was all Jack's way.

Next morning we started to work. We were to build the buggy-house at the back near the end of the old house, but first we had to take down a rotten old place that might have been the original hut in the Bush before the old house was built. There was a window in it, opposite the laundry window in the old place, and the first thing I did was to take out the sash. I'd noticed Jack yarning with 'Possum before he started work. While I was at work at the window he called me round to the other end of the hut to help him lift a grindstone out of the way; and when we'd done it, he took the tips of my ear between his fingers and thumb and stretched it and whispered into it—

'Don't hurry with that window, Joe; the strips are hardwood and hard to get off—you'll have to take the sash out very carefully so as not to break the glass.' Then he stretched my ear a little more and put his mouth closer—

'Make a looking-glass of that window, Joe,' he said.

I was used to Jack, and when I went back to the window I started to puzzle out what he meant, and presently I saw it by chance.

That window reflected the laundry window: the room was dark inside and there was a good clear reflection; and presently I saw Mary come to the laundry window and stand with her hands behind her back, thoughtfully watching me. The laundry window had an old-fashioned hinged sash, and I like that sort of window—there's more romance about it, I think. There was thick dark-green ivy all round the window, and Mary looked prettier than a picture. I squared up my shoulders and put my heels together and put as much style as I could into the work. I couldn't have turned round to save my life.

Presently Jack came round, and Mary disappeared.

'Well?' he whispered.

'You're a fool, Jack,' I said. 'She's only interested in the old house being pulled down.'

'That's all right,' he said. 'I've been keeping an eye on the business round the corner, and she ain't interested when I'M round this end.'

'You seem mighty interested in the business,' I said.

'Yes,' said Jack. 'This sort of thing just suits a man of my rank in times of peace.'

'What made you think of the window?' I asked.

'Oh, that's as simple as striking matches. I'm up to all those dodges. Why, where there wasn't a window, I've fixed up a piece of looking-glass to see if a girl was taking any notice of me when she thought I wasn't looking.'

He went away, and presently Mary was at the window again, and this time she had a tray with cups of tea and a plate of cake and bread-and-butter. I was prizing off the strips that held the sash, very carefully, and my heart suddenly commenced to gallop, without any reference to me. I'd never felt like that before, except once or twice. It was just as if I'd swallowed some clockwork arrangement, unconsciously, and it had started to go, without warning. I reckon it was all on account of that blarsted Jack working me up. He had a quiet way of working you up to a thing, that made you want to hit him sometimes—after you'd made an ass of yourself.

I didn't hear Mary at first. I hoped Jack would come round and help me out of the fix, but he didn't.

'Mr—Mr Wilson!' said Mary. She had a sweet voice.

I turned round.

'I thought you and Mr Barnes might like a cup of tea.'

'Oh, thank you!' I said, and I made a dive for the window, as if hurry would help it. I trod on an old cask-hoop; it sprang up and dinted my shin and I stumbled—and that didn't help matters much.

'Oh! did you hurt yourself, Mr Wilson?' cried Mary.

'Hurt myself! Oh no, not at all, thank you,' I blurted out. 'It takes more than that to hurt me.'

I was about the reddest shy lanky fool of a Bushman that was ever taken at a disadvantage on foot, and when I took the tray my hands shook so that a lot of the tea was spilt into the saucers. I embarrassed her too, like the damned fool I was, till she must have been as red as I was, and it's a wonder we didn't spill the whole lot between us. I got away from the window in as much of a hurry as if Jack had cut his leg with a chisel and fainted, and I was running with whisky for him. I blundered round to where he was, feeling like a man feels when he's just made an ass of himself in public. The memory of that sort of thing hurts you worse and makes you jerk your head more impatiently than the thought of a past crime would, I think.

I pulled myself together when I got to where Jack was.

'Here, Jack!' I said. 'I've struck something all right; here's some tea and brownie—we'll hang out here all right.'

Jack took a cup of tea and a piece of cake and sat down to enjoy it, just as if he'd paid for it and ordered it to be sent out about that time.

He was silent for a while, with the sort of silence that always made me wild at him. Presently he said, as if he'd just thought of it—

'That's a very pretty little girl, 'Possum, isn't she, Joe? Do you notice how she dresses?—always fresh and trim. But she's got on her best bib-and-tucker to-day, and a pinafore with frills to it. And it's ironing-day, too. It can't be on your account. If it was Saturday or Sunday afternoon, or some holiday, I could understand it. But perhaps one of her admirers is going to take her to the church bazaar in Solong to-night. That's what it is.'

He gave me time to think over that.

'But yet she seems interested in you, Joe,' he said. 'Why didn't you offer to take her to the bazaar instead of letting another chap get in ahead of you? You miss all your chances, Joe.'

Then a thought struck me. I ought to have known Jack well enough to have thought of it before.

'Look here, Jack,' I said. 'What have you been saying to that girl about me?'

'Oh, not much,' said Jack. 'There isn't much to say about you.'

'What did you tell her?'

'Oh, nothing in particular. She'd heard all about you before.'

'She hadn't heard much good, I suppose,' I said.

'Well, that's true, as far as I could make out. But you've only got yourself to blame. I didn't have the breeding and rearing of you. I smoothed over matters with her as much as I could.'

'What did you tell her?' I said. 'That's what I want to know.'

'Well, to tell the truth, I didn't tell her anything much. I only answered questions.'

'And what questions did she ask?'

'Well, in the first place, she asked if your name wasn't Joe Wilson; and I said it was, as far as I knew. Then she said she heard that you wrote poetry, and I had to admit that that was true.'

'Look here, Jack,' I said, 'I've two minds to punch your head.'

'And she asked me if it was true that you were wild,' said Jack, 'and I said you was, a bit. She said it seemed a pity. She asked me if it was true that you drank, and I drew a long face and said that I was sorry to say it was true. She asked me if you had any friends, and I said none that I knew of, except me. I said that you'd lost all your friends; they stuck to you as long as they could, but they had to give you best, one after the other.'

'What next?'

'She asked me if you were delicate, and I said no, you were as tough as fencing-wire. She said you looked rather pale and thin, and asked me if you'd had an illness lately. And I said no—it was all on account of the wild, dissipated life you'd led. She said it was a pity you hadn't a mother or a sister to look after you—it was a pity that something couldn't be done for you, and I said it was, but I was afraid that nothing could be done. I told her that I was doing all I could to keep you straight.'

I knew enough of Jack to know that most of this was true. And so she only pitied me after all. I felt as if I'd been courting her for six months and she'd thrown me over—but I didn't know anything about women yet.

'Did you tell her I was in jail?' I growled.

'No, by Gum! I forgot that. But never mind I'll fix that up all right. I'll tell her that you got two years' hard for horse-stealing. That ought to make her interested in you, if she isn't already.'

We smoked a while.

'And was that all she said?' I asked.

'Who?—Oh! 'Possum,' said Jack rousing himself. 'Well—no; let me think— We got chatting of other things—you know a married man's privileged, and can say a lot more to a girl than a single man can. I got talking nonsense about sweethearts, and one thing led to another till at last she said, "I suppose Mr Wilson's got a sweetheart, Mr Barnes?"'

'And what did you say?' I growled.

'Oh, I told her that you were a holy terror amongst the girls,' said Jack. 'You'd better take back that tray, Joe, and let us get to work.'

I wouldn't take back the tray—but that didn't mend matters, for Jack took it back himself.

I didn't see Mary's reflection in the window again, so I took the window out. I reckoned that she was just a big-hearted, impulsive little thing, as many Australian girls are, and I reckoned that I was a fool for thinking for a moment that she might give me a second thought, except by way of kindness. Why! young Black and half a dozen better men than me were sweet on her, and young Black was to get his father's station and the money—or rather his mother's money, for she held the stuff (she kept it close too, by all accounts). Young Black was away at the time, and his mother was dead against him about Mary, but that didn't make any difference, as far as I could see. I reckoned that it was only just going to be a hopeless, heart-breaking, stand-far-off-and-worship affair, as far as I was concerned—like my first love affair, that I haven't told you about yet. I was tired of being pitied by good girls. You see, I didn't know women then. If I had known, I think I might have made more than one mess of my life.

Jack rode home to Solong every night. I was staying at a pub some distance out of town, between Solong and Haviland. There were three or four wet days, and we didn't get on with the work. I fought shy of Mary till one day she was hanging out clothes and the line broke. It was the old-style sixpenny clothes-line. The clothes were all down, but it was clean grass, so it didn't matter much. I looked at Jack.

'Go and help her, you capital Idiot!' he said, and I made the plunge.

'Oh, thank you, Mr Wilson!' said Mary, when I came to help. She had the broken end of the line and was trying to hold some of the clothes off the ground, as if she could pull it an inch with the heavy wet sheets and table-cloths and things on it, or as if it would do any good if she did. But that's the way with women—especially little women—some of 'em would try to pull a store bullock if they got the end of the rope on the right side of the fence. I took the line from Mary, and accidentally touched her soft, plump little hand as I did so: it sent a thrill right through me. She seemed a lot cooler than I was.

Now, in cases like this, especially if you lose your head a bit, you get hold of the loose end of the rope that's hanging from the post with one hand, and the end of the line with the clothes on with the other, and try to pull 'em far enough together to make a knot. And that's about all you do for the present, except look like a fool. Then I took off the post end, spliced the line, took it over the fork, and pulled, while Mary helped me with the prop. I thought Jack might have come and taken the prop from her, but he didn't; he just went on with his work as if nothing was happening inside the horizon.

She'd got the line about two-thirds full of clothes, it was a bit short now, so she had to jump and catch it with one hand and hold it down while she pegged a sheet she'd thrown over. I'd made the plunge now, so I volunteered to help her. I held down the line while she threw the things over and pegged out. As we got near the post and higher I straightened out some ends and pegged myself. Bushmen are handy at most things. We laughed, and now and again Mary would say, 'No, that's not the way, Mr Wilson; that's not right; the sheet isn't far enough over; wait till I fix it,' &c. I'd a reckless idea once of holding her up while she pegged, and I was glad afterwards that I hadn't made such a fool of myself.

'There's only a few more things in the basket, Miss Brand,' I said. 'You can't reach—I'll fix 'em up.'

She seemed to give a little gasp.

'Oh, those things are not ready yet,' she said, 'they're not rinsed,' and she grabbed the basket and held it away from me. The things looked the same to me as the rest on the line; they looked rinsed enough and blued too. I reckoned that she didn't want me to take the trouble, or thought that I mightn't like to be seen hanging out clothes, and was only doing it out of kindness.

'Oh, it's no trouble,' I said, 'let me hang 'em out. I like it. I've hung out clothes at home on a windy day,' and I made a reach into the basket. But she flushed red, with temper I thought, and snatched the basket away.

'Excuse me, Mr Wilson,' she said, 'but those things are not ready yet!' and she marched into the wash-house.

'Ah well! you've got a little temper of your own,' I thought to myself.

When I told Jack, he said that I'd made another fool of myself. He said I'd both disappointed and offended her. He said that my line was to stand off a bit and be serious and melancholy in the background.

That evening when we'd started home, we stopped some time yarning with a chap we met at the gate; and I happened to look back, and saw Mary hanging out the rest of the things—she thought that we were out of sight. Then I understood why those things weren't ready while we were round.

For the next day or two Mary didn't take the slightest notice of me, and I kept out of her way. Jack said I'd disillusioned her—and hurt her dignity—which was a thousand times worse. He said I'd spoilt the thing altogether. He said that she'd got an idea that I was shy and poetic, and I'd only shown myself the usual sort of Bush-whacker.

I noticed her talking and chatting with other fellows once or twice, and it made me miserable. I got drunk two evenings running, and then, as it appeared afterwards, Mary consulted Jack, and at last she said to him, when we were together—

'Do you play draughts, Mr Barnes?'

'No,' said Jack.

'Do you, Mr Wilson?' she asked, suddenly turning her big, bright eyes on me, and speaking to me for the first time since last washing-day.

'Yes,' I said, 'I do a little.' Then there was a silence, and I had to say something else.

'Do you play draughts, Miss Brand?' I asked.

'Yes,' she said, 'but I can't get any one to play with me here of an evening, the men are generally playing cards or reading.' Then she said, 'It's very dull these long winter evenings when you've got nothing to do. Young Mr Black used to play draughts, but he's away.'

I saw Jack winking at me urgently.

'I'll play a game with you, if you like,' I said, 'but I ain't much of a player.'

'Oh, thank you, Mr Wilson! When shall you have an evening to spare?'

We fixed it for that same evening. We got chummy over the draughts. I had a suspicion even then that it was a put-up job to keep me away from the pub.

Perhaps she found a way of giving a hint to old Black without committing herself. Women have ways— or perhaps Jack did it. Anyway, next day the Boss came round and said to me—

'Look here, Joe, you've got no occasion to stay at the pub. Bring along your blankets and camp in one of the spare rooms of the old house. You can have your tucker here.'

He was a good sort, was Black the squatter: a squatter of the old school, who'd shared the early hardships with his men, and couldn't see why he should not shake hands and have a smoke and a yarn over old times with any of his old station hands that happened to come along. But he'd married an Englishwoman after the hardships were over, and she'd never got any Australian notions.

Next day I found one of the skillion rooms scrubbed out and a bed fixed up for me. I'm not sure to this day who did it, but I supposed that good-natured old Black had given one of the women a hint. After tea I had a yarn with Mary, sitting on a log of the wood-heap. I don't remember exactly how we both came to be there, or who sat down first. There was about two feet between us. We got very chummy and confidential. She told me about her childhood and her father.

He'd been an old mate of Black's, a younger son of a well-to-do English family (with blue blood in it, I believe), and sent out to Australia with a thousand pounds to make his way, as many younger sons are, with more or less. They think they're hard done by; they blue their thousand pounds in Melbourne or Sydney, and they don't make any more nowadays, for the Roarin' Days have been dead these thirty years. I wish I'd had a thousand pounds to start on!

Mary's mother was the daughter of a German immigrant, who selected up there in the old days. She had a will of her own as far as I could understand, and bossed the home till the day of her death. Mary's father made money, and lost it, and drank—and died. Mary remembered him sitting on the verandah one evening with his hand on her head, and singing a German song (the 'Lorelei', I think it was) softly, as if to himself. Next day he stayed in bed, and the children were kept out of the room; and, when he died, the children were adopted round (there was a little money coming from England).

Mary told me all about her girlhood. She went first to live with a sort of cousin in town, in a house where they took in cards on a tray, and then she came to live with Mrs Black, who took a fancy to her at first. I'd had no boyhood to speak of, so I gave her some of my ideas of what the world ought to be, and she seemed interested.

Next day there were sheets on my bed, and I felt pretty cocky until I remembered that I'd told her I had no one to care for me; then I suspected pity again.

But next evening we remembered that both our fathers and mothers were dead, and discovered that we had no friends except Jack and old Black, and things went on very satisfactorily.

And next day there was a little table in my room with a crocheted cover and a looking-glass.

I noticed the other girls began to act mysterious and giggle when I was round, but Mary didn't seem aware of it.

We got very chummy. Mary wasn't comfortable at Haviland. Old Black was very fond of her and always took her part, but she wanted to be independent. She had a great idea of going to Sydney and getting into the hospital as a nurse. She had friends in Sydney, but she had no money. There was a little money coming to her when she was twenty-one—a few pounds—and she was going to try and get it before that time.

'Look here, Miss Brand,' I said, after we'd watched the moon rise. 'I'll lend you the money. I've got plenty—more than I know what to do with.'

But I saw I'd hurt her. She sat up very straight for a while, looking before her; then she said it was time to go in, and said 'Good-night, Mr Wilson.'

I reckoned I'd done it that time; but Mary told me afterwards that she was only hurt because it struck her that what she said about money might have been taken for a hint. She didn't understand me yet, and I didn't know human nature. I didn't say anything to Jack—in fact about this time I left off telling him about things. He didn't seem hurt; he worked hard and seemed happy.

I really meant what I said to Mary about the money. It was pure good nature. I'd be a happier man now, I think, and richer man perhaps, if I'd never grown any more selfish than I was that night on the wood-heap with Mary. I felt a great sympathy for her—but I got to love her. I went through all the ups and downs of it. One day I was having tea in the kitchen, and Mary and another girl, named Sarah, reached me a clean plate at the same time: I took Sarah's plate because she was first, and Mary seemed very nasty about it, and that gave me great hopes. But all next evening she played draughts with a drover that she'd chummed up with. I pretended to be interested in Sarah's talk, but it didn't seem to work.

A few days later a Sydney Jackaroo visited the station. He had a good pea-rifle, and one afternoon he started to teach Mary to shoot at a target. They seemed to get very chummy. I had a nice time for three or four days, I can tell you. I was worse than a wall-eyed bullock with the pleuro. The other chaps had a shot out of the rifle. Mary called 'Mr Wilson' to have a shot, and I made a worse fool of myself by sulking. If it hadn't been a blooming Jackaroo I wouldn't have minded so much.

Next evening the Jackaroo and one or two other chaps and the girls went out 'possum-shooting. Mary went. I could have gone, but I didn't. I mooched round all the evening like an orphan bandicoot on a burnt ridge, and then I went up to the pub and filled myself with beer, and damned the world, and came home and went to bed. I think that evening was the only time I ever wrote poetry down on a piece of paper. I got so miserable that I enjoyed it.

I felt better next morning, and reckoned I was cured. I ran against Mary accidentally and had to say something.

'How did you enjoy yourself yesterday evening, Miss Brand?' I asked.

'Oh, very well, thank you, Mr Wilson,' she said. Then she asked, 'How did you enjoy yourself, Mr Wilson?'

I puzzled over that afterwards, but couldn't make anything out of it. Perhaps she only said it for the sake of saying something. But about this time my handkerchiefs and collars disappeared from the room and turned up washed and ironed and laid tidily on my table. I used to keep an eye out, but could never catch anybody near my room. I straightened up, and kept my room a bit tidy, and when my handkerchief got too dirty, and I was ashamed of letting it go to the wash, I'd slip down to the river after dark and wash it out, and dry it next day, and rub it up to look as if it hadn't been washed, and leave it on my table. I felt so full of hope and joy that I worked twice as hard as Jack, till one morning he remarked casually—

'I see you've made a new mash, Joe. I saw the half-caste cook tidying up your room this morning and taking your collars and things to the wash-house.'

I felt very much off colour all the rest of the day, and I had such a bad night of it that I made up my mind next morning to look the hopelessness square in the face and live the thing down.

It was the evening before Anniversary Day. Jack and I had put in a good day's work to get the job finished, and Jack was having a smoke and a yarn with the chaps before he started home. We sat on an old log along by the fence at the back of the house. There was Jimmy Nowlett the bullock-driver, and long Dave Regan the drover, and big Jim Bullock the fencer, and one or two others. Mary and the station girls and one or two visitors were sitting under the old verandah. The Jackaroo was there too, so I felt happy. It was the girls who used to bring the chaps hanging round. They were getting up a dance party for Anniversary night. Along in the evening another chap came riding up to the station: he was a big shearer, a dark, handsome fellow, who looked like a gipsy: it was reckoned that there was foreign blood in him. He went by the name of Romany. He was supposed to be shook after Mary too. He had the nastiest temper and the best violin in the district, and the chaps put up with him a lot because they wanted him to play at Bush dances. The moon had risen over Pine Ridge, but it was dusky where we were. We saw Romany loom up, riding in from the gate; he rode round the end of the coach-house and across towards where we were—I suppose he was going to tie up his horse at the fence; but about half-way across the grass he disappeared. It struck me that there was something peculiar about the way he got down, and I heard a sound like a horse stumbling.

'What the hell's Romany trying to do?' said Jimmy Nowlett. 'He couldn't have fell off his horse—or else he's drunk.'

A couple of chaps got up and went to see. Then there was that waiting, mysterious silence that comes when something happens in the dark and nobody knows what it is. I went over, and the thing dawned on me. I'd stretched a wire clothes-line across there during the day, and had forgotten all about it for the moment. Romany had no idea of the line, and, as he rode up, it caught him on a level with his elbows and scraped him off his horse. He was sitting on the grass, swearing in a surprised voice, and the horse looked surprised too. Romany wasn't hurt, but the sudden shock had spoilt his temper. He wanted to know who'd put up that bloody line. He came over and sat on the log. The chaps smoked a while.

'What did you git down so sudden for, Romany?' asked Jim Bullock presently. 'Did you hurt yerself on the pommel?'

'Why didn't you ask the horse to go round?' asked Dave Regan.

'I'd only like to know who put up that bleeding wire!' growled Romany.

'Well,' said Jimmy Nowlett, 'if we'd put up a sign to beware of the line you couldn't have seen it in the dark.'

'Unless it was a transparency with a candle behind it,' said Dave Regan. 'But why didn't you get down on one end, Romany, instead of all along? It wouldn't have jolted yer so much.'

All this with the Bush drawl, and between the puffs of their pipes. But I didn't take any interest in it. I was brooding over Mary and the Jackaroo.

'I've heard of men getting down over their horse's head,' said Dave presently, in a reflective sort of way—'in fact I've done it myself—but I never saw a man get off backwards over his horse's rump.'

But they saw that Romany was getting nasty, and they wanted him to play the fiddle next night, so they dropped it.

Mary was singing an old song. I always thought she had a sweet voice, and I'd have enjoyed it if that damned Jackaroo hadn't been listening too. We listened in silence until she'd finished.

'That gal's got a nice voice,' said Jimmy Nowlett.

'Nice voice!' snarled Romany, who'd been waiting for a chance to be nasty. 'Why, I've heard a tom-cat sing better.'

I moved, and Jack, he was sitting next me, nudged me to keep quiet. The chaps didn't like Romany's talk about 'Possum at all. They were all fond of her: she wasn't a pet or a tomboy, for she wasn't built that way, but they were fond of her in such a way that they didn't like to hear anything said about her. They said nothing for a while, but it meant a lot. Perhaps the single men didn't care to speak for fear that it would be said that they were gone on Mary. But presently Jimmy Nowlett gave a big puff at his pipe and spoke—

'I suppose you got bit too in that quarter, Romany?'

'Oh, she tried it on, but it didn't go,' said Romany. 'I've met her sort before. She's setting her cap at that Jackaroo now. Some girls will run after anything with trousers on,' and he stood up.

Jack Barnes must have felt what was coming, for he grabbed my arm, and whispered, 'Sit still, Joe, damn you! He's too good for you!' but I was on my feet and facing Romany as if a giant hand had reached down and wrenched me off the log and set me there.

'You're a damned crawler, Romany!' I said.

Little Jimmy Nowlett was between us and the other fellows round us before a blow got home. 'Hold on, you damned fools!' they said. 'Keep quiet till we get away from the house!' There was a little clear flat down by the river and plenty of light there, so we decided to go down there and have it out.

Now I never was a fighting man; I'd never learnt to use my hands. I scarcely knew how to put them up. Jack often wanted to teach me, but I wouldn't bother about it. He'd say, 'You'll get into a fight some day, Joe, or out of one, and shame me;' but I hadn't the patience to learn. He'd wanted me to take lessons at the station after work, but he used to get excited, and I didn't want Mary to see him knocking me about. Before he was married Jack was always getting into fights—he generally tackled a better man and got a hiding; but he didn't seem to care so long as he made a good show—though he used to explain the thing away from a scientific point of view for weeks after. To tell the truth, I had a horror of fighting; I had a horror of being marked about the face; I think I'd sooner stand off and fight a man with revolvers than fight him with fists; and then I think I would say, last thing, 'Don't shoot me in the face!' Then again I hated the idea of hitting a man. It seemed brutal to me. I was too sensitive and sentimental, and that was what the matter was. Jack seemed very serious on it as we walked down to the river, and he couldn't help hanging out blue lights.

'Why didn't you let me teach you to use your hands?' he said. 'The only chance now is that Romany can't fight after all. If you'd waited a minute I'd have been at him.' We were a bit behind the rest, and Jack started giving me points about lefts and rights, and 'half-arms', and that sort of thing. 'He's left-handed, and that's the worst of it,' said Jack. 'You must only make as good a show as you can, and one of us will take him on afterwards.'

But I just heard him and that was all. It was to be my first fight since I was a boy, but, somehow, I felt cool about it—sort of dulled. If the chaps had known all they would have set me down as a cur. I thought of that, but it didn't make any difference with me then; I knew it was a thing they couldn't understand. I knew I was reckoned pretty soft. But I knew one thing that they didn't know. I knew that it was going to be a fight to a finish, one way or the other. I had more brains and imagination than the rest put together, and I suppose that that was the real cause of most of my trouble. I kept saying to myself, 'You'll have to go through with it now, Joe, old man! It's the turning-point of your life.' If I won the fight, I'd set to work and win Mary; if I lost, I'd leave the district for ever. A man thinks a lot in a flash sometimes; I used to get excited over little things, because of the very paltriness of them, but I was mostly cool in a crisis—Jack was the reverse. I looked ahead: I wouldn't be able to marry a girl who could look back and remember when her husband was beaten by another man—no matter what sort of brute the other man was.

I never in my life felt so cool about a thing. Jack kept whispering instructions, and showing with his hands, up to the last moment, but it was all lost on me.

Looking back, I think there was a bit of romance about it: Mary singing under the vines to amuse a Jackaroo dude, and a coward going down to the river in the moonlight to fight for her.

It was very quiet in the little moonlit flat by the river. We took off our coats and were ready. There was no swearing or barracking. It seemed an understood thing with the men that if I went out first round Jack would fight Romany; and if Jack knocked him out somebody else would fight Jack to square matters. Jim Bullock wouldn't mind obliging for one; he was a mate of Jack's, but he didn't mind who he fought so long as it was for the sake of fair play—or 'peace and quietness', as he said. Jim was very good-natured. He backed Romany, and of course Jack backed me.

As far as I could see, all Romany knew about fighting was to jerk one arm up in front of his face and duck his head by way of a feint, and then rush and lunge out. But he had the weight and strength and length of reach, and my first lesson was a very short one. I went down early in the round. But it did me good; the blow and the look I'd seen in Romany's eyes knocked all the sentiment out of me. Jack said nothing,—he seemed to regard it as a hopeless job from the first. Next round I tried to remember some things Jack had told me, and made a better show, but I went down in the end.

I felt Jack breathing quick and trembling as he lifted me up.

'How are you, Joe?' he whispered.

'I'm all right,' I said.

'It's all right,' whispered Jack in a voice as if I was going to be hanged, but it would soon be all over. 'He can't use his hands much more than you can—take your time, Joe—try to remember something I told you, for God's sake!'

When two men fight who don't know how to use their hands, they stand a show of knocking each other about a lot. I got some awful thumps, but mostly on the body. Jimmy Nowlett began to get excited and jump round—he was an excitable little fellow.

'Fight! you—!' he yelled. 'Why don't you fight? That ain't fightin'. Fight, and don't try to murder each other. Use your crimson hands or, by God, I'll chip you! Fight, or I'll blanky well bullock-whip the pair of you;' then his language got awful. They said we went like windmills, and that nearly every one of the blows we made was enough to kill a bullock if it had got home. Jimmy stopped us once, but they held him back.

Presently I went down pretty flat, but the blow was well up on the head and didn't matter much—I had a good thick skull. And I had one good eye yet.

'For God's sake, hit him!' whispered Jack—he was trembling like a leaf. 'Don't mind what I told you. I wish I was fighting him myself! Get a blow home, for God's sake! Make a good show this round and I'll stop the fight.'

That showed how little even Jack, my old mate, understood me.

I had the Bushman up in me now, and wasn't going to be beaten while I could think. I was wonderfully cool, and learning to fight. There's nothing like a fight to teach a man. I was thinking fast, and learning more in three seconds than Jack's sparring could have taught me in three weeks. People think that blows hurt in a fight, but they don't—not till afterwards. I fancy that a fighting man, if he isn't altogether an animal, suffers more mentally than he does physically.

While I was getting my wind I could hear through the moonlight and still air the sound of Mary's voice singing up at the house. I thought hard into the future, even as I fought. The fight only seemed something that was passing.

I was on my feet again and at it, and presently I lunged out and felt such a jar in my arm that I thought it was telescoped. I thought I'd put out my wrist and elbow. And Romany was lying on the broad of his back.

I heard Jack draw three breaths of relief in one. He said nothing as he straightened me up, but I could feel his heart beating. He said afterwards that he didn't speak because he thought a word might spoil it.

I went down again, but Jack told me afterwards that he FELT I was all right when he lifted me.

Then Romany went down, then we fell together, and the chaps separated us. I got another knock-down blow in, and was beginning to enjoy the novelty of it, when Romany staggered and limped.

'I've done,' he said. 'I've twisted my ankle.' He'd caught his heel against a tuft of grass.

'Shake hands,' yelled Jimmy Nowlett.

I stepped forward, but Romany took his coat and limped to his horse.

'If yer don't shake hands with Wilson, I'll lamb yer!' howled Jimmy; but Jack told him to let the man alone, and Romany got on his horse somehow and rode off.

I saw Jim Bullock stoop and pick up something from the grass, and heard him swear in surprise. There was some whispering, and presently Jim said—

'If I thought that, I'd kill him.'

'What is it?' asked Jack.

Jim held up a butcher's knife. It was common for a man to carry a butcher's knife in a sheath fastened to his belt.

'Why did you let your man fight with a butcher's knife in his belt?' asked Jimmy Nowlett.

But the knife could easily have fallen out when Romany fell, and we decided it that way.

'Any way,' said Jimmy Nowlett, 'if he'd stuck Joe in hot blood before us all it wouldn't be so bad as if he sneaked up and stuck him in the back in the dark. But you'd best keep an eye over yer shoulder for a year or two, Joe. That chap's got Eye-talian blood in him somewhere. And now the best thing you chaps can do is to keep your mouth shut and keep all this dark from the gals.'

Jack hurried me on ahead. He seemed to act queer, and when I glanced at him I could have sworn that there was water in his eyes. I said that Jack had no sentiment except for himself, but I forgot, and I'm sorry I said it.

'What's up, Jack?' I asked.

'Nothing,' said Jack.

'What's up, you old fool?' I said.

'Nothing,' said Jack, 'except that I'm damned proud of you, Joe, you old ass!' and he put his arm round my shoulders and gave me a shake. 'I didn't know it was in you, Joe—I wouldn't have said it before, or listened to any other man say it, but I didn't think you had the pluck—God's truth, I didn't. Come along and get your face fixed up.'

We got into my room quietly, and Jack got a dish of water, and told one of the chaps to sneak a piece of fresh beef from somewhere.

Jack was as proud as a dog with a tin tail as he fussed round me. He fixed up my face in the best style he knew, and he knew a good many—he'd been mended himself so often.

While he was at work we heard a sudden hush and a scraping of feet amongst the chaps that Jack had kicked out of the room, and a girl's voice whispered, 'Is he hurt? Tell me. I want to know,—I might be able to help.'

It made my heart jump, I can tell you. Jack went out at once, and there was some whispering. When he came back he seemed wild.

'What is it, Jack?' I asked.

'Oh, nothing,' he said, 'only that damned slut of a half-caste cook overheard some of those blanky fools arguing as to how Romany's knife got out of the sheath, and she's put a nice yarn round amongst the girls. There's a regular bobbery, but it's all right now. Jimmy Nowlett's telling 'em lies at a great rate.'

Presently there was another hush outside, and a saucer with vinegar and brown paper was handed in.

One of the chaps brought some beer and whisky from the pub, and we had a quiet little time in my room. Jack wanted to stay all night, but I reminded him that his little wife was waiting for him in Solong, so he said he'd be round early in the morning, and went home.

I felt the reaction pretty bad. I didn't feel proud of the affair at all. I thought it was a low, brutal business all round. Romany was a quiet chap after all, and the chaps had no right to chyack him. Perhaps he'd had a hard life, and carried a big swag of trouble that we didn't know anything about. He seemed a lonely man. I'd gone through enough myself to teach me not to judge men. I made up my mind to tell him how I felt about the matter next time we met. Perhaps I made my usual mistake of bothering about 'feelings' in another party that hadn't any feelings at all—perhaps I didn't; but it's generally best to chance it on the kind side in a case like this. Altogether I felt as if I'd made another fool of myself and been a weak coward. I drank the rest of the beer and went to sleep.

About daylight I woke and heard Jack's horse on the gravel. He came round the back of the buggy-shed and up to my door, and then, suddenly, a girl screamed out. I pulled on my trousers and 'lastic-side boots and hurried out. It was Mary herself, dressed, and sitting on an old stone step at the back of the kitchen with her face in her hands, and Jack was off his horse and stooping by her side with his hand on her shoulder. She kept saying, 'I thought you were—! I thought you were—!' I didn't catch the name. An old single-barrel, muzzle-loader shot-gun was lying in the grass at her feet. It was the gun they used to keep loaded and hanging in straps in a room of the kitchen ready for a shot at a cunning old hawk that they called "Tarnal Death", and that used to be always after the chickens.

When Mary lifted her face it was as white as note-paper, and her eyes seemed to grow wilder when she caught sight of me.

'Oh, you did frighten me, Mr Barnes,' she gasped. Then she gave a little ghost of a laugh and stood up, and some colour came back.

'Oh, I'm a little fool!' she said quickly. 'I thought I heard old 'Tarnal Death at the chickens, and I thought it would be a great thing if I got the gun and brought him down; so I got up and dressed quietly so as not to wake Sarah. And then you came round the corner and frightened me. I don't know what you must think of me, Mr Barnes.'

'Never mind,' said Jack. 'You go and have a sleep, or you won't be able to dance to-night. Never mind the gun—I'll put that away.' And he steered her round to the door of her room off the brick verandah where she slept with one of the other girls.

'Well, that's a rum start!' I said.

'Yes, it is,' said Jack; 'it's very funny. Well, how's your face this morning, Joe?'

He seemed a lot more serious than usual.

We were hard at work all the morning cleaning out the big wool-shed and getting it ready for the dance, hanging hoops for the candles, making seats, &c. I kept out of sight of the girls as much as I could. One side of my face was a sight and the other wasn't too classical. I felt as if I had been stung by a swarm of bees.

'You're a fresh, sweet-scented beauty now, and no mistake, Joe,' said Jimmy Nowlett—he was going to play the accordion that night. 'You ought to fetch the girls now, Joe. But never mind, your face'll go down in about three weeks. My lower jaw is crooked yet; but that fight straightened my nose, that had been knocked crooked when I was a boy—so I didn't lose much beauty by it.'

When we'd done in the shed, Jack took me aside and said—

'Look here, Joe! if you won't come to the dance to-night—and I can't say you'd ornament it—I tell you what you'll do. You get little Mary away on the quiet and take her out for a stroll—and act like a man. The job's finished now, and you won't get another chance like this.'

'But how am I to get her out?' I said.

'Never you mind. You be mooching round down by the big peppermint-tree near the river-gate, say about half-past ten.'

'What good'll that do?'

'Never you mind. You just do as you're told, that's all you've got to do,' said Jack, and he went home to get dressed and bring his wife.

After the dancing started that night I had a peep in once or twice. The first time I saw Mary dancing with Jack, and looking serious; and the second time she was dancing with the blarsted Jackaroo dude, and looking excited and happy. I noticed that some of the girls, that I could see sitting on a stool along the opposite wall, whispered, and gave Mary black looks as the Jackaroo swung her past. It struck me pretty forcibly that I should have taken fighting lessons from him instead of from poor Romany. I went away and walked about four miles down the river road, getting out of the way into the Bush whenever I saw any chap riding along. I thought of poor Romany and wondered where he was, and thought that there wasn't much to choose between us as far as happiness was concerned. Perhaps he was walking by himself in the Bush, and feeling like I did. I wished I could shake hands with him.

But somehow, about half-past ten, I drifted back to the river slip-rails and leant over them, in the shadow of the peppermint-tree, looking at the rows of river-willows in the moonlight. I didn't expect anything, in spite of what Jack said.

I didn't like the idea of hanging myself: I'd been with a party who found a man hanging in the Bush, and it was no place for a woman round where he was. And I'd helped drag two bodies out of the

Cudgeegong river in a flood, and they weren't sleeping beauties. I thought it was a pity that a chap couldn't lie down on a grassy bank in a graceful position in the moonlight and die just by thinking of it—and die with his eyes and mouth shut. But then I remembered that I wouldn't make a beautiful corpse, anyway it went, with the face I had on me.

I was just getting comfortably miserable when I heard a step behind me, and my heart gave a jump. And I gave a start too.

'Oh, is that you, Mr Wilson?' said a timid little voice.

'Yes,' I said. 'Is that you, Mary?'

And she said yes. It was the first time I called her Mary, but she did not seem to notice it.

'Did I frighten you?' I asked.

'No—yes—just a little,' she said. 'I didn't know there was any one—' then she stopped.

'Why aren't you dancing?' I asked her.

'Oh, I'm tired,' she said. 'It was too hot in the wool-shed. I thought I'd like to come out and get my head cool and be quiet a little while.'

'Yes,' I said, 'it must be hot in the wool-shed.'

She stood looking out over the willows. Presently she said, 'It must be very dull for you, Mr Wilson—you must feel lonely. Mr Barnes said—' Then she gave a little gasp and stopped—as if she was just going to put her foot in it.

'How beautiful the moonlight looks on the willows!' she said.

'Yes,' I said, 'doesn't it? Supposing we have a stroll by the river.'

'Oh, thank you, Mr Wilson. I'd like it very much.'

I didn't notice it then, but, now I come to think of it, it was a beautiful scene: there was a horseshoe of high blue hills round behind the house, with the river running round under the slopes, and in front was a rounded hill covered with pines, and pine ridges, and a soft blue peak away over the ridges ever so far in the distance.

I had a handkerchief over the worst of my face, and kept the best side turned to her. We walked down by the river, and didn't say anything for a good while. I was thinking hard. We came to a white smooth log in a quiet place out of sight of the house.

'Suppose we sit down for a while, Mary,' I said.

'If you like, Mr Wilson,' she said.

There was about a foot of log between us.

'What a beautiful night!' she said.

'Yes,' I said, 'isn't it?'

Presently she said, 'I suppose you know I'm going away next month, Mr Wilson?'

I felt suddenly empty. 'No,' I said, 'I didn't know that.'

'Yes,' she said, 'I thought you knew. I'm going to try and get into the hospital to be trained for a nurse, and if that doesn't come off I'll get a place as assistant public-school teacher.'

We didn't say anything for a good while.

'I suppose you won't be sorry to go, Miss Brand?' I said.

'I—I don't know,' she said. 'Everybody's been so kind to me here.'

She sat looking straight before her, and I fancied her eyes glistened. I put my arm round her shoulders, but she didn't seem to notice it. In fact, I scarcely noticed it myself at the time.

'So you think you'll be sorry to go away?' I said.

'Yes, Mr Wilson. I suppose I'll fret for a while. It's been my home, you know.'

I pressed my hand on her shoulder, just a little, so as she couldn't pretend not to know it was there. But she didn't seem to notice.

'Ah, well,' I said, 'I suppose I'll be on the wallaby again next week.'

'Will you, Mr Wilson?' she said. Her voice seemed very soft.

I slipped my arm round her waist, under her arm. My heart was going like clockwork now.

Presently she said—

'Don't you think it's time to go back now, Mr Wilson?'

'Oh, there's plenty of time!' I said. I shifted up, and put my arm farther round, and held her closer. She sat straight up, looking right in front of her, but she began to breathe hard.

'Mary,' I said.

'Yes,' she said.

'Call me Joe,' I said.

'I—I don't like to,' she said. 'I don't think it would be right.'

So I just turned her face round and kissed her. She clung to me and cried.

'What is it, Mary?' I asked.

She only held me tighter and cried.

'What is it, Mary?' I said. 'Ain't you well? Ain't you happy?'

'Yes, Joe,' she said, 'I'm very happy.' Then she said, 'Oh, your poor face! Can't I do anything for it?'

'No,' I said. 'That's all right. My face doesn't hurt me a bit now.'

But she didn't seem right.

'What is it, Mary?' I said. 'Are you tired? You didn't sleep last night—' Then I got an inspiration.

'Mary,' I said, 'what were you doing out with the gun this morning?'

And after some coaxing it all came out, a bit hysterical.

'I couldn't sleep—I was frightened. Oh! I had such a terrible dream about you, Joe! I thought Romany came back and got into your room and stabbed you with his knife. I got up and dressed, and about daybreak I heard a horse at the gate; then I got the gun down from the wall—and—and Mr Barnes came round the corner and frightened me. He's something like Romany, you know.'

Then I got as much of her as I could into my arms.

And, oh, but wasn't I happy walking home with Mary that night! She was too little for me to put my arm round her waist, so I put it round her shoulder, and that felt just as good. I remember I asked her who'd cleaned up my room and washed my things, but she wouldn't tell.

She wouldn't go back to the dance yet; she said she'd go into her room and rest a while. There was no one near the old verandah; and when she stood on the end of the floor she was just on a level with my shoulder.

'Mary,' I whispered, 'put your arms round my neck and kiss me.'

She put her arms round my neck, but she didn't kiss me; she only hid her face.

'Kiss me, Mary!' I said.

'I—I don't like to,' she whispered.

'Why not, Mary?'

Then I felt her crying or laughing, or half crying and half laughing. I'm not sure to this day which it was.

'Why won't you kiss me, Mary? Don't you love me?'

'Because,' she said, 'because—because I—I don't—I don't think it's right for—for a girl to—to kiss a man unless she's going to be his wife.'

Then it dawned on me! I'd forgot all about proposing.

'Mary,' I said, 'would you marry a chap like me?'

And that was all right.

Next morning Mary cleared out my room and sorted out my things, and didn't take the slightest notice of the other girls' astonishment.

But she made me promise to speak to old Black, and I did the same evening. I found him sitting on the log by the fence, having a yarn on the quiet with an old Bushman; and when the old Bushman got up and went away, I sat down.

'Well, Joe,' said Black, 'I see somebody's been spoiling your face for the dance.' And after a bit he said, 'Well, Joe, what is it? Do you want another job? If you do, you'll have to ask Mrs Black, or Bob' (Bob was his eldest son); 'they're managing the station for me now, you know.' He could be bitter sometimes in his quiet way.

'No,' I said; 'it's not that, Boss.'

'Well, what is it, Joe?'

'I—well the fact is, I want little Mary.'

He puffed at his pipe for a long time, then I thought he spoke.

'What did you say, Boss?' I said.

'Nothing, Joe,' he said. 'I was going to say a lot, but it wouldn't be any use. My father used to say a lot to me before I was married.'

I waited a good while for him to speak.

'Well, Boss,' I said, 'what about Mary?'

'Oh! I suppose that's all right, Joe,' he said. 'I—I beg your pardon. I got thinking of the days when I was courting Mrs Black.'

Brighten's Sister-In-Law

Jim was born on Gulgong, New South Wales. We used to say 'on' Gulgong—and old diggers still talked of being 'on th' Gulgong'—though the goldfield there had been worked out for years, and the place was only a dusty little pastoral town in the scrubs. Gulgong was about the last of the great alluvial 'rushes' of the 'roaring days'—and dreary and dismal enough it looked when I was there. The expression 'on' came from being on the 'diggings' or goldfield—the workings or the goldfield was all underneath, of course, so we lived (or starved) ON them—not in nor at 'em.

Mary and I had been married about two years when Jim came—His name wasn't 'Jim', by the way, it was 'John Henry', after an uncle godfather; but we called him Jim from the first—(and before it)—because Jim was a popular Bush name, and most of my old mates were Jims. The Bush is full of good-hearted scamps called Jim.

We lived in an old weather-board shanty that had been a sly-grog-shop, and the Lord knows what else! in the palmy days of Gulgong; and I did a bit of digging ['fossicking', rather), a bit of shearing, a bit of fencing, a bit of Bush-carpentering, tank-sinking,—anything, just to keep the billy boiling.

We had a lot of trouble with Jim with his teeth. He was bad with every one of them, and we had most of them lanced—couldn't pull him through without. I remember we got one lanced and the gum healed over before the tooth came through, and we had to get it cut again. He was a plucky little chap, and after the first time he never whimpered when the doctor was lancing his gum: he used to say 'tar' afterwards, and want to bring the lance home with him.

The first turn we got with Jim was the worst. I had had the wife and Jim out camping with me in a tent at a dam I was making at Cattle Creek; I had two men working for me, and a boy to drive one of the tip-drays, and I took Mary out to cook for us. And it was lucky for us that the contract was finished and we got back to Gulgong, and within reach of a doctor, the day we did. We were just camping in the house, with our goods and chattels anyhow, for the night; and we were hardly back home an hour when Jim took convulsions for the first time.

Did you ever see a child in convulsions? You wouldn't want to see it again: it plays the devil with a man's nerves. I'd got the beds fixed up on the floor, and the billies on the fire—I was going to make some tea, and put a piece of corned beef on to boil over night—when Jim (he'd been queer all day, and his mother was trying to hush him to sleep)—Jim, he screamed out twice. He'd been crying a good deal, and I was dog-tired and worried (over some money a man owed me) or I'd have noticed at once that there was something unusual in the way the child cried out: as it was I didn't turn round till Mary screamed 'Joe! Joe!' You know how a woman cries out when her child is in danger or dying—short, and sharp, and terrible. 'Joe! Look! look! Oh, my God! our child! Get the bath, quick! quick! it's convulsions!'

Jim was bent back like a bow, stiff as a bullock-yoke, in his mother's arms, and his eyeballs were turned up and fixed—a thing I saw twice afterwards, and don't want ever to see again.

I was falling over things getting the tub and the hot water, when the woman who lived next door rushed in. She called to her husband to run for the doctor, and before the doctor came she and Mary had got Jim into a hot bath and pulled him through.

The neighbour woman made me up a shake-down in another room, and stayed with Mary that night; but it was a long while before I got Jim and Mary's screams out of my head and fell asleep.

You may depend I kept the fire in, and a bucket of water hot over it, for a good many nights after that; but (it always happens like this) there came a night, when the fright had worn off, when I was too tired to bother about the fire, and that night Jim took us by surprise. Our wood-heap was done, and I broke up a new chair to get a fire, and had to run a quarter of a mile for water; but this turn wasn't so bad as the first, and we pulled him through.

You never saw a child in convulsions? Well, you don't want to. It must be only a matter of seconds, but it seems long minutes; and half an hour afterwards the child might be laughing and playing with you, or stretched out dead. It shook me up a lot. I was always pretty high-strung and sensitive. After Jim took the first fit, every time he cried, or turned over, or stretched out in the night, I'd jump: I was always feeling his forehead in the dark to see if he was feverish, or feeling his limbs to see if he was 'limp' yet. Mary and I often laughed about it—afterwards. I tried sleeping in another room, but for nights after Jim's first attack I'd be just dozing off into a sound sleep, when I'd hear him scream, as plain as could be, and I'd hear Mary cry, 'Joe!—Joe!'—short, sharp, and terrible—and I'd be up and into their room like a shot, only to find them sleeping peacefully. Then I'd feel Jim's head and his breathing for signs of convulsions, see to the fire and water, and go back to bed and try to sleep. For the first few nights I was like that all night, and I'd feel relieved when daylight came. I'd be in first thing to see if they were all right; then I'd sleep till dinner-time if it was Sunday or I had no work. But then I was run down about that time: I was worried about some money for a wool-shed I put up and never got paid for; and, besides, I'd been pretty wild before I met Mary.

I was fighting hard then—struggling for something better. Both Mary and I were born to better things, and that's what made the life so hard for us.

Jim got on all right for a while: we used to watch him well, and have his teeth lanced in time.

It used to hurt and worry me to see how—just as he was getting fat and rosy and like a natural happy child, and I'd feel proud to take him out—a tooth would come along, and he'd get thin and white and pale and bigger-eyed and old-fashioned. We'd say, 'He'll be safe when he gets his eye-teeth': but he didn't get them till he was two; then, 'He'll be safe when he gets his two-year-old teeth': they didn't come till he was going on for three.

He was a wonderful little chap—Yes, I know all about parents thinking that their child is the best in the world. If your boy is small for his age, friends will say that small children make big men; that he's a very bright, intelligent child, and that it's better to have a bright, intelligent child than a big, sleepy lump of fat. And if your boy is dull and sleepy, they say that the dullest boys make the cleverest men—and all the rest of it. I never took any notice of that sort of clatter—took it for what it was worth; but, all the same, I don't think I ever saw such a child as Jim was when he turned two. He was everybody's favourite. They spoilt him rather. I had my own ideas about bringing up a child. I reckoned Mary was too soft with Jim. She'd say, 'Put that' (whatever it was) 'out of Jim's reach, will you, Joe?' and I'd say, 'No! leave it there, and make him understand he's not to have it. Make him have his meals without any nonsense, and go to bed at a regular hour,' I'd say. Mary and I had many a breeze over Jim. She'd say that I forgot he was only a baby: but I held that a baby could be trained from the first week; and I believe I was right.

But, after all, what are you to do? You'll see a boy that was brought up strict turn out a scamp; and another that was dragged up anyhow (by the hair of the head, as the saying is) turn out well. Then, again, when a child is delicate—and you might lose him any day—you don't like to spank him, though he might be turning out a little fiend, as delicate children often do. Suppose you gave a child a hammering, and the same night he took convulsions, or something, and died—how'd you feel about it? You never know what a child is going to take, any more than you can tell what some women are going to say or do.

I was very fond of Jim, and we were great chums. Sometimes I'd sit and wonder what the deuce he was thinking about, and often, the way he talked, he'd make me uneasy. When he was two he wanted a pipe above all things, and I'd get him a clean new clay and he'd sit by my side, on the edge of the verandah, or on a log of the wood-heap, in the cool of the evening, and suck away at his pipe, and try to spit when he saw me do it. He seemed to understand that a cold empty pipe wasn't quite the thing, yet to have the sense to know that he couldn't smoke tobacco yet: he made the best he could of things. And if he broke a clay pipe he wouldn't have a new one, and there'd be a row; the old one had to be mended up, somehow, with string or wire. If I got my hair cut, he'd want his cut too; and it always troubled him to see me shave—as if he thought there must be something wrong somewhere, else he ought to have to be shaved too. I lathered him one day, and pretended to shave him: he sat through it as solemn as an owl, but didn't seem to appreciate it—perhaps he had sense enough to know that it couldn't possibly be the real thing. He felt his face, looked very hard at the lather I scraped off, and whimpered, 'No blood, daddy!'

I used to cut myself a good deal: I was always impatient over shaving.

Then he went in to interview his mother about it. She understood his lingo better than I did.

But I wasn't always at ease with him. Sometimes he'd sit looking into the fire, with his head on one side, and I'd watch him and wonder what he was thinking about (I might as well have wondered what a Chinaman was thinking about) till he seemed at least twenty years older than me: sometimes, when I moved or spoke, he'd glance round just as if to see what that old fool of a dadda of his was doing now.

I used to have a fancy that there was something Eastern, or Asiatic—something older than our civilisation or religion—about old-fashioned children. Once I started to explain my idea to a woman I thought would understand—and as it happened she had an old-fashioned child, with very slant eyes—a little tartar he was too. I suppose it was the sight of him that unconsciously reminded me of my internal theory, and set me off on it, without warning me. Anyhow, it got me mixed up in an awful row with the woman and her husband—and all their tribe. It wasn't an easy thing to explain myself out of it, and the row hasn't been fixed up yet. There were some Chinamen in the district.

I took a good-size fencing contract, the frontage of a ten-mile paddock, near Gulgong, and did well out of it. The railway had got as far as the Cudgeegong river—some twenty miles from Gulgong and two hundred from the coast—and 'carrying' was good then. I had a couple of draught-horses, that I worked in the tip-drays when I was tank-sinking, and one or two others running in the Bush. I bought a broken-down waggon cheap, tinkered it up myself—christened it 'The Same Old Thing'—and started carrying from the railway terminus through Gulgong and along the bush roads and tracks that branch out fanlike through the scrubs to the one-pub towns and sheep and cattle stations out there in the howling wilderness. It wasn't much of a team. There were the two heavy horses for 'shafters'; a stunted colt, that I'd bought out of the pound for thirty shillings; a light, spring-cart horse; an old grey mare, with points like a big red-and-white Australian store bullock, and with the grit of an old washerwoman to work; and a horse that had spanked along in Cob & Co.'s mail-coach in his time. I had a couple there that didn't belong to me: I worked them for the feeding of them in the dry weather. And I had all sorts of harness, that I mended and fixed up myself. It was a mixed team, but I took light stuff, got through pretty quick, and freight rates were high. So I got along.

Before this, whenever I made a few pounds I'd sink a shaft somewhere, prospecting for gold; but Mary never let me rest till she talked me out of that.

I made up my mind to take on a small selection farm—that an old mate of mine had fenced in and cleared, and afterwards chucked up—about thirty miles out west of Gulgong, at a place called Lahey's Creek. (The places were all called Lahey's Creek, or Spicer's Flat, or Murphy's Flat, or Ryan's Crossing, or some such name—round there.) I reckoned I'd have a run for the horses and be able to grow a bit of feed. I always had a dread of taking Mary and the children too far away from a doctor—or a good woman neighbour; but there were some people came to live on Lahey's Creek, and besides, there was a young brother of Mary's—a young scamp (his name was Jim, too, and we called him 'Jimmy' at first to make room for our Jim—he hated the name 'Jimmy' or James). He came to live with us—without asking—and I thought he'd find enough work at Lahey's Creek to keep him out of mischief. He wasn't to be depended on much—he thought nothing of riding off, five hundred miles or so, 'to have a look at the country'—but he was fond of Mary, and he'd stay by her till I got some one else to keep her company while I was on the road. He would be a protection against 'sundowners' or any shearers who happened to wander that way in the 'D.T.'s' after a spree. Mary had a married sister come to live at Gulgong just before we left, and nothing would suit her and her husband but we must leave little Jim with them for a month or so—till we got settled down at Lahey's Creek. They were newly married.

Mary was to have driven into Gulgong, in the spring-cart, at the end of the month, and taken Jim home; but when the time came she wasn't too well—and, besides, the tyres of the cart were loose, and I hadn't time to get them cut, so we let Jim's time run on a week or so longer, till I happened to come out through Gulgong from the river with a small load of flour for Lahey's Creek way. The roads were good, the weather grand—no chance of it raining, and I had a spare tarpaulin if it did—I would only camp out one night; so I decided to take Jim home with me.

Jim was turning three then, and he was a cure. He was so old-fashioned that he used to frighten me sometimes—I'd almost think that there was something supernatural about him; though, of course, I never took any notice of that rot about some children being too old-fashioned to live. There's always the ghoulish old hag (and some not so old nor haggish either) who'll come round and shake up young parents with such croaks as, 'You'll never rear that child—he's too bright for his age.' To the devil with them! I say.

But I really thought that Jim was too intelligent for his age, and I often told Mary that he ought to be kept back, and not let talk too much to old diggers and long lanky jokers of Bushmen who rode in and hung their horses outside my place on Sunday afternoons.

I don't believe in parents talking about their own children everlastingly—you get sick of hearing them; and their kids are generally little devils, and turn out larrikins as likely as not.

But, for all that, I really think that Jim, when he was three years old, was the most wonderful little chap, in every way, that I ever saw.

For the first hour or so, along the road, he was telling me all about his adventures at his auntie's.

'But they spoilt me too much, dad,' he said, as solemn as a native bear. 'An' besides, a boy ought to stick to his parrans!'

I was taking out a cattle-pup for a drover I knew, and the pup took up a good deal of Jim's time.

Sometimes he'd jolt me, the way he talked; and other times I'd have to turn away my head and cough, or shout at the horses, to keep from laughing outright. And once, when I was taken that way, he said—

'What are you jerking your shoulders and coughing, and grunting, and going on that way for, dad? Why don't you tell me something?'

'Tell you what, Jim?'

'Tell me some talk.'

So I told him all the talk I could think of. And I had to brighten up, I can tell you, and not draw too much on my imagination—for Jim was a terror at cross-examination when the fit took him; and he didn't think twice about telling you when he thought you were talking nonsense. Once he said—

'I'm glad you took me home with you, dad. You'll get to know Jim.'

'What!' I said.

'You'll get to know Jim.'

'But don't I know you already?'

'No, you don't. You never has time to know Jim at home.'

And, looking back, I saw that it was cruel true. I had known in my heart all along that this was the truth; but it came to me like a blow from Jim. You see, it had been a hard struggle for the last year or so; and when I was home for a day or two I was generally too busy, or too tired and worried, or full of schemes for the future, to take much notice of Jim. Mary used to speak to me about it sometimes. 'You never take notice of the child,' she'd say. 'You could surely find a few minutes of an evening. What's the use of always worrying and brooding? Your brain will go with a snap some day, and, if you get over it, it will teach you a lesson. You'll be an old man, and Jim a young one, before you realise that you had a child once. Then it will be too late.'

This sort of talk from Mary always bored me and made me impatient with her, because I knew it all too well. I never worried for myself—only for Mary and the children. And often, as the days went by, I said to myself, 'I'll take more notice of Jim and give Mary more of my time, just as soon as I can see things clear ahead a bit.' And the hard days went on, and the weeks, and the months, and the years— Ah, well!

Mary used to say, when things would get worse, 'Why don't you talk to me, Joe? Why don't you tell me your thoughts, instead of shutting yourself up in yourself and brooding—eating your heart out? It's hard for me: I get to think you're tired of me, and selfish. I might be cross and speak sharp to you when you are in trouble. How am I to know, if you don't tell me?'

But I didn't think she'd understand.

And so, getting acquainted, and chumming and dozing, with the gums closing over our heads here and there, and the ragged patches of sunlight and shade passing up, over the horses, over us, on the front of the load, over the load, and down on to the white, dusty road again—Jim and I got along the lonely Bush road and over the ridges, some fifteen miles before sunset, and camped at Ryan's Crossing on Sandy Creek for the night. I got the horses out and took the harness off. Jim wanted badly to help me, but I made him stay on the load; for one of the horses—a vicious, red-eyed chestnut—was a kicker: he'd broken a man's leg. I got the feed-bags stretched across the shafts, and the chaff-and-corn into them; and there stood the horses all round with their rumps north, south, and west, and their heads between the shafts, munching and switching their tails. We use double shafts, you know, for horse-teams—two pairs side by side,—and prop them up, and stretch bags between them, letting the bags sag to serve as feed-boxes. I threw the spare tarpaulin over the wheels on one side, letting about half of it lie on the ground in case of damp, and so making a floor and a break-wind. I threw down bags and the blankets and 'possum rug against the wheel to make a camp for Jim and the cattle-pup, and got a gin-case we used for a tucker-box, the frying-pan and billy down, and made a good fire at a log close handy, and soon everything was comfortable. Ryan's Crossing was a grand camp. I stood with my pipe in my mouth, my hands behind my back, and my back to the fire, and took the country in.

Reedy Creek came down along a western spur of the range: the banks here were deep and green, and the water ran clear over the granite bars, boulders, and gravel. Behind us was a dreary flat covered with those gnarled, grey-barked, dry-rotted 'native apple-trees' (about as much like apple-trees as the native bear is like any other), and a nasty bit of sand-dusty road that I was always glad to get over in wet weather. To the left on our side of the creek were reedy marshes, with frogs croaking, and across the creek the dark box-scrub-covered ridges ended in steep 'sidings' coming down to the creek-bank, and to the main road that skirted them, running on west up over a 'saddle' in the ridges and on towards Dubbo. The road by Lahey's Creek to a place called Cobborah branched off, through dreary apple-tree and stringy-bark flats, to the left, just beyond the crossing: all these fanlike branch tracks from the Cudgeegong were inside a big horse-shoe in the Great Western Line, and so they gave small carriers a chance, now that Cob & Co.'s coaches and the big teams and vans had shifted out of the main western terminus. There were tall she-oaks all along the creek, and a clump of big ones over a deep water-hole just above the crossing. The creek oaks have rough barked trunks, like English elms, but are much taller, and higher to the branches—and the leaves are reedy; Kendel, the Australian poet, calls them the 'she-oak harps Aeolian'. Those trees are always sigh-sigh-sighing—more of a sigh than a sough or the 'whoosh' of gum-trees in the wind. You always hear them sighing, even when you can't feel any wind. It's the same with telegraph wires: put your head against a telegraph-post on a dead, still day, and you'll hear and feel the far-away roar of the wires. But then the oaks are not connected with the distance, where there might be wind; and they don't ROAR in a gale, only sigh louder and softer according to the wind, and never seem to go above or below a certain pitch,—like a big harp with all the strings the same. I used to have a theory that those creek oaks got the wind's voice telephoned to them, so to speak, through the ground.

I happened to look down, and there was Jim (I thought he was on the tarpaulin, playing with the pup): he was standing close beside me with his legs wide apart, his hands behind his back, and his back to the fire.

He held his head a little on one side, and there was such an old, old, wise expression in his big brown eyes—just as if he'd been a child for a hundred years or so, or as though he were listening to those oaks and understanding them in a fatherly sort of way.

'Dad!' he said presently—'Dad! do you think I'll ever grow up to be a man?'

'Wh—why, Jim?' I gasped.

'Because I don't want to.'

I couldn't think of anything against this. It made me uneasy. But I remembered 'I' used to have a childish dread of growing up to be a man.

'Jim,' I said, to break the silence, 'do you hear what the she-oaks say?'

'No, I don't. Is they talking?'

'Yes,' I said, without thinking.

'What is they saying?' he asked.

I took the bucket and went down to the creek for some water for tea. I thought Jim would follow with a little tin billy he had, but he didn't: when I got back to the fire he was again on the 'possum rug, comforting the pup. I fried some bacon and eggs that I'd brought out with me. Jim sang out from the waggon—

'Don't cook too much, dad—I mightn't be hungry.'

I got the tin plates and pint-pots and things out on a clean new flour-bag, in honour of Jim, and dished up. He was leaning back on the rug looking at the pup in a listless sort of way. I reckoned he was tired out, and pulled the gin-case up close to him for a table and put his plate on it. But he only tried a mouthful or two, and then he said—

'I ain't hungry, dad! You'll have to eat it all.'

It made me uneasy—I never liked to see a child of mine turn from his food. They had given him some tinned salmon in Gulgong, and I was afraid that that was upsetting him. I was always against tinned muck.

'Sick, Jim?' I asked.

'No, dad, I ain't sick; I don't know what's the matter with me.'

'Have some tea, sonny?'

'Yes, dad.'

I gave him some tea, with some milk in it that I'd brought in a bottle from his aunt's for him. He took a sip or two and then put the pint-pot on the gin-case.

'Jim's tired, dad,' he said.

I made him lie down while I fixed up a camp for the night. It had turned a bit chilly, so I let the big tarpaulin down all round—it was made to cover a high load, the flour in the waggon didn't come above the rail, so the tarpaulin came down well on to the ground. I fixed Jim up a comfortable bed under the tail-end of the waggon: when I went to lift him in he was lying back, looking up at the stars in a half-dreamy, half-fascinated way that I didn't like. Whenever Jim was extra old-fashioned, or affectionate, there was danger.

'How do you feel now, sonny?'

It seemed a minute before he heard me and turned from the stars.

'Jim's better, dad.' Then he said something like, 'The stars are looking at me.' I thought he was half asleep. I took off his jacket and boots, and carried him in under the waggon and made him comfortable for the night.

'Kiss me 'night-night, daddy,' he said.

I'd rather he hadn't asked me—it was a bad sign. As I was going to the fire he called me back.

'What is it, Jim?'

'Get me my things and the cattle-pup, please, daddy.'

I was scared now. His things were some toys and rubbish he'd brought from Gulgong, and I remembered, the last time he had convulsions, he took all his toys and a kitten to bed with him. And "night-night' and 'daddy' were two-year-old language to Jim. I'd thought he'd forgotten those words— he seemed to be going back.

'Are you quite warm enough, Jim?'

'Yes, dad.'

I started to walk up and down—I always did this when I was extra worried.

I was frightened now about Jim, though I tried to hide the fact from myself. Presently he called me again.

'What is it, Jim?'

'Take the blankets off me, fahver—Jim's sick!' (They'd been teaching him to say father.)

I was scared now. I remembered a neighbour of ours had a little girl die (she swallowed a pin), and when she was going she said—

'Take the blankets off me, muvver—I'm dying.'

And I couldn't get that out of my head

I threw back a fold of the 'possum rug, and felt Jim's head—he seemed cool enough.

'Where do you feel bad, sonny?'

No answer for a while; then he said suddenly, but in a voice as if he were talking in his sleep—

'Put my boots on, please, daddy. I want to go home to muvver!'

I held his hand, and comforted him for a while; then he slept—in a restless, feverish sort of way.

I got the bucket I used for water for the horses and stood it over the fire; I ran to the creek with the big kerosene-tin bucket and got it full of cold water and stood it handy. I got the spade (we always carried one to dig wheels out of bogs in wet weather) and turned a corner of the tarpaulin back, dug a hole, and trod the tarpaulin down into the hole, to serve for a bath, in case of the worst. I had a tin of mustard, and meant to fight a good round for Jim, if death came along.

I stooped in under the tail-board of the waggon and felt Jim. His head was burning hot, and his skin parched and dry as a bone.

Then I lost nerve and started blundering backward and forward between the waggon and the fire, and repeating what I'd heard Mary say the last time we fought for Jim: 'God! don't take my child! God! don't take my boy!' I'd never had much faith in doctors, but, my God! I wanted one then. The nearest was fifteen miles away.

I threw back my head and stared up at the branches, in desperation; and—Well, I don't ask you to take much stock in this, though most old Bushmen will believe anything of the Bush by night; and—Now, it might have been that I was all unstrung, or it might have been a patch of sky outlined in the gently moving branches, or the blue smoke rising up. But I saw the figure of a woman, all white, come down, down, nearly to the limbs of the trees, point on up the main road, and then float up and up and vanish, still pointing. I thought Mary was dead! Then it flashed on me—

Four or five miles up the road, over the 'saddle', was an old shanty that had been a half-way inn before the Great Western Line got round as far as Dubbo and took the coach traffic off those old Bush roads. A man named Brighten lived there. He was a selector; did a little farming, and as much sly-grog selling as he could. He was married—but it wasn't that: I'd thought of them, but she was a childish, worn-out, spiritless woman, and both were pretty 'ratty' from hardship and loneliness—they weren't likely to be of any use to me. But it was this: I'd heard talk, among some women in Gulgong, of a sister of Brighten's wife who'd gone out to live with them lately: she'd been a hospital matron in the city, they said; and there were yarns about her. Some said she got the sack for exposing the doctors—or carrying on with them—I didn't remember which. The fact of a city woman going out to live in such a place, with such people, was enough to make talk among women in a town twenty miles away, but then there must have been something extra about her, else Bushmen wouldn't have talked and carried her name so far; and I wanted a woman out of the ordinary now. I even reasoned this way, thinking like lightning, as I knelt over Jim between the big back wheels of the waggon.

I had an old racing mare that I used as a riding hack, following the team. In a minute I had her saddled and bridled; I tied the end of a half-full chaff-bag, shook the chaff into each end and dumped it on to the pommel as a cushion or buffer for Jim; I wrapped him in a blanket, and scrambled into the saddle with him.

The next minute we were stumbling down the steep bank, clattering and splashing over the crossing, and struggling up the opposite bank to the level. The mare, as I told you, was an old racer, but broken-winded—she must have run without wind after the first half mile. She had the old racing instinct in her strong, and whenever I rode in company I'd have to pull her hard else she'd race the other horse or burst. She ran low fore and aft, and was the easiest horse I ever rode. She ran like wheels on rails, with a bit of a tremble now and then—like a railway carriage—when she settled down to it.

The chaff-bag had slipped off, in the creek I suppose, and I let the bridle-rein go and held Jim up to me like a baby the whole way. Let the strongest man, who isn't used to it, hold a baby in one position for five minutes—and Jim was fairly heavy. But I never felt the ache in my arms that night—it must have gone before I was in a fit state of mind to feel it. And at home I'd often growled about being asked to hold the baby for a few minutes. I could never brood comfortably and nurse a baby at the same time. It was a ghostly moonlight night. There's no timber in the world so ghostly as the Australian Bush in moonlight—or just about daybreak. The all-shaped patches of moonlight falling between ragged, twisted boughs; the ghostly blue-white bark of the 'white-box' trees; a dead naked white ring-barked tree, or dead white stump starting out here and there, and the ragged patches of shade and light on the road that made anything, from the shape of a spotted bullock to a naked corpse laid out stark. Roads and tracks through the Bush made by moonlight—every one seeming straighter and clearer than the real one: you have to trust to your horse then. Sometimes the naked white trunk of a red stringy-bark tree, where a sheet of bark had been taken off, would start out like a ghost from the dark Bush. And dew or frost glistening on these things, according to the season. Now and again a great grey kangaroo, that had been feeding on a green patch down by the road, would start with a 'thump-thump', and away up the siding.

The Bush seemed full of ghosts that night—all going my way—and being left behind by the mare. Once I stopped to look at Jim: I just sat back and the mare 'propped'—she'd been a stock-horse, and was used to 'cutting-out'. I felt Jim's hands and forehead; he was in a burning fever. I bent forward, and the old mare settled down to it again. I kept saying out loud—and Mary and me often laughed about it (afterwards): 'He's limp yet!—Jim's limp yet!' (the words seemed jerked out of me by sheer fright)— 'He's limp yet!' till the mare's feet took it up. Then, just when I thought she was doing her best and racing her hardest, she suddenly started forward, like a cable tram gliding along on its own and the grip put on suddenly. It was just what she'd do when I'd be riding alone and a strange horse drew up from behind—the old racing instinct. I FELT the thing too! I felt as if a strange horse WAS there! And then— the words just jerked out of me by sheer funk—I started saying, 'Death is riding to-night!... Death is racing to-night!... Death is riding to-night!' till the hoofs took that up. And I believe the old mare felt the black horse at her side and was going to beat him or break her heart.

I was mad with anxiety and fright: I remember I kept saying, 'I'll be kinder to Mary after this! I'll take more notice of Jim!' and the rest of it.

I don't know how the old mare got up the last 'pinch'. She must have slackened pace, but I never noticed it: I just held Jim up to me and gripped the saddle with my knees—I remember the saddle jerked from the desperate jumps of her till I thought the girth would go. We topped the gap and were going down into a gully they called Dead Man's Hollow, and there, at the back of a ghostly clearing that opened from the road where there were some black-soil springs, was a long, low, oblong weatherboard-

and-shingle building, with blind, broken windows in the gable-ends, and a wide steep verandah roof slanting down almost to the level of the window-sills—there was something sinister about it, I thought—like the hat of a jail-bird slouched over his eyes. The place looked both deserted and haunted. I saw no light, but that was because of the moonlight outside. The mare turned in at the corner of the clearing to take a short cut to the shanty, and, as she struggled across some marshy ground, my heart kept jerking out the words, 'It's deserted! They've gone away! It's deserted!' The mare went round to the back and pulled up between the back door and a big bark-and-slab kitchen. Some one shouted from inside—

'Who's there?'

'It's me. Joe Wilson. I want your sister-in-law—I've got the boy—he's sick and dying!'

Brighten came out, pulling up his moleskins. 'What boy?' he asked.

'Here, take him,' I shouted, 'and let me get down.'

'What's the matter with him?' asked Brighten, and he seemed to hang back. And just as I made to get my leg over the saddle, Jim's head went back over my arm, he stiffened, and I saw his eyeballs turned up and glistening in the moonlight.

I felt cold all over then and sick in the stomach—but CLEAR-HEADED in a way: strange, wasn't it? I don't know why I didn't get down and rush into the kitchen to get a bath ready. I only felt as if the worst had come, and I wished it were over and gone. I even thought of Mary and the funeral.

Then a woman ran out of the house—a big, hard-looking woman. She had on a wrapper of some sort, and her feet were bare. She laid her hand on Jim, looked at his face, and then snatched him from me and ran into the kitchen—and me down and after her. As great good luck would have it, they had some dirty clothes on to boil in a kerosene tin—dish-cloths or something.

Brighten's sister-in-law dragged a tub out from under the table, wrenched the bucket off the hook, and dumped in the water, dish-cloths and all, snatched a can of cold water from a corner, dashed that in, and felt the water with her hand—holding Jim up to her hip all the time—and I won't say how he looked. She stood him in the tub and started dashing water over him, tearing off his clothes between the splashes.

'Here, that tin of mustard—there on the shelf!' she shouted to me.

She knocked the lid off the tin on the edge of the tub, and went on splashing and spanking Jim.

It seemed an eternity. And I? Why, I never thought clearer in my life. I felt cold-blooded—I felt as if I'd like an excuse to go outside till it was all over. I thought of Mary and the funeral—and wished that that was past. All this in a flash, as it were. I felt that it would be a great relief, and only wished the funeral was months past. I felt—well, altogether selfish. I only thought for myself.

Brighten's sister-in-law splashed and spanked him hard—hard enough to break his back I thought, and—after about half an hour it seemed—the end came: Jim's limbs relaxed, he slipped down into the tub, and the pupils of his eyes came down. They seemed dull and expressionless, like the eyes of a new baby, but he was back for the world again.

I dropped on the stool by the table.

'It's all right,' she said. 'It's all over now. I wasn't going to let him die.' I was only thinking, 'Well it's over now, but it will come on again. I wish it was over for good. I'm tired of it.'

She called to her sister, Mrs Brighten, a washed-out, helpless little fool of a woman, who'd been running in and out and whimpering all the time—

'Here, Jessie! bring the new white blanket off my bed. And you, Brighten, take some of that wood off the fire, and stuff something in that hole there to stop the draught.'

Brighten—he was a nuggety little hairy man with no expression to be seen for whiskers—had been running in with sticks and back logs from the wood-heap. He took the wood out, stuffed up the crack, and went inside and brought out a black bottle—got a cup from the shelf, and put both down near my elbow.

Mrs Brighten started to get some supper or breakfast, or whatever it was, ready. She had a clean cloth, and set the table tidily. I noticed that all the tins were polished bright (old coffee- and mustard-tins and the like, that they used instead of sugar-basins and tea-caddies and salt-cellars), and the kitchen was kept as clean as possible. She was all right at little things. I knew a haggard, worked-out Bushwoman who put her whole soul—or all she'd got left—into polishing old tins till they dazzled your eyes.

I didn't feel inclined for corned beef and damper, and post-and-rail tea. So I sat and squinted, when I thought she wasn't looking, at Brighten's sister-in-law. She was a big woman, her hands and feet were big, but well-shaped and all in proportion—they fitted her. She was a handsome woman—about forty I should think. She had a square chin, and a straight thin-lipped mouth—straight save for a hint of a turn down at the corners, which I fancied (and I have strange fancies) had been a sign of weakness in the days before she grew hard. There was no sign of weakness now. She had hard grey eyes and blue-black hair. She hadn't spoken yet. She didn't ask me how the boy took ill or I got there, or who or what I was— at least not until the next evening at tea-time.

She sat upright with Jim wrapped in the blanket and laid across her knees, with one hand under his neck and the other laid lightly on him, and she just rocked him gently.

She sat looking hard and straight before her, just as I've seen a tired needlewoman sit with her work in her lap, and look away back into the past. And Jim might have been the work in her lap, for all she seemed to think of him. Now and then she knitted her forehead and blinked.

Suddenly she glanced round and said—in a tone as if I was her husband and she didn't think much of me—

'Why don't you eat something?'

'Beg pardon?'

'Eat something!'

I drank some tea, and sneaked another look at her. I was beginning to feel more natural, and wanted Jim again, now that the colour was coming back into his face, and he didn't look like an unnaturally stiff and staring corpse. I felt a lump rising, and wanted to thank her. I sneaked another look at her.

She was staring straight before her,—I never saw a woman's face change so suddenly—I never saw a woman's eyes so haggard and hopeless. Then her great chest heaved twice, I heard her draw a long shuddering breath, like a knocked-out horse, and two great tears dropped from her wide open eyes down her cheeks like rain-drops on a face of stone. And in the firelight they seemed tinged with blood.

I looked away quick, feeling full up myself. And presently (I hadn't seen her look round) she said—

'Go to bed.'

'Beg pardon?' (Her face was the same as before the tears.)

'Go to bed. There's a bed made for you inside on the sofa.'

'But—the team—I must—'

'What?'

'The team. I left it at the camp. I must look to it.'

'Oh! Well, Brighten will ride down and bring it up in the morning—or send the half-caste. Now you go to bed, and get a good rest. The boy will be all right. I'll see to that.'

I went out—it was a relief to get out—and looked to the mare. Brighten had got her some corn* and chaff in a candle-box, but she couldn't eat yet. She just stood or hung resting one hind-leg and then the other, with her nose over the box—and she sobbed. I put my arms round her neck and my face down on her ragged mane, and cried for the second time since I was a boy.

* Maize or Indian corn—wheat is never called corn in Australia.—

As I started to go in I heard Brighten's sister-in-law say, suddenly and sharply—

'Take THAT away, Jessie.'

And presently I saw Mrs Brighten go into the house with the black bottle.

The moon had gone behind the range. I stood for a minute between the house and the kitchen and peeped in through the kitchen window.

She had moved away from the fire and sat near the table. She bent over Jim and held him up close to her and rocked herself to and fro.

I went to bed and slept till the next afternoon. I woke just in time to hear the tail-end of a conversation between Jim and Brighten's sister-in-law. He was asking her out to our place and she promising to come.

'And now,' says Jim, 'I want to go home to "muffer" in "The Same Ol' Fling".'

'What?'

Jim repeated.

'Oh! "The Same Old Thing",—the waggon.'

The rest of the afternoon I poked round the gullies with old Brighten, looking at some 'indications' (of the existence of gold) he had found. It was no use trying to 'pump' him concerning his sister-in-law; Brighten was an 'old hand', and had learned in the old Bush-ranging and cattle-stealing days to know nothing about other people's business. And, by the way, I noticed then that the more you talk and listen to a bad character, the more you lose your dislike for him.

I never saw such a change in a woman as in Brighten's sister-in-law that evening. She was bright and jolly, and seemed at least ten years younger. She bustled round and helped her sister to get tea ready. She rooted out some old china that Mrs Brighten had stowed away somewhere, and set the table as I seldom saw it set out there. She propped Jim up with pillows, and laughed and played with him like a great girl. She described Sydney and Sydney life as I'd never heard it described before; and she knew as much about the Bush and old digging days as I did. She kept old Brighten and me listening and laughing till nearly midnight. And she seemed quick to understand everything when I talked. If she wanted to explain anything that we hadn't seen, she wouldn't say that it was 'like a—like a'—and hesitate (you know what I mean); she'd hit the right thing on the head at once. A squatter with a very round, flaming red face and a white cork hat had gone by in the afternoon: she said it was 'like a mushroom on the rising moon.' She gave me a lot of good hints about children.

But she was quiet again next morning. I harnessed up, and she dressed Jim and gave him his breakfast, and made a comfortable place for him on the load with the 'possum rug and a spare pillow. She got up on the wheel to do it herself. Then was the awkward time. I'd half start to speak to her, and then turn away and go fixing up round the horses, and then make another false start to say good-bye. At last she took Jim up in her arms and kissed him, and lifted him on the wheel; but he put his arms tight round her neck, and kissed her—a thing Jim seldom did with anybody, except his mother, for he wasn't what you'd call an affectionate child,—he'd never more than offer his cheek to me, in his old-fashioned way. I'd got up the other side of the load to take him from her.

'Here, take him,' she said.

I saw his mouth twitching as I lifted him. Jim seldom cried nowadays—no matter how much he was hurt. I gained some time fixing Jim comfortable.

'You'd better make a start,' she said. 'You want to get home early with that boy.'

I got down and went round to where she stood. I held out my hand and tried to speak, but my voice went like an ungreased waggon wheel, and I gave it up, and only squeezed her hand.

'That's all right,' she said; then tears came into her eyes, and she suddenly put her hand on my shoulder and kissed me on the cheek. 'You be off—you're only a boy yourself. Take care of that boy; be kind to your wife, and take care of yourself.'

'Will you come to see us?'

'Some day,' she said.

I started the horses, and looked round once more. She was looking up at Jim, who was waving his hand to her from the top of the load. And I saw that haggard, hungry, hopeless look come into her eyes in spite of the tears.

I smoothed over that story and shortened it a lot, when I told it to Mary—I didn't want to upset her. But, some time after I brought Jim home from Gulgong, and while I was at home with the team for a few days, nothing would suit Mary but she must go over to Brighten's shanty and see Brighten's sister-in-law. So James drove her over one morning in the spring-cart: it was a long way, and they stayed at Brighten's overnight and didn't get back till late the next afternoon. I'd got the place in a pig-muck, as Mary said, 'doing for' myself, and I was having a snooze on the sofa when they got back. The first thing I remember was some one stroking my head and kissing me, and I heard Mary saying, 'My poor boy! My poor old boy!'

I sat up with a jerk. I thought that Jim had gone off again. But it seems that Mary was only referring to me. Then she started to pull grey hairs out of my head and put 'em in an empty match-box—to see how many she'd get. She used to do this when she felt a bit soft. I don't know what she said to Brighten's sister-in-law or what Brighten's sister-in-law said to her, but Mary was extra gentle for the next few days.

'Water Them Geraniums'

I

A Lonely Track

The time Mary and I shifted out into the Bush from Gulgong to 'settle on the land' at Lahey's Creek.

I'd sold the two tip-drays that I used for tank-sinking and dam-making, and I took the traps out in the waggon on top of a small load of rations and horse-feed that I was taking to a sheep-station out that way. Mary drove out in the spring-cart. You remember we left little Jim with his aunt in Gulgong till we got settled down. I'd sent James (Mary's brother) out the day before, on horseback, with two or three cows and some heifers and steers and calves we had, and I'd told him to clean up a bit, and make the hut as bright and cheerful as possible before Mary came.

We hadn't much in the way of furniture. There was the four-poster cedar bedstead that I bought before we were married, and Mary was rather proud of it: it had 'turned' posts and joints that bolted together. There was a plain hardwood table, that Mary called her 'ironing-table', upside down on top of the load, with the bedding and blankets between the legs; there were four of those common black kitchen-chairs—with apples painted on the hard board backs—that we used for the parlour; there was a cheap batten sofa with arms at the ends and turned rails between the uprights of the arms (we were a little proud of the turned rails); and there was the camp-oven, and the three-legged pot, and pans and buckets, stuck about the load and hanging under the tail-board of the waggon.

There was the little Wilcox & Gibb's sewing-machine—my present to Mary when we were married (and what a present, looking back to it!). There was a cheap little rocking-chair, and a looking-glass and some pictures that were presents from Mary's friends and sister. She had her mantel-shelf ornaments and crockery and nick-nacks packed away, in the linen and old clothes, in a big tub made of half a cask, and a box that had been Jim's cradle. The live stock was a cat in one box, and in another an old rooster, and three hens that formed cliques, two against one, turn about, as three of the same sex will do all over the world. I had my old cattle-dog, and of course a pup on the load—I always had a pup that I gave away, or sold and didn't get paid for, or had 'touched' (stolen) as soon as it was old enough. James had his three spidery, sneaking, thieving, cold-blooded kangaroo-dogs with him. I was taking out three months' provisions in the way of ration-sugar, tea, flour, and potatoes, &c.

I started early, and Mary caught up to me at Ryan's Crossing on Sandy Creek, where we boiled the billy and had some dinner.

Mary bustled about the camp and admired the scenery and talked too much, for her, and was extra cheerful, and kept her face turned from me as much as possible. I soon saw what was the matter. She'd been crying to herself coming along the road. I thought it was all on account of leaving little Jim behind for the first time. She told me that she couldn't make up her mind till the last moment to leave him, and that, a mile or two along the road, she'd have turned back for him, only that she knew her sister would laugh at her. She was always terribly anxious about the children.

We cheered each other up, and Mary drove with me the rest of the way to the creek, along the lonely branch track, across native-apple-tree flats. It was a dreary, hopeless track. There was no horizon, nothing but the rough ashen trunks of the gnarled and stunted trees in all directions, little or no undergrowth, and the ground, save for the coarse, brownish tufts of dead grass, as bare as the road, for it was a dry season: there had been no rain for months, and I wondered what I should do with the cattle if there wasn't more grass on the creek.

In this sort of country a stranger might travel for miles without seeming to have moved, for all the difference there is in the scenery. The new tracks were 'blazed'—that is, slices of bark cut off from both sides of trees, within sight of each other, in a line, to mark the track until the horses and wheel-marks made it plain. A smart Bushman, with a sharp tomahawk, can blaze a track as he rides. But a Bushman a little used to the country soon picks out differences amongst the trees, half unconsciously as it were, and so finds his way about.

Mary and I didn't talk much along this track—we couldn't have heard each other very well, anyway, for the 'clock-clock' of the waggon and the rattle of the cart over the hard lumpy ground. And I suppose we both began to feel pretty dismal as the shadows lengthened. I'd noticed lately that Mary and I had got out of the habit of talking to each other—noticed it in a vague sort of way that irritated me (as vague things will irritate one) when I thought of it. But then I thought, 'It won't last long—I'll make life brighter for her by-and-by.'

As we went along—and the track seemed endless—I got brooding, of course, back into the past. And I feel now, when it's too late, that Mary must have been thinking that way too. I thought of my early boyhood, of the hard life of 'grubbin'' and 'milkin'' and 'fencin'' and 'ploughin'' and 'ring-barkin'', &c.,

and all for nothing. The few months at the little bark-school, with a teacher who couldn't spell. The cursed ambition or craving that tortured my soul as a boy—ambition or craving for—I didn't know what for! For something better and brighter, anyhow. And I made the life harder by reading at night.

It all passed before me as I followed on in the waggon, behind Mary in the spring-cart. I thought of these old things more than I thought of her. She had tried to help me to better things. And I tried too—I had the energy of half-a-dozen men when I saw a road clear before me, but shied at the first check. Then I brooded, or dreamed of making a home—that one might call a home—for Mary—some day. Ah, well!—

And what was Mary thinking about, along the lonely, changeless miles? I never thought of that. Of her kind, careless, gentleman father, perhaps. Of her girlhood. Of her homes—not the huts and camps she lived in with me. Of our future?—she used to plan a lot, and talk a good deal of our future—but not lately. These things didn't strike me at the time—I was so deep in my own brooding. Did she think now—did she begin to feel now that she had made a great mistake and thrown away her life, but must make the best of it? This might have roused me, had I thought of it. But whenever I thought Mary was getting indifferent towards me, I'd think, 'I'll soon win her back. We'll be sweethearts again—when things brighten up a bit.'

It's an awful thing to me, now I look back to it, to think how far apart we had grown, what strangers we were to each other. It seems, now, as though we had been sweethearts long years before, and had parted, and had never really met since.

The sun was going down when Mary called out—

'There's our place, Joe!'

She hadn't seen it before, and somehow it came new and with a shock to me, who had been out here several times. Ahead, through the trees to the right, was a dark green clump of the oaks standing out of the creek, darker for the dead grey grass and blue-grey bush on the barren ridge in the background. Across the creek (it was only a deep, narrow gutter—a water-course with a chain of water-holes after rain), across on the other bank, stood the hut, on a narrow flat between the spur and the creek, and a little higher than this side. The land was much better than on our old selection, and there was good soil along the creek on both sides: I expected a rush of selectors out here soon. A few acres round the hut was cleared and fenced in by a light two-rail fence of timber split from logs and saplings. The man who took up this selection left it because his wife died here.

It was a small oblong hut built of split slabs, and he had roofed it with shingles which he split in spare times. There was no verandah, but I built one later on. At the end of the house was a big slab-and-bark shed, bigger than the hut itself, with a kitchen, a skillion for tools, harness, and horse-feed, and a spare bedroom partitioned off with sheets of bark and old chaff-bags. The house itself was floored roughly, with cracks between the boards; there were cracks between the slabs all round—though he'd nailed strips of tin, from old kerosene-tins, over some of them; the partitioned-off bedroom was lined with old chaff-bags with newspapers pasted over them for wall-paper. There was no ceiling, calico or otherwise, and we could see the round pine rafters and battens, and the under ends of the shingles. But ceilings make a hut hot and harbour insects and reptiles—snakes sometimes. There was one small glass window in the 'dining-room' with three panes and a sheet of greased paper, and the rest were rough wooden shutters. There was a pretty good cow-yard and calf-pen, and—that was about all. There was no dam or tank (I made one later on); there was a water-cask, with the hoops falling off and the staves gaping, at the corner of the house, and spouting, made of lengths of bent tin, ran round under the eaves. Water from a new shingle roof is wine-red for a year or two, and water from a stringy-bark roof is like tan-water for years. In dry weather the selector had got his house water from a cask sunk in the gravel at the bottom of the deepest water-hole in the creek. And the longer the drought lasted, the farther he had to go down the creek for his water, with a cask on a cart, and take his cows to drink, if he had any. Four, five, six, or seven miles—even ten miles to water is nothing in some places.

James hadn't found himself called upon to do more than milk old 'Spot' (the grandmother cow of our mob), pen the calf at night, make a fire in the kitchen, and sweep out the house with a bough. He helped me unharness and water and feed the horses, and then started to get the furniture off the waggon and into the house. James wasn't lazy—so long as one thing didn't last too long; but he was too uncomfortably practical and matter-of-fact for me. Mary and I had some tea in the kitchen. The kitchen was permanently furnished with a table of split slabs, adzed smooth on top, and supported by four stakes driven into the ground, a three-legged stool and a block of wood, and two long stools made of half-round slabs (sapling trunks split in halves) with auger-holes bored in the round side and sticks stuck into them for legs. The floor was of clay; the chimney of slabs and tin; the fireplace was about eight feet wide, lined with clay, and with a blackened pole across, with sooty chains and wire hooks on it for the pots.

Mary didn't seem able to eat. She sat on the three-legged stool near the fire, though it was warm weather, and kept her face turned from me. Mary was still pretty, but not the little dumpling she had been: she was thinner now. She had big dark hazel eyes that shone a little too much when she was pleased or excited. I thought at times that there was something very German about her expression; also something aristocratic about the turn of her nose, which nipped in at the nostrils when she spoke. There was nothing aristocratic about me. Mary was German in figure and walk. I used sometimes to call her 'Little Duchy' and 'Pigeon Toes'. She had a will of her own, as shown sometimes by the obstinate knit in her forehead between the eyes.

Mary sat still by the fire, and presently I saw her chin tremble.

'What is it, Mary?'

She turned her face farther from me. I felt tired, disappointed, and irritated—suffering from a reaction.

'Now, what is it, Mary?' I asked; 'I'm sick of this sort of thing. Haven't you got everything you wanted? You've had your own way. What's the matter with you now?'

'You know very well, Joe.'

'But I DON'T know,' I said. I knew too well.

She said nothing.

'Look here, Mary,' I said, putting my hand on her shoulder, 'don't go on like that; tell me what's the matter?'

'It's only this,' she said suddenly, 'I can't stand this life here; it will kill me!'

I had a pannikin of tea in my hand, and I banged it down on the table.

'This is more than a man can stand!' I shouted. 'You know very well that it was you that dragged me out here. You run me on to this! Why weren't you content to stay in Gulgong?'

'And what sort of a place was Gulgong, Joe?' asked Mary quietly.

(I thought even then in a flash what sort of a place Gulgong was. A wretched remnant of a town on an abandoned goldfield. One street, each side of the dusty main road; three or four one-storey square brick cottages with hip roofs of galvanised iron that glared in the heat—four rooms and a passage—the police-station, bank-manager and schoolmaster's cottages, &c. Half-a-dozen tumble-down weather-board shanties—the three pubs., the two stores, and the post-office. The town tailing off into weather-board boxes with tin tops, and old bark huts—relics of the digging days—propped up by many rotting poles. The men, when at home, mostly asleep or droning over their pipes or hanging about the verandah posts of the pubs., saying, "Ullo, Bill!" or "Ullo, Jim!"—or sometimes drunk. The women, mostly hags, who blackened each other's and girls' characters with their tongues, and criticised the aristocracy's washing hung out on the line: 'And the colour of the clothes! Does that woman wash her clothes at all? or only soak 'em and hang 'em out?'—that was Gulgong.)

'Well, why didn't you come to Sydney, as I wanted you to?' I asked Mary.

'You know very well, Joe,' said Mary quietly.

(I knew very well, but the knowledge only maddened me. I had had an idea of getting a billet in one of the big wool-stores—I was a fair wool expert—but Mary was afraid of the drink. I could keep well away from it so long as I worked hard in the Bush. I had gone to Sydney twice since I met Mary, once before we were married, and she forgave me when I came back; and once afterwards. I got a billet there then, and was going to send for her in a month. After eight weeks she raised the money somehow and came to Sydney and brought me home. I got pretty low down that time.)

'But, Mary,' I said, 'it would have been different this time. You would have been with me. I can take a glass now or leave it alone.'

'As long as you take a glass there is danger,' she said.

'Well, what did you want to advise me to come out here for, if you can't stand it? Why didn't you stay where you were?' I asked.

'Well,' she said, 'why weren't you more decided?'

I'd sat down, but I jumped to my feet then.

'Good God!' I shouted, 'this is more than any man can stand. I'll chuck it all up! I'm damned well sick and tired of the whole thing.'

'So am I, Joe,' said Mary wearily.

We quarrelled badly then—that first hour in our new home. I know now whose fault it was.

I got my hat and went out and started to walk down the creek. I didn't feel bitter against Mary—I had spoken too cruelly to her to feel that way. Looking back, I could see plainly that if I had taken her advice all through, instead of now and again, things would have been all right with me. I had come away and left her crying in the hut, and James telling her, in a brotherly way, that it was all her fault. The trouble was that I never liked to 'give in' or go half-way to make it up—not half-way—it was all the way or nothing with our natures.

'If I don't make a stand now,' I'd say, 'I'll never be master. I gave up the reins when I got married, and I'll have to get them back again.'

What women some men are! But the time came, and not many years after, when I stood by the bed where Mary lay, white and still; and, amongst other things, I kept saying, 'I'll give in, Mary—I'll give in,' and then I'd laugh. They thought that I was raving mad, and took me from the room. But that time was to come.

As I walked down the creek track in the moonlight the question rang in my ears again, as it had done when I first caught sight of the house that evening—

'Why did I bring her here?'

I was not fit to 'go on the land'. The place was only fit for some stolid German, or Scotsman, or even Englishman and his wife, who had no ambition but to bullock and make a farm of the place. I had only drifted here through carelessness, brooding, and discontent.

I walked on and on till I was more than half-way to the only neighbours—a wretched selector's family, about four miles down the creek,—and I thought I'd go on to the house and see if they had any fresh meat.

A mile or two farther I saw the loom of the bark hut they lived in, on a patchy clearing in the scrub, and heard the voice of the selector's wife—I had seen her several times: she was a gaunt, haggard Bushwoman, and, I supposed, the reason why she hadn't gone mad through hardship and loneliness was that she hadn't either the brains or the memory to go farther than she could see through the trunks of the 'apple-trees'.

'You, An-nay!' (Annie.)

'Ye-es' (from somewhere in the gloom).

'Didn't I tell yer to water them geraniums!'

'Well, didn't I?'

'Don't tell lies or I'll break yer young back!'

'I did, I tell yer—the water won't soak inter the ashes.'

Geraniums were the only flowers I saw grow in the drought out there. I remembered this woman had a few dirty grey-green leaves behind some sticks against the bark wall near the door; and in spite of the sticks the fowls used to get in and scratch beds under the geraniums, and scratch dust over them, and ashes were thrown there—with an idea of helping the flower, I suppose; and greasy dish-water, when fresh water was scarce—till you might as well try to water a dish of fat.

Then the woman's voice again—

'You, Tom-may!' (Tommy.)

Silence, save for an echo on the ridge.

'Y-o-u, T-o-m-MAY!'

'Ye-e-s!' shrill shriek from across the creek.

'Didn't I tell you to ride up to them new people and see if they want any meat or any think?' in one long screech.

'Well—I karnt find the horse.'

'Well-find-it-first-think-in-the-morning and. And-don't-forgit-to-tell-Mrs-Wi'son-that-mother'll-be-up-as-soon-as-she-can.'

I didn't feel like going to the woman's house that night. I felt—and the thought came like a whip-stroke on my heart—that this was what Mary would come to if I left her here.

I turned and started to walk home, fast. I'd made up my mind. I'd take Mary straight back to Gulgong in the morning—I forgot about the load I had to take to the sheep station. I'd say, 'Look here, Girlie' (that's what I used to call her), 'we'll leave this wretched life; we'll leave the Bush for ever! We'll go to Sydney, and I'll be a man! and work my way up.' And I'd sell waggon, horses, and all, and go.

When I got to the hut it was lighted up. Mary had the only kerosene lamp, a slush lamp, and two tallow candles going. She had got both rooms washed out—to James's disgust, for he had to move the furniture and boxes about. She had a lot of things unpacked on the table; she had laid clean newspapers on the mantel-shelf—a slab on two pegs over the fireplace—and put the little wooden clock in the centre and some of the ornaments on each side, and was tacking a strip of vandyked American oil-cloth round the rough edge of the slab.

'How does that look, Joe? We'll soon get things ship-shape.'

I kissed her, but she had her mouth full of tacks. I went out in the kitchen, drank a pint of cold tea, and sat down.

Somehow I didn't feel satisfied with the way things had gone.

II

'Past Carin''

Next morning things looked a lot brighter. Things always look brighter in the morning—more so in the Australian Bush, I should think, than in most other places. It is when the sun goes down on the dark bed of the lonely Bush, and the sunset flashes like a sea of fire and then fades, and then glows out again, like a bank of coals, and then burns away to ashes—it is then that old things come home to one. And strange, new-old things too, that haunt and depress you terribly, and that you can't understand. I often think how, at sunset, the past must come home to new-chum blacksheep, sent out to Australia and drifted into the Bush. I used to think that they couldn't have much brains, or the loneliness would drive them mad.

I'd decided to let James take the team for a trip or two. He could drive alright; he was a better business man, and no doubt would manage better than me—as long as the novelty lasted; and I'd stay at home for a week or so, till Mary got used to the place, or I could get a girl from somewhere to come and stay with her. The first weeks or few months of loneliness are the worst, as a rule, I believe, as they say the first weeks in jail are—I was never there. I know it's so with tramping or hard graft*: the first day or two are twice as hard as any of the rest. But, for my part, I could never get used to loneliness and dulness; the last days used to be the worst with me: then I'd have to make a move, or drink. When you've been too much and too long alone in a lonely place, you begin to do queer things and think queer thoughts— provided you have any imagination at all. You'll sometimes sit of an evening and watch the lonely track, by the hour, for a horseman or a cart or some one that's never likely to come that way—some one, or a stranger, that you can't and don't really expect to see. I think that most men who have been alone in the Bush for any length of time—and married couples too—are more or less mad. With married couples it is generally the husband who is painfully shy and awkward when strangers come. The woman seems to stand the loneliness better, and can hold her own with strangers, as a rule. It's only afterwards, and looking back, that you see how queer you got. Shepherds and boundary-riders, who are alone for months, MUST have their periodical spree, at the nearest shanty, else they'd go raving mad. Drink is the only break in the awful monotony, and the yearly or half-yearly spree is the only thing they've got to look forward to: it keeps their minds fixed on something definite ahead.

* 'Graft', work. The term is now applied, in Australia, to all sorts of work, from bullock-driving to writing poetry.

But Mary kept her head pretty well through the first months of loneliness. WEEKS, rather, I should say, for it wasn't as bad as it might have been farther up-country: there was generally some one came of a Sunday afternoon—a spring-cart with a couple of women, or maybe a family,—or a lanky shy Bush native or two on lanky shy horses. On a quiet Sunday, after I'd brought Jim home, Mary would dress him and herself—just the same as if we were in town—and make me get up on one end and put on a collar and take her and Jim for a walk along the creek. She said she wanted to keep me civilised. She tried to make a gentleman of me for years, but gave it up gradually.

Well. It was the first morning on the creek: I was greasing the waggon-wheels, and James out after the horse, and Mary hanging out clothes, in an old print dress and a big ugly white hood, when I heard her being hailed as 'Hi, missus!' from the front slip-rails.

It was a boy on horseback. He was a light-haired, very much freckled boy of fourteen or fifteen, with a small head, but with limbs, especially his bare sun-blotched shanks, that might have belonged to a grown man. He had a good face and frank grey eyes. An old, nearly black cabbage-tree hat rested on the butts of his ears, turning them out at right angles from his head, and rather dirty sprouts they were. He wore a dirty torn Crimean shirt; and a pair of man's moleskin trousers rolled up above the knees, with the wide waistband gathered under a greenhide belt. I noticed, later on, that, even when he wore trousers short enough for him, he always rolled 'em up above the knees when on horseback, for some reason of his own: to suggest leggings, perhaps, for he had them rolled up in all weathers, and he wouldn't have bothered to save them from the sweat of the horse, even if that horse ever sweated.

He was seated astride a three-bushel bag thrown across the ridge-pole of a big grey horse, with a coffin-shaped head, and built astern something after the style of a roughly put up hip-roofed box-bark humpy.* His colour was like old box-bark, too, a dirty bluish-grey; and, one time, when I saw his rump looming out of the scrub, I really thought it was some old shepherd's hut that I hadn't noticed there before. When he cantered it was like the humpy starting off on its corner-posts.

* 'Humpy', a rough hut.

'Are you Mrs Wilson?' asked the boy.

'Yes,' said Mary.

'Well, mother told me to ride acrost and see if you wanted anythink. We killed lars' night, and I've fetched a piece er cow.'

'Piece of WHAT?' asked Mary.

He grinned, and handed a sugar-bag across the rail with something heavy in the bottom of it, that nearly jerked Mary's arm out when she took it. It was a piece of beef, that looked as if it had been cut off with a wood-axe, but it was fresh and clean.

'Oh, I'm so glad!' cried Mary. She was always impulsive, save to me sometimes. 'I was just wondering where we were going to get any fresh meat. How kind of your mother! Tell her I'm very much obliged to her indeed.' And she felt behind her for a poor little purse she had. 'And now—how much did your mother say it would be?'

The boy blinked at her, and scratched his head.

'How much will it be,' he repeated, puzzled. 'Oh—how much does it weigh I-s'pose-yer-mean. Well, it ain't been weighed at all—we ain't got no scales. A butcher does all that sort of think. We just kills it, and cooks it, and eats it—and goes by guess. What won't keep we salts down in the cask. I reckon it weighs about a ton by the weight of it if yer wanter know. Mother thought that if she sent any more it would go bad before you could scoff it. I can't see—'

'Yes, yes,' said Mary, getting confused. 'But what I want to know is, how do you manage when you sell it?'

He glared at her, and scratched his head. 'Sell it? Why, we only goes halves in a steer with some one, or sells steers to the butcher—or maybe some meat to a party of fencers or surveyors, or tank-sinkers, or them sorter people—'

'Yes, yes; but what I want to know is, how much am I to send your mother for this?'

'How much what?'

'Money, of course, you stupid boy,' said Mary. 'You seem a very stupid boy.'

Then he saw what she was driving at. He began to fling his heels convulsively against the sides of his horse, jerking his body backward and forward at the same time, as if to wind up and start some clockwork machinery inside the horse, that made it go, and seemed to need repairing or oiling.

'We ain't that sorter people, missus,' he said. 'We don't sell meat to new people that come to settle here.' Then, jerking his thumb contemptuously towards the ridges, 'Go over ter Wall's if yer wanter buy meat; they sell meat ter strangers.' (Wall was the big squatter over the ridges.)

'Oh!' said Mary, 'I'm SO sorry. Thank your mother for me. She IS kind.'

'Oh, that's nothink. She said to tell yer she'll be up as soon as she can. She'd have come up yisterday evening—she thought yer'd feel lonely comin' new to a place like this—but she couldn't git up.'

The machinery inside the old horse showed signs of starting. You almost heard the wooden joints CREAK as he lurched forward, like an old propped-up humpy when the rotting props give way; but at the sound of Mary's voice he settled back on his foundations again. It must have been a very poor selection that couldn't afford a better spare horse than that.

'Reach me that lump er wood, will yer, missus?' said the boy, and he pointed to one of my 'spreads' (for the team-chains) that lay inside the fence. 'I'll fling it back agin over the fence when I git this ole cow started.'

'But wait a minute—I've forgotten your mother's name,' said Mary.

He grabbed at his thatch impatiently. 'Me mother—oh!—the old woman's name's Mrs Spicer. (Git up, karnt yer!)' He twisted himself round, and brought the stretcher down on one of the horse's 'points' (and he had many) with a crack that must have jarred his wrist.

'Do you go to school?' asked Mary. There was a three-days-a-week school over the ridges at Wall's station.

'No!' he jerked out, keeping his legs going. 'Me—why I'm going on fur fifteen. The last teacher at Wall's finished me. I'm going to Queensland next month drovin'.' (Queensland border was over three hundred miles away.)

'Finished you? How?' asked Mary.

'Me edgercation, of course! How do yer expect me to start this horse when yer keep talkin'?'

He split the 'spread' over the horse's point, threw the pieces over the fence, and was off, his elbows and legs flinging wildly, and the old saw-stool lumbering along the road like an old working bullock trying a canter. That horse wasn't a trotter.

And next month he DID start for Queensland. He was a younger son and a surplus boy on a wretched, poverty-stricken selection; and as there was 'northin' doin'' in the district, his father (in a burst of fatherly kindness, I suppose) made him a present of the old horse and a new pair of Blucher boots, and I gave him an old saddle and a coat, and he started for the Never-Never Country.

And I'll bet he got there. But I'm doubtful if the old horse did.

Mary gave the boy five shillings, and I don't think he had anything more except a clean shirt and an extra pair of white cotton socks.

'Spicer's farm' was a big bark humpy on a patchy clearing in the native apple-tree scrub. The clearing was fenced in by a light 'dog-legged' fence (a fence of sapling poles resting on forks and X-shaped uprights), and the dusty ground round the house was almost entirely covered with cattle-dung. There was no attempt at cultivation when I came to live on the creek; but there were old furrow-marks amongst the stumps of another shapeless patch in the scrub near the hut. There was a wretched sapling cow-yard and calf-pen, and a cow-bail with one sheet of bark over it for shelter. There was no dairy to be seen, and I suppose the milk was set in one of the two skillion rooms, or lean-to's behind the hut,— the other was 'the boys' bedroom'. The Spicers kept a few cows and steers, and had thirty or forty sheep. Mrs Spicer used to drive down the creek once a-week, in her rickety old spring-cart, to Cobborah, with butter and eggs. The hut was nearly as bare inside as it was out—just a frame of 'round-timber' (sapling poles) covered with bark. The furniture was permanent (unless you rooted it up), like in our kitchen: a rough slab table on stakes driven into the ground, and seats made the same way. Mary told me afterwards that the beds in the bag-and-bark partitioned-off room ['mother's bedroom'] were simply poles laid side by side on cross-pieces supported by stakes driven into the ground, with straw mattresses and some worn-out bed-clothes. Mrs Spicer had an old patchwork quilt, in rags, and the remains of a white one, and Mary said it was pitiful to see how these things would be spread over the beds—to hide them as much as possible—when she went down there. A packing-case, with something like an old print skirt draped round it, and a cracked looking-glass (without a frame) on top, was the dressing-table. There were a couple of gin-cases for a wardrobe. The boys' beds were three-bushel bags stretched between poles fastened to uprights. The floor was the original surface, tramped hard, worn uneven with much sweeping, and with puddles in rainy weather where the roof leaked. Mrs Spicer used to stand old tins, dishes, and buckets under as many of the leaks as she could. The saucepans, kettles, and boilers were old kerosene-tins and billies. They used kerosene-tins, too, cut longways in halves, for setting the milk in. The plates and cups were of tin; there were two or three cups without saucers, and a crockery plate or two—also two mugs, cracked and without handles, one with 'For a Good Boy' and the other with 'For a Good Girl' on it; but all these were kept on the mantel-shelf for ornament and for company. They were the only ornaments in the house, save a little wooden clock that hadn't gone for years. Mrs Spicer had a superstition that she had 'some things packed away from the children.'

The pictures were cut from old copies of the 'Illustrated Sydney News' and pasted on to the bark. I remember this, because I remembered, long ago, the Spencers, who were our neighbours when I was a boy, had the walls of their bedroom covered with illustrations of the American Civil War, cut from illustrated London papers, and I used to 'sneak' into 'mother's bedroom' with Fred Spencer whenever we got the chance, and gloat over the prints. I gave him a blade of a pocket-knife once, for taking me in there.

I saw very little of Spicer. He was a big, dark, dark-haired and whiskered man. I had an idea that he wasn't a selector at all, only a 'dummy' for the squatter of the Cobborah run. You see, selectors were allowed to take up land on runs, or pastoral leases. The squatters kept them off as much as possible, by all manner of dodges and paltry persecution. The squatter would get as much freehold as he could afford, 'select' as much land as the law allowed one man to take up, and then employ dummies (dummy selectors) to take up bits of land that he fancied about his run, and hold them for him.

Spicer seemed gloomy and unsociable. He was seldom at home. He was generally supposed to be away shearin', or fencin', or workin' on somebody's station. It turned out that the last six months he was away it was on the evidence of a cask of beef and a hide with the brand cut out, found in his camp on a fencing contract up-country, and which he and his mates couldn't account for satisfactorily, while the squatter could. Then the family lived mostly on bread and honey, or bread and treacle, or bread and dripping, and tea. Every ounce of butter and every egg was needed for the market, to keep them in flour, tea, and sugar. Mary found that out, but couldn't help them much—except by 'stuffing' the children with bread and meat or bread and jam whenever they came up to our place—for Mrs Spicer was proud with the pride that lies down in the end and turns its face to the wall and dies.

Once, when Mary asked Annie, the eldest girl at home, if she was hungry, she denied it—but she looked it. A ragged mite she had with her explained things. The little fellow said—

'Mother told Annie not to say we was hungry if yer asked; but if yer give us anythink to eat, we was to take it an' say thenk yer, Mrs Wilson.'

'I wouldn't 'a' told yer a lie; but I thought Jimmy would split on me, Mrs Wilson,' said Annie. 'Thenk yer, Mrs Wilson.'

She was not a big woman. She was gaunt and flat-chested, and her face was 'burnt to a brick', as they say out there. She had brown eyes, nearly red, and a little wild-looking at times, and a sharp face—ground sharp by hardship—the cheeks drawn in. She had an expression like—well, like a woman who had been very curious and suspicious at one time, and wanted to know everybody's business and hear everything, and had lost all her curiosity, without losing the expression or the quick suspicious movements of the head. I don't suppose you understand. I can't explain it any other way. She was not more than forty.

I remember the first morning I saw her. I was going up the creek to look at the selection for the first time, and called at the hut to see if she had a bit of fresh mutton, as I had none and was sick of 'corned beef'.

'Yes—of—course,' she said, in a sharp nasty tone, as if to say, 'Is there anything more you want while the shop's open?' I'd met just the same sort of woman years before while I was carrying swag between the shearing-sheds in the awful scrubs out west of the Darling river, so I didn't turn on my heels and walk away. I waited for her to speak again.

'Come—inside,' she said, 'and sit down. I see you've got the waggon outside. I s'pose your name's Wilson, ain't it? You're thinkin' about takin' on Harry Marshfield's selection up the creek, so I heard. Wait till I fry you a chop and boil the billy.'

Her voice sounded, more than anything else, like a voice coming out of a phonograph—I heard one in Sydney the other day—and not like a voice coming out of her. But sometimes when she got outside her everyday life on this selection she spoke in a sort of—in a sort of lost groping-in-the-dark kind of voice.

She didn't talk much this time—just spoke in a mechanical way of the drought, and the hard times, 'an' butter 'n' eggs bein' down, an' her husban' an' eldest son bein' away, an' that makin' it so hard for her.'

I don't know how many children she had. I never got a chance to count them, for they were nearly all small, and shy as piccaninnies, and used to run and hide when anybody came. They were mostly nearly as black as piccaninnies too. She must have averaged a baby a-year for years—and God only knows how she got over her confinements! Once, they said, she only had a black gin with her. She had an elder boy and girl, but she seldom spoke of them. The girl, 'Liza', was 'in service in Sydney.' I'm afraid I knew what that meant. The elder son was 'away'. He had been a bit of a favourite round there, it seemed.

Some one might ask her, 'How's your son Jack, Mrs Spicer?' or, 'Heard of Jack lately? and where is he now?'

'Oh, he's somewheres up country,' she'd say in the 'groping' voice, or 'He's drovin' in Queenslan',' or 'Shearin' on the Darlin' the last time I heerd from him.' 'We ain't had a line from him since—les' see—since Chris'mas 'fore last.'

And she'd turn her haggard eyes in a helpless, hopeless sort of way towards the west—towards 'up-country' and 'Out-Back'.*

* 'Out-Back' is always west of the Bushman, no matter how far out he be.

The eldest girl at home was nine or ten, with a little old face and lines across her forehead: she had an older expression than her mother. Tommy went to Queensland, as I told you. The eldest son at home, Bill (older than Tommy), was 'a bit wild.'

I've passed the place in smothering hot mornings in December, when the droppings about the cow-yard had crumpled to dust that rose in the warm, sickly, sunrise wind, and seen that woman at work in the cow-yard, 'bailing up' and leg-roping cows, milking, or hauling at a rope round the neck of a half-grown calf that was too strong for her (and she was tough as fencing-wire), or humping great buckets of sour milk to the pigs or the 'poddies' (hand-fed calves) in the pen. I'd get off the horse and give her a hand sometimes with a young steer, or a cranky old cow that wouldn't 'bail-up' and threatened her with her horns. She'd say—

'Thenk yer, Mr Wilson. Do yer think we're ever goin' to have any rain?'

I've ridden past the place on bitter black rainy mornings in June or July, and seen her trudging about the yard—that was ankle-deep in black liquid filth—with an old pair of Blucher boots on, and an old coat of her husband's, or maybe a three-bushel bag over her shoulders. I've seen her climbing on the roof by means of the water-cask at the corner, and trying to stop a leak by shoving a piece of tin in under the bark. And when I'd fixed the leak—

'Thenk yer, Mr Wilson. This drop of rain's a blessin'! Come in and have a dry at the fire and I'll make yer a cup of tea.' And, if I was in a hurry, 'Come in, man alive! Come in! and dry yerself a bit till the rain holds up. Yer can't go home like this! Yer'll git yer death o' cold.'

I've even seen her, in the terrible drought, climbing she-oaks and apple-trees by a makeshift ladder, and awkwardly lopping off boughs to feed the starving cattle.

'Jist tryin' ter keep the milkers alive till the rain comes.'

They said that when the pleuro-pneumonia was in the district and amongst her cattle she bled and physicked them herself, and fed those that were down with slices of half-ripe pumpkins (from a crop that had failed).

'An', one day,' she told Mary, 'there was a big barren heifer (that we called Queen Elizabeth) that was down with the ploorer. She'd been down for four days and hadn't moved, when one mornin' I dumped some wheaten chaff—we had a few bags that Spicer brought home—I dumped it in front of her nose, an'—would yer b'lieve me, Mrs Wilson?—she stumbled onter her feet an' chased me all the way to the house! I had to pick up me skirts an' run! Wasn't it redic'lus?'

They had a sense of the ridiculous, most of those poor sun-dried Bushwomen. I fancy that that helped save them from madness.

'We lost nearly all our milkers,' she told Mary. 'I remember one day Tommy came running to the house and screamed: 'Marther! [mother] there's another milker down with the ploorer!' Jist as if it was great news. Well, Mrs Wilson, I was dead-beat, an' I giv' in. I jist sat down to have a good cry, and felt for my han'kerchief—it WAS a rag of a han'kerchief, full of holes (all me others was in the wash). Without seein' what I was doin' I put me finger through one hole in the han'kerchief an' me thumb through the other, and poked me fingers into me eyes, instead of wipin' them. Then I had to laugh.'

There's a story that once, when the Bush, or rather grass, fires were out all along the creek on Spicer's side, Wall's station hands were up above our place, trying to keep the fire back from the boundary, and towards evening one of the men happened to think of the Spicers: they saw smoke down that way. Spicer was away from home, and they had a small crop of wheat, nearly ripe, on the selection.

'My God! that poor devil of a woman will be burnt out, if she ain't already!' shouted young Billy Wall. 'Come along, three or four of you chaps'—(it was shearing-time, and there were plenty of men on the station).

They raced down the creek to Spicer's, and were just in time to save the wheat. She had her sleeves tucked up, and was beating out the burning grass with a bough. She'd been at it for an hour, and was as black as a gin, they said. She only said when they'd turned the fire: 'Thenk yer! Wait an' I'll make some tea.'

After tea the first Sunday she came to see us, Mary asked—

'Don't you feel lonely, Mrs Spicer, when your husband goes away?'

'Well—no, Mrs Wilson,' she said in the groping sort of voice. 'I uster, once. I remember, when we lived on the Cudgeegong river—we lived in a brick house then—the first time Spicer had to go away from home I nearly fretted my eyes out. And he was only goin' shearin' for a month. I muster bin a fool; but then we were only jist married a little while. He's been away drovin' in Queenslan' as long as eighteen months at a time since then. But' (her voice seemed to grope in the dark more than ever) 'I don't mind,—I somehow seem to have got past carin'. Besides—besides, Spicer was a very different man then to what he is now. He's got so moody and gloomy at home, he hardly ever speaks.'

Mary sat silent for a minute thinking. Then Mrs Spicer roused herself—

'Oh, I don't know what I'm talkin' about! You mustn't take any notice of me, Mrs Wilson,—I don't often go on like this. I do believe I'm gittin' a bit ratty at times. It must be the heat and the dulness.'

But once or twice afterwards she referred to a time 'when Spicer was a different man to what he was now.'

I walked home with her a piece along the creek. She said nothing for a long time, and seemed to be thinking in a puzzled way. Then she said suddenly—

'What-did-you-bring-her-here-for? She's only a girl.'

'I beg pardon, Mrs Spicer.'

'Oh, I don't know what I'm talkin' about! I b'lieve I'm gittin' ratty. You mustn't take any notice of me, Mr Wilson.'

She wasn't much company for Mary; and often, when she had a child with her, she'd start taking notice of the baby while Mary was talking, which used to exasperate Mary. But poor Mrs Spicer couldn't help it, and she seemed to hear all the same.

Her great trouble was that she 'couldn't git no reg'lar schoolin' for the children.'

'I learns 'em at home as much as I can. But I don't git a minute to call me own; an' I'm ginerally that dead-beat at night that I'm fit for nothink.'

Mary had some of the children up now and then later on, and taught them a little. When she first offered to do so, Mrs Spicer laid hold of the handiest youngster and said—

'There—do you hear that? Mrs Wilson is goin' to teach yer, an' it's more than yer deserve!' (the youngster had been 'cryin'' over something). 'Now, go up an' say "Thenk yer, Mrs Wilson." And if yer ain't good, and don't do as she tells yer, I'll break every bone in yer young body!'

The poor little devil stammered something, and escaped.

The children were sent by turns over to Wall's to Sunday-school. When Tommy was at home he had a new pair of elastic-side boots, and there was no end of rows about them in the family—for the mother made him lend them to his sister Annie, to go to Sunday-school in, in her turn. There were only about three pairs of anyway decent boots in the family, and these were saved for great occasions. The children were always as clean and tidy as possible when they came to our place.

And I think the saddest and most pathetic sight on the face of God's earth is the children of very poor people made to appear well: the broken worn-out boots polished or greased, the blackened (inked) pieces of string for laces; the clean patched pinafores over the wretched threadbare frocks. Behind the little row of children hand-in-hand—and no matter where they are—I always see the worn face of the mother.

Towards the end of the first year on the selection our little girl came. I'd sent Mary to Gulgong for four months that time, and when she came back with the baby Mrs Spicer used to come up pretty often. She came up several times when Mary was ill, to lend a hand. She wouldn't sit down and condole with Mary, or waste her time asking questions, or talking about the time when she was ill herself. She'd take off her hat—a shapeless little lump of black straw she wore for visiting—give her hair a quick brush back with the palms of her hands, roll up her sleeves, and set to work to 'tidy up'. She seemed to take most pleasure in sorting out our children's clothes, and dressing them. Perhaps she used to dress her own like that in the days when Spicer was a different man from what he was now. She seemed interested in the fashion-plates of some women's journals we had, and used to study them with an interest that puzzled me, for she was not likely to go in for fashion. She never talked of her early girlhood; but Mary, from some things she noticed, was inclined to think that Mrs Spicer had been fairly well brought up. For instance, Dr Balanfantie, from Cudgeegong, came out to see Wall's wife, and drove up the creek to our place on his way back to see how Mary and the baby were getting on. Mary got out some crockery and some table-napkins that she had packed away for occasions like this; and she said that the way Mrs Spicer handled the things, and helped set the table (though she did it in a mechanical sort of way), convinced her that she had been used to table-napkins at one time in her life.

Sometimes, after a long pause in the conversation, Mrs Spicer would say suddenly—

'Oh, I don't think I'll come up next week, Mrs Wilson.'

'Why, Mrs Spicer?'

'Because the visits doesn't do me any good. I git the dismals afterwards.'

'Why, Mrs Spicer? What on earth do you mean?'

'Oh,-I-don't-know-what-I'm-talkin'-about. You mustn't take any notice of me.' And she'd put on her hat, kiss the children—and Mary too, sometimes, as if she mistook her for a child—and go.

Mary thought her a little mad at times. But I seemed to understand.

Once, when Mrs Spicer was sick, Mary went down to her, and down again next day. As she was coming away the second time, Mrs Spicer said—

'I wish you wouldn't come down any more till I'm on me feet, Mrs Wilson. The children can do for me.'

'Why, Mrs Spicer?'

'Well, the place is in such a muck, and it hurts me.'

We were the aristocrats of Lahey's Creek. Whenever we drove down on Sunday afternoon to see Mrs Spicer, and as soon as we got near enough for them to hear the rattle of the cart, we'd see the children running to the house as fast as they could split, and hear them screaming—

'Oh, marther! Here comes Mr and Mrs Wilson in their spring-cart.'

And we'd see her bustle round, and two or three fowls fly out the front door, and she'd lay hold of a broom (made of a bound bunch of 'broom-stuff'—coarse reedy grass or bush from the ridges—with a stick stuck in it) and flick out the floor, with a flick or two round in front of the door perhaps. The floor nearly always needed at least one flick of the broom on account of the fowls. Or she'd catch a youngster and scrub his face with a wet end of a cloudy towel, or twist the towel round her finger and dig out his ears—as if she was anxious to have him hear every word that was going to be said.

No matter what state the house would be in she'd always say, 'I was jist expectin' yer, Mrs Wilson.' And she was original in that, anyway.

She had an old patched and darned white table-cloth that she used to spread on the table when we were there, as a matter of course ['The others is in the wash, so you must excuse this, Mrs Wilson'], but I saw by the eyes of the children that the cloth was rather a wonderful thing to them. 'I must really git some more knives an' forks next time I'm in Cobborah,' she'd say. 'The children break an' lose 'em till I'm ashamed to ask Christians ter sit down ter the table.'

She had many Bush yarns, some of them very funny, some of them rather ghastly, but all interesting, and with a grim sort of humour about them. But the effect was often spoilt by her screaming at the children to 'Drive out them fowls, karnt yer,' or 'Take yer maulies [hands] outer the sugar,' or 'Don't touch Mrs Wilson's baby with them dirty maulies,' or 'Don't stand starin' at Mrs Wilson with yer mouth an' ears in that vulgar way.'

Poor woman! she seemed everlastingly nagging at the children. It was a habit, but they didn't seem to mind. Most Bushwomen get the nagging habit. I remember one, who had the prettiest, dearest, sweetest, most willing, and affectionate little girl I think I ever saw, and she nagged that child from daylight till dark—and after it. Taking it all round, I think that the nagging habit in a mother is often worse on ordinary children, and more deadly on sensitive youngsters, than the drinking habit in a father.

One of the yarns Mrs Spicer told us was about a squatter she knew who used to go wrong in his head every now and again, and try to commit suicide. Once, when the station-hand, who was watching him, had his eye off him for a minute, he hanged himself to a beam in the stable. The men ran in and found him hanging and kicking. 'They let him hang for a while,' said Mrs Spicer, 'till he went black in the face and stopped kicking. Then they cut him down and threw a bucket of water over him.'

'Why! what on earth did they let the man hang for?' asked Mary.

'To give him a good bellyful of it: they thought it would cure him of tryin' to hang himself again.'

'Well, that's the coolest thing I ever heard of,' said Mary.

'That's jist what the magistrate said, Mrs Wilson,' said Mrs Spicer.

'One morning,' said Mrs Spicer, 'Spicer had gone off on his horse somewhere, and I was alone with the children, when a man came to the door and said—

'"For God's sake, woman, give me a drink!"

'Lord only knows where he came from! He was dressed like a new chum—his clothes was good, but he looked as if he'd been sleepin' in them in the Bush for a month. He was very shaky. I had some coffee that mornin', so I gave him some in a pint pot; he drank it, and then he stood on his head till he tumbled over, and then he stood up on his feet and said, "Thenk yer, mum."

'I was so surprised that I didn't know what to say, so I jist said, "Would you like some more coffee?"

'"Yes, thenk yer," he said—"about two quarts."

'I nearly filled the pint pot, and he drank it and stood on his head as long as he could, and when he got right end up he said, "Thenk yer, mum—it's a fine day," and then he walked off. He had two saddle-straps in his hands.'

'Why, what did he stand on his head for?' asked Mary.

'To wash it up and down, I suppose, to get twice as much taste of the coffee. He had no hat. I sent Tommy across to Wall's to tell them that there was a man wanderin' about the Bush in the horrors of drink, and to get some one to ride for the police. But they was too late, for he hanged himself that night.'

'O Lord!' cried Mary.

'Yes, right close to here, jist down the creek where the track to Wall's branches off. Tommy found him while he was out after the cows. Hangin' to the branch of a tree with the two saddle-straps.'

Mary stared at her, speechless.

'Tommy came home yellin' with fright. I sent him over to Wall's at once. After breakfast, the minute my eyes was off them, the children slipped away and went down there. They came back screamin' at the tops of their voices. I did give it to them. I reckon they won't want ter see a dead body again in a hurry. Every time I'd mention it they'd huddle together, or ketch hold of me skirts and howl.

'"Yer'll go agen when I tell yer not to," I'd say.

'"Oh no, mother," they'd howl.

'"Yer wanted ter see a man hangin'," I said.

'"Oh, don't, mother! Don't talk about it."

'"Yer wouldn't be satisfied till yer see it," I'd say; "yer had to see it or burst. Yer satisfied now, ain't yer?"

'"Oh, don't, mother!"

'"Yer run all the way there, I s'pose?"

'"Don't, mother!"

'"But yer run faster back, didn't yer?"

'"Oh, don't, mother."

'But,' said Mrs Spicer, in conclusion, 'I'd been down to see it myself before they was up.'

'And ain't you afraid to live alone here, after all these horrible things?' asked Mary.

'Well, no; I don't mind. I seem to have got past carin' for anythink now. I felt it a little when Tommy went away—the first time I felt anythink for years. But I'm over that now.'

'Haven't you got any friends in the district, Mrs Spicer?'

'Oh yes. There's me married sister near Cobborah, and a married brother near Dubbo; he's got a station. They wanted to take me an' the children between them, or take some of the younger children. But I couldn't bring my mind to break up the home. I want to keep the children together as much as possible. There's enough of them gone, God knows. But it's a comfort to know that there's some one to see to them if anythink happens to me.'

One day—I was on my way home with the team that day—Annie Spicer came running up the creek in terrible trouble.

'Oh, Mrs Wilson! something terribl's happened at home! A trooper' (mounted policeman—they called them 'mounted troopers' out there), 'a trooper's come and took Billy!' Billy was the eldest son at home.

'What?'

'It's true, Mrs Wilson.'

'What for? What did the policeman say?'

'He—he—he said, "I—I'm very sorry, Mrs Spicer; but—I—I want William."'

It turned out that William was wanted on account of a horse missed from Wall's station and sold down-country.

'An' mother took on awful,' sobbed Annie; 'an' now she'll only sit stock-still an' stare in front of her, and won't take no notice of any of us. Oh! it's awful, Mrs Wilson. The policeman said he'd tell Aunt Emma' (Mrs Spicer's sister at Cobborah), 'and send her out. But I had to come to you, an' I've run all the way.'

James put the horse to the cart and drove Mary down.

Mary told me all about it when I came home.

'I found her just as Annie said; but she broke down and cried in my arms. Oh, Joe! it was awful! She didn't cry like a woman. I heard a man at Haviland cry at his brother's funeral, and it was just like that. She came round a bit after a while. Her sister's with her now.... Oh, Joe! you must take me away from the Bush.'

Later on Mary said—

'How the oaks are sighing to-night, Joe!'

Next morning I rode across to Wall's station and tackled the old man; but he was a hard man, and wouldn't listen to me—in fact, he ordered me off the station. I was a selector, and that was enough for him. But young Billy Wall rode after me.

'Look here, Joe!' he said, 'it's a blanky shame. All for the sake of a horse! And as if that poor devil of a woman hasn't got enough to put up with already! I wouldn't do it for twenty horses. I'LL tackle the boss, and if he won't listen to me, I'll walk off the run for the last time, if I have to carry my swag.'

Billy Wall managed it. The charge was withdrawn, and we got young Billy Spicer off up-country.

But poor Mrs Spicer was never the same after that. She seldom came up to our place unless Mary dragged her, so to speak; and then she would talk of nothing but her last trouble, till her visits were painful to look forward to.

'If it only could have been kep' quiet—for the sake of the other children; they are all I think of now. I tried to bring 'em all up decent, but I s'pose it was my fault, somehow. It's the disgrace that's killin' me—I can't bear it.'

I was at home one Sunday with Mary and a jolly Bush-girl named Maggie Charlsworth, who rode over sometimes from Wall's station (I must tell you about her some other time; James was 'shook after her'), and we got talkin' about Mrs Spicer. Maggie was very warm about old Wall.

'I expected Mrs Spicer up to-day,' said Mary. 'She seems better lately.'

'Why!' cried Maggie Charlsworth, 'if that ain't Annie coming running up along the creek. Something's the matter!'

We all jumped up and ran out.

'What is it, Annie?' cried Mary.

'Oh, Mrs Wilson! Mother's asleep, and we can't wake her!'

'What?'

'It's—it's the truth, Mrs Wilson.'

'How long has she been asleep?'

'Since lars' night.'

'My God!' cried Mary, 'SINCE LAST NIGHT?'

'No, Mrs Wilson, not all the time; she woke wonst, about daylight this mornin'. She called me and said she didn't feel well, and I'd have to manage the milkin'.'

'Was that all she said?'

'No. She said not to go for you; and she said to feed the pigs and calves; and she said to be sure and water them geraniums.'

Mary wanted to go, but I wouldn't let her. James and I saddled our horses and rode down the creek.

Mrs Spicer looked very little different from what she did when I last saw her alive. It was some time before we could believe that she was dead. But she was 'past carin'' right enough.

A Double Buggy at Lahey's Creek

I

Spuds, and a Woman's Obstinacy

Ever since we were married it had been Mary's great ambition to have a buggy. The house or furniture didn't matter so much—out there in the Bush where we were—but, where there were no railways or coaches, and the roads were long, and mostly hot and dusty, a buggy was the great thing. I had a few pounds when we were married, and was going to get one then; but new buggies went high, and another party got hold of a second-hand one that I'd had my eye on, so Mary thought it over and at last she said, 'Never mind the buggy, Joe; get a sewing-machine and I'll be satisfied. I'll want the machine more than the buggy, for a while. Wait till we're better off.'

After that, whenever I took a contract—to put up a fence or wool-shed, or sink a dam or something— Mary would say, 'You ought to knock a buggy out of this job, Joe;' but something always turned up—bad weather or sickness. Once I cut my foot with the adze and was laid up; and, another time, a dam I was making was washed away by a flood before I finished it. Then Mary would say, 'Ah, well—never mind, Joe. Wait till we are better off.' But she felt it hard the time I built a wool-shed and didn't get paid for it, for we'd as good as settled about another second-hand buggy then.

I always had a fancy for carpentering, and was handy with tools. I made a spring-cart—body and wheels—in spare time, out of colonial hardwood, and got Little the blacksmith to do the ironwork; I painted the cart myself. It wasn't much lighter than one of the tip-drays I had, but it WAS a spring-cart, and Mary pretended to be satisfied with it: anyway, I didn't hear any more of the buggy for a while.

I sold that cart, for fourteen pounds, to a Chinese gardener who wanted a strong cart to carry his vegetables round through the Bush. It was just before our first youngster came: I told Mary that I wanted the money in case of extra expense—and she didn't fret much at losing that cart. But the fact was, that I was going to make another try for a buggy, as a present for Mary when the child was born. I thought of getting the turn-out while she was laid up, keeping it dark from her till she was on her feet again, and then showing her the buggy standing in the shed. But she had a bad time, and I had to have the doctor regularly, and get a proper nurse, and a lot of things extra; so the buggy idea was knocked on the head. I was set on it, too: I'd thought of how, when Mary was up and getting strong, I'd say one morning, 'Go round and have a look in the shed, Mary; I've got a few fowls for you,' or something like that—and follow her round to watch her eyes when she saw the buggy. I never told Mary about that—it wouldn't have done any good.

Later on I got some good timber—mostly scraps that were given to me—and made a light body for a spring-cart. Galletly, the coach-builder at Cudgeegong, had got a dozen pairs of American hickory wheels up from Sydney, for light spring-carts, and he let me have a pair for cost price and carriage. I got him to iron the cart, and he put it through the paint-shop for nothing. He sent it out, too, at the tail of Tom Tarrant's big van—to increase the surprise. We were swells then for a while; I heard no more of a buggy until after we'd been settled at Lahey's Creek for a couple of years.

I told you how I went into the carrying line, and took up a selection at Lahey's Creek—for a run for the horses and to grow a bit of feed—and shifted Mary and little Jim out there from Gulgong, with Mary's young scamp of a brother James to keep them company while I was on the road. The first year I did well enough carrying, but I never cared for it—it was too slow; and, besides, I was always anxious when I was away from home. The game was right enough for a single man—or a married one whose wife had got the nagging habit (as many Bushwomen have—God help 'em!), and who wanted peace and quietness sometimes. Besides, other small carriers started (seeing me getting on); and Tom Tarrant, the coach-driver at Cudgeegong, had another heavy spring-van built, and put it on the roads, and he took a lot of the light stuff.

The second year I made a rise—out of 'spuds', of all the things in the world. It was Mary's idea. Down at the lower end of our selection—Mary called it 'the run'—was a shallow watercourse called Snake's Creek, dry most of the year, except for a muddy water-hole or two; and, just above the junction, where it ran into Lahey's Creek, was a low piece of good black-soil flat, on our side—about three acres. The flat was fairly clear when I came to the selection—save for a few logs that had been washed up there in some big 'old man' flood, way back in black-fellows' times; and one day, when I had a spell at home, I got the horses and trace-chains and dragged the logs together—those that wouldn't split for fencing timber—and burnt them off. I had a notion to get the flat ploughed and make a lucern-paddock of it. There was a good water-hole, under a clump of she-oak in the bend, and Mary used to take her stools and tubs and boiler down there in the spring-cart in hot weather, and wash the clothes under the shade of the trees—it was cooler, and saved carrying water to the house. And one evening after she'd done the washing she said to me—

'Look here, Joe; the farmers out here never seem to get a new idea: they don't seem to me ever to try and find out beforehand what the market is going to be like—they just go on farming the same old way and putting in the same old crops year after year. They sow wheat, and, if it comes on anything like the thing, they reap and thresh it; if it doesn't, they mow it for hay—and some of 'em don't have the brains to do that in time. Now, I was looking at that bit of flat you cleared, and it struck me that it wouldn't be a half bad idea to get a bag of seed-potatoes, and have the land ploughed—old Corny George would do it cheap—and get them put in at once. Potatoes have been dear all round for the last couple of years.'

I told her she was talking nonsense, that the ground was no good for potatoes, and the whole district was too dry. 'Everybody I know has tried it, one time or another, and made nothing of it,' I said.

'All the more reason why you should try it, Joe,' said Mary. 'Just try one crop. It might rain for weeks, and then you'll be sorry you didn't take my advice.'

'But I tell you the ground is not potato-ground,' I said.

'How do you know? You haven't sown any there yet.'

'But I've turned up the surface and looked at it. It's not rich enough, and too dry, I tell you. You need swampy, boggy ground for potatoes. Do you think I don't know land when I see it?'

'But you haven't TRIED to grow potatoes there yet, Joe. How do you know—'

I didn't listen to any more. Mary was obstinate when she got an idea into her head. It was no use arguing with her. All the time I'd be talking she'd just knit her forehead and go on thinking straight ahead, on the track she'd started,—just as if I wasn't there,—and it used to make me mad. She'd keep driving at me till I took her advice or lost my temper,—I did both at the same time, mostly.

I took my pipe and went out to smoke and cool down.

A couple of days after the potato breeze, I started with the team down to Cudgeegong for a load of fencing-wire I had to bring out; and after I'd kissed Mary good-bye, she said—

'Look here, Joe, if you bring out a bag of seed-potatoes, James and I will slice them, and old Corny George down the creek would bring his plough up in the dray and plough the ground for very little. We could put the potatoes in ourselves if the ground were only ploughed.'

I thought she'd forgotten all about it. There was no time to argue—I'd be sure to lose my temper, and then I'd either have to waste an hour comforting Mary or go off in a 'huff', as the women call it, and be miserable for the trip. So I said I'd see about it. She gave me another hug and a kiss. 'Don't forget, Joe,' she said as I started. 'Think it over on the road.' I reckon she had the best of it that time.

About five miles along, just as I turned into the main road, I heard some one galloping after me, and I saw young James on his hack. I got a start, for I thought that something had gone wrong at home. I remember, the first day I left Mary on the creek, for the first five or six miles I was half-a-dozen times on the point of turning back—only I thought she'd laugh at me.

'What is it, James?' I shouted, before he came up—but I saw he was grinning.

'Mary says to tell you not to forget to bring a hoe out with you.'

'You clear off home!' I said, 'or I'll lay the whip about your young hide; and don't come riding after me again as if the run was on fire.'

'Well, you needn't get shirty with me!' he said. 'I don't want to have anything to do with a hoe.' And he rode off.

I DID get thinking about those potatoes, though I hadn't meant to. I knew of an independent man in that district who'd made his money out of a crop of potatoes; but that was away back in the roaring 'Fifties— '54—when spuds went up to twenty-eight shillings a hundredweight (in Sydney), on account of the gold rush. We might get good rain now, and, anyway, it wouldn't cost much to put the potatoes in. If they came on well, it would be a few pounds in my pocket; if the crop was a failure, I'd have a better show with Mary next time she was struck by an idea outside housekeeping, and have something to grumble about when I felt grumpy.

I got a couple of bags of potatoes—we could use those that were left over; and I got a small iron plough and a harrow that Little the blacksmith had lying in his yard and let me have cheap—only about a pound more than I told Mary I gave for them. When I took advice, I generally made the mistake of taking more than was offered, or adding notions of my own. It was vanity, I suppose. If the crop came on well I could claim the plough-and-harrow part of the idea, anyway. (It didn't strike me that if the crop failed Mary would have the plough and harrow against me, for old Corny would plough the ground for ten or fifteen shillings.) Anyway, I'd want a plough and harrow later on, and I might as well get it now; it would give James something to do.

I came out by the western road, by Guntawang, and up the creek home; and the first thing I saw was old Corny George ploughing the flat. And Mary was down on the bank superintending. She'd got James with the trace-chains and the spare horses, and had made him clear off every stick and bush where another furrow might be squeezed in. Old Corny looked pretty grumpy on it—he'd broken all his ploughshares but one, in the roots; and James didn't look much brighter. Mary had an old felt hat and a new pair of 'lastic-side boots of mine on, and the boots were covered with clay, for she'd been down hustling James to get a rotten old stump out of the way by the time Corny came round with his next furrow.

'I thought I'd make the boots easy for you, Joe,' said Mary.

'It's all right, Mary,' I said. 'I'm not going to growl.' Those boots were a bone of contention between us; but she generally got them off before I got home.

Her face fell a little when she saw the plough and harrow in the waggon, but I said that would be all right—we'd want a plough anyway.

'I thought you wanted old Corny to plough the ground,' she said.

'I never said so.'

'But when I sent Jim after you about the hoe to put the spuds in, you didn't say you wouldn't bring it,' she said.

I had a few days at home, and entered into the spirit of the thing. When Corny was done, James and I cross-ploughed the land, and got a stump or two, a big log, and some scrub out of the way at the upper end and added nearly an acre, and ploughed that. James was all right at most Bushwork: he'd bullock so long as the novelty lasted; he liked ploughing or fencing, or any graft he could make a show at. He didn't care for grubbing out stumps, or splitting posts and rails. We sliced the potatoes of an evening—and there was trouble between Mary and James over cutting through the 'eyes'. There was no time for the hoe—and besides it wasn't a novelty to James—so I just ran furrows and they dropped the spuds in behind me, and I turned another furrow over them, and ran the harrow over the ground. I think I hilled those spuds, too, with furrows—or a crop of Indian corn I put in later on.

It rained heavens-hard for over a week: we had regular showers all through, and it was the finest crop of potatoes ever seen in the district. I believe at first Mary used to slip down at daybreak to see if the potatoes were up; and she'd write to me about them, on the road. I forget how many bags I got; but the few who had grown potatoes in the district sent theirs to Sydney, and spuds went up to twelve and fifteen shillings a hundredweight in that district. I made a few quid out of mine—and saved carriage too, for I could take them out on the waggon. Then Mary began to hear (through James) of a buggy that some one had for sale cheap, or a dogcart that somebody else wanted to get rid of—and let me know about it, in an offhand way.

II

Joe Wilson's Luck

There was good grass on the selection all the year. I'd picked up a small lot—about twenty head—of half-starved steers for next to nothing, and turned them on the run; they came on wonderfully, and my brother-in-law (Mary's sister's husband), who was running a butchery at Gulgong, gave me a good price for them. His carts ran out twenty or thirty miles, to little bits of gold-rushes that were going on at th' Home Rule, Happy Valley, Guntawang, Tallawang, and Cooyal, and those places round there, and he was doing well.

Mary had heard of a light American waggonette, when the steers went—a tray-body arrangement, and she thought she'd do with that. 'It would be better than the buggy, Joe,' she said—'there'd be more room for the children, and, besides, I could take butter and eggs to Gulgong, or Cobborah, when we get a few more cows.' Then James heard of a small flock of sheep that a selector—who was about starved off his selection out Talbragar way—wanted to get rid of. James reckoned he could get them for less than half-a-crown a-head. We'd had a heavy shower of rain, that came over the ranges and didn't seem to go beyond our boundaries. Mary said, 'It's a pity to see all that grass going to waste, Joe. Better get those sheep and try your luck with them. Leave some money with me, and I'll send James over for them. Never mind about the buggy—we'll get that when we're on our feet.'

So James rode across to Talbragar and drove a hard bargain with that unfortunate selector, and brought the sheep home. There were about two hundred, wethers and ewes, and they were young and looked a good breed too, but so poor they could scarcely travel; they soon picked up, though. The drought was blazing all round and Out-Back, and I think that my corner of the ridges was the only place where there was any grass to speak of. We had another shower or two, and the grass held out. Chaps began to talk of 'Joe Wilson's luck'.

I would have liked to shear those sheep; but I hadn't time to get a shed or anything ready—along towards Christmas there was a bit of a boom in the carrying line. Wethers in wool were going as high as thirteen to fifteen shillings at the Homebush yards at Sydney, so I arranged to truck the sheep down from the river by rail, with another small lot that was going, and I started James off with them. He took the west road, and down Guntawang way a big farmer who saw James with the sheep (and who was speculating, or adding to his stock, or took a fancy to the wool) offered James as much for them as he reckoned I'd get in Sydney, after paying the carriage and the agents and the auctioneer. James put the sheep in a paddock and rode back to me. He was all there where riding was concerned. I told him to let the sheep go. James made a Greener shot-gun, and got his saddle done up, out of that job.

I took up a couple more forty-acre blocks—one in James's name, to encourage him with the fencing. There was a good slice of land in an angle between the range and the creek, farther down, which everybody thought belonged to Wall, the squatter, but Mary got an idea, and went to the local land office and found out that it was 'unoccupied Crown land', and so I took it up on pastoral lease, and got a few more sheep—I'd saved some of the best-looking ewes from the last lot.

One evening—I was going down next day for a load of fencing-wire for myself—Mary said,—

'Joe! do you know that the Matthews have got a new double buggy?'

The Matthews were a big family of cockatoos, along up the main road, and I didn't think much of them. The sons were all 'bad-eggs', though the old woman and girls were right enough.

'Well, what of that?' I said. 'They're up to their neck in debt, and camping like black-fellows in a big bark humpy. They do well to go flashing round in a double buggy.'

'But that isn't what I was going to say,' said Mary. 'They want to sell their old single buggy, James says. I'm sure you could get it for six or seven pounds; and you could have it done up.'

'I wish James to the devil!' I said. 'Can't he find anything better to do than ride round after cock-and-bull yarns about buggies?'

'Well,' said Mary, 'it was James who got the steers and the sheep.'

Well, one word led to another, and we said things we didn't mean—but couldn't forget in a hurry. I remember I said something about Mary always dragging me back just when I was getting my head above water and struggling to make a home for her and the children; and that hurt her, and she spoke of the 'homes' she'd had since she was married. And that cut me deep.

It was about the worst quarrel we had. When she began to cry I got my hat and went out and walked up and down by the creek. I hated anything that looked like injustice—I was so sensitive about it that it made me unjust sometimes. I tried to think I was right, but I couldn't—it wouldn't have made me feel any better if I could have thought so. I got thinking of Mary's first year on the selection and the life she'd had since we were married.

When I went in she'd cried herself to sleep. I bent over and, 'Mary,' I whispered.

She seemed to wake up.

'Joe—Joe!' she said.

'What is it Mary?' I said.

'I'm pretty well sure that old Spot's calf isn't in the pen. Make James go at once!'

Old Spot's last calf was two years old now; so Mary was talking in her sleep, and dreaming she was back in her first year.

We both laughed when I told her about it afterwards; but I didn't feel like laughing just then.

Later on in the night she called out in her sleep,—

'Joe—Joe! Put that buggy in the shed, or the sun will blister the varnish!'

I wish I could say that that was the last time I ever spoke unkindly to Mary.

Next morning I got up early and fried the bacon and made the tea, and took Mary's breakfast in to her—like I used to do, sometimes, when we were first married. She didn't say anything—just pulled my head down and kissed me.

When I was ready to start Mary said,—

'You'd better take the spring-cart in behind the dray and get the tyres cut and set. They're ready to drop off, and James has been wedging them up till he's tired of it. The last time I was out with the children I had to knock one of them back with a stone: there'll be an accident yet.'

So I lashed the shafts of the cart under the tail of the waggon, and mean and ridiculous enough the cart looked, going along that way. It suggested a man stooping along handcuffed, with his arms held out and down in front of him.

It was dull weather, and the scrubs looked extra dreary and endless—and I got thinking of old things. Everything was going all right with me, but that didn't keep me from brooding sometimes—trying to hatch out stones, like an old hen we had at home. I think, taking it all round, I used to be happier when I was mostly hard-up—and more generous. When I had ten pounds I was more likely to listen to a chap who said, 'Lend me a pound-note, Joe,' than when I had fifty; THEN I fought shy of careless chaps—and lost mates that I wanted afterwards—and got the name of being mean. When I got a good cheque I'd be as miserable as a miser over the first ten pounds I spent; but when I got down to the last I'd buy things for the house. And now that I was getting on, I hated to spend a pound on anything. But then, the farther I got away from poverty the greater the fear I had of it—and, besides, there was always before us all the thought of the terrible drought, with blazing runs as bare and dusty as the road, and dead stock rotting every yard, all along the barren creeks.

I had a long yarn with Mary's sister and her husband that night in Gulgong, and it brightened me up. I had a fancy that that sort of a brother-in-law made a better mate than a nearer one; Tom Tarrant had one, and he said it was sympathy. But while we were yarning I couldn't help thinking of Mary, out there in the hut on the Creek, with no one to talk to but the children, or James, who was sulky at home, or Black Mary or Black Jimmy (our black boy's father and mother), who weren't oversentimental. Or maybe a selector's wife (the nearest was five miles away), who could talk only of two or three things—'lambin'' and 'shearin'' and 'cookin' for the men', and what she said to her old man, and what he said to her—and her own ailments—over and over again.

It's a wonder it didn't drive Mary mad!—I know I could never listen to that woman more than an hour. Mary's sister said,—

'Now if Mary had a comfortable buggy, she could drive in with the children oftener. Then she wouldn't feel the loneliness so much.'

I said 'Good night' then and turned in. There was no getting away from that buggy. Whenever Mary's sister started hinting about a buggy, I reckoned it was a put-up job between them.

III

The Ghost of Mary's Sacrifice

When I got to Gudgeegong I stopped at Galletly's coach-shop to leave the cart. The Galletlys were good fellows: there were two brothers—one was a saddler and harness-maker. Big brown-bearded men—the biggest men in the district, 'twas said.

Their old man had died lately and left them some money; they had men, and only worked in their shops when they felt inclined, or there was a special work to do; they were both first-class tradesmen. I went into the painter's shop to have a look at a double buggy that Galletly had built for a man who couldn't pay cash for it when it was finished—and Galletly wouldn't trust him.

There it stood, behind a calico screen that the coach-painters used to keep out the dust when they were varnishing. It was a first-class piece of work—pole, shafts, cushions, whip, lamps, and all complete. If you only wanted to drive one horse you could take out the pole and put in the shafts, and there you were. There was a tilt over the front seat; if you only wanted the buggy to carry two, you could fold down the back seat, and there you had a handsome, roomy, single buggy. It would go near fifty pounds.

While I was looking at it, Bill Galletly came in, and slapped me on the back.

'Now, there's a chance for you, Joe!' he said. 'I saw you rubbing your head round that buggy the last time you were in. You wouldn't get a better one in the colonies, and you won't see another like it in the district again in a hurry—for it doesn't pay to build 'em. Now you're a full-blown squatter, and it's time you took little Mary for a fly round in her own buggy now and then, instead of having her stuck out there in the scrub, or jolting through the dust in a cart like some old Mother Flourbag.'

He called her 'little Mary' because the Galletly family had known her when she was a girl.

I rubbed my head and looked at the buggy again. It was a great temptation.

'Look here, Joe,' said Bill Galletly in a quieter tone. 'I'll tell you what I'll do. I'll let YOU have the buggy. You can take it out and send along a bit of a cheque when you feel you can manage it, and the rest later on,—a year will do, or even two years. You've had a hard pull, and I'm not likely to be hard up for money in a hurry.'

They were good fellows the Galletlys, but they knew their men. I happened to know that Bill Galletly wouldn't let the man he built the buggy for take it out of the shop without cash down, though he was a big-bug round there. But that didn't make it easier for me.

Just then Robert Galletly came into the shop. He was rather quieter than his brother, but the two were very much alike.

'Look here, Bob,' said Bill; 'here's a chance for you to get rid of your harness. Joe Wilson's going to take that buggy off my hands.'

Bob Galletly put his foot up on a saw-stool, took one hand out of his pockets, rested his elbow on his knee and his chin on the palm of his hand, and bunched up his big beard with his fingers, as he always did when he was thinking. Presently he took his foot down, put his hand back in his pocket, and said to me, 'Well, Joe, I've got a double set of harness made for the man who ordered that damned buggy, and if you like I'll let you have it. I suppose when Bill there has squeezed all he can out of you I'll stand a show of getting something. He's a regular Shylock, he is.'

I pushed my hat forward and rubbed the back of my head and stared at the buggy.

'Come across to the Royal, Joe,' said Bob.

But I knew that a beer would settle the business, so I said I'd get the wool up to the station first and think it over, and have a drink when I came back.

I thought it over on the way to the station, but it didn't seem good enough. I wanted to get some more sheep, and there was the new run to be fenced in, and the instalments on the selections. I wanted lots of things that I couldn't well do without. Then, again, the farther I got away from debt and hard-upedness the greater the horror I had of it. I had two horses that would do; but I'd have to get another later on, and altogether the buggy would run me nearer a hundred than fifty pounds. Supposing a dry season threw me back with that buggy on my hands. Besides, I wanted a spell. If I got the buggy it would only mean an extra turn of hard graft for me. No, I'd take Mary for a trip to Sydney, and she'd have to be satisfied with that.

I'd got it settled, and was just turning in through the big white gates to the goods-shed when young Black, the squatter, dashed past the station in his big new waggonette, with his wife and a driver and a lot of portmanteaus and rugs and things. They were going to do the grand in Sydney over Christmas. Now it was young Black who was so shook after Mary when she was in service with the Blacks before the old man died, and if I hadn't come along—and if girls never cared for vagabonds—Mary would have been mistress of Haviland homestead, with servants to wait on her; and she was far better fitted for it than the one that was there. She would have been going to Sydney every holiday and putting up at the old Royal, with every comfort that a woman could ask for, and seeing a play every night. And I'd have been knocking around amongst the big stations Out-Back, or maybe drinking myself to death at the shanties.

The Blacks didn't see me as I went by, ragged and dusty, and with an old, nearly black, cabbage-tree hat drawn over my eyes. I didn't care a damn for them, or any one else, at most times, but I had moods when I felt things.

One of Black's big wool teams was just coming away from the shed, and the driver, a big, dark, rough fellow, with some foreign blood in him, didn't seem inclined to wheel his team an inch out of the middle of the road. I stopped my horses and waited. He looked at me and I looked at him—hard. Then he wheeled off, scowling, and swearing at his horses. I'd given him a hiding, six or seven years before, and he hadn't forgotten it. And I felt then as if I wouldn't mind trying to give some one a hiding.

The goods clerk must have thought that Joe Wilson was pretty grumpy that day. I was thinking of Mary, out there in the lonely hut on a barren creek in the Bush—for it was little better—with no one to speak to except a haggard, worn-out Bushwoman or two, that came to see her on Sunday. I thought of the hardships she went through in the first year—that I haven't told you about yet; of the time she was ill, and I away, and no one to understand; of the time she was alone with James and Jim sick; and of the loneliness she fought through out there. I thought of Mary, outside in the blazing heat, with an old print dress and a felt hat, and a pair of 'lastic-siders of mine on, doing the work of a station manager as well as that of a housewife and mother. And her cheeks were getting thin, and her colour was going: I thought of the gaunt, brick-brown, saw-file voiced, hopeless and spiritless Bushwomen I knew—and some of them not much older than Mary.

When I went back down into the town, I had a drink with Bill Galletly at the Royal, and that settled the buggy; then Bob shouted,* and I took the harness. Then I shouted, to wet the bargain. When I was going, Bob said, 'Send in that young scamp of a brother of Mary's with the horses: if the collars don't fit I'll fix up a pair of makeshifts, and alter the others.' I thought they both gripped my hand harder than usual, but that might have been the beer.

* 'Shout', to buy a round of drinks.

IV

The Buggy Comes Home

I 'whipped the cat' a bit, the first twenty miles or so, but then, I thought, what did it matter? What was the use of grinding to save money until we were too old to enjoy it. If we had to go down in the world again, we might as well fall out of a buggy as out of a dray—there'd be some talk about it, anyway, and perhaps a little sympathy. When Mary had the buggy she wouldn't be tied down so much to that wretched hole in the Bush; and the Sydney trips needn't be off either. I could drive down to Wallerawang on the main line, where Mary had some people, and leave the buggy and horses there, and take the train to Sydney; or go right on, by the old coach-road, over the Blue Mountains: it would be a grand drive. I thought best to tell Mary's sister at Gulgong about the buggy; I told her I'd keep it dark from Mary till the buggy came home. She entered into the spirit of the thing, and said she'd give the world to be able to go out with the buggy, if only to see Mary open her eyes when she saw it; but she couldn't go, on account of a new baby she had. I was rather glad she couldn't, for it would spoil the surprise a little, I thought. I wanted that all to myself.

I got home about sunset next day, and, after tea, when I'd finished telling Mary all the news, and a few lies as to why I didn't bring the cart back, and one or two other things, I sat with James, out on a log of the wood-heap, where we generally had our smokes and interviews, and told him all about the buggy. He whistled, then he said—

'But what do you want to make it such a Bushranging business for? Why can't you tell Mary now? It will cheer her up. She's been pretty miserable since you've been away this trip.'

'I want it to be a surprise,' I said.

'Well, I've got nothing to say against a surprise, out in a hole like this; but it 'ud take a lot to surprise me. What am I to say to Mary about taking the two horses in? I'll only want one to bring the cart out, and she's sure to ask.'

'Tell her you're going to get yours shod.'

'But he had a set of slippers only the other day. She knows as much about horses as we do. I don't mind telling a lie so long as a chap has only got to tell a straight lie and be done with it. But Mary asks so many questions.'

'Well, drive the other horse up the creek early, and pick him up as you go.'

'Yes. And she'll want to know what I want with two bridles. But I'll fix her—YOU needn't worry.'

'And, James,' I said, 'get a chamois leather and sponge—we'll want 'em anyway—and you might give the buggy a wash down in the creek, coming home. It's sure to be covered with dust.'

'Oh!—orlright.'

'And if you can, time yourself to get here in the cool of the evening, or just about sunset.'

'What for?'

I'd thought it would be better to have the buggy there in the cool of the evening, when Mary would have time to get excited and get over it—better than in the blazing hot morning, when the sun rose as hot as at noon, and we'd have the long broiling day before us.

'What do you want me to come at sunset for?' asked James. 'Do you want me to camp out in the scrub and turn up like a blooming sundowner?'

'Oh well,' I said, 'get here at midnight if you like.'

We didn't say anything for a while—just sat and puffed at our pipes. Then I said,—

'Well, what are you thinking about?'

I'm thinking it's time you got a new hat, the sun seems to get in through your old one too much,' and he got out of my reach and went to see about penning the calves. Before we turned in he said,—

'Well, what am I to get out of the job, Joe?'

He had his eye on a double-barrel gun that Franca the gunsmith in Cudgeegong had—one barrel shot, and the other rifle; so I said,—

'How much does Franca want for that gun?'

'Five-ten; but I think he'd take my single barrel off it. Anyway, I can squeeze a couple of quid out of Phil Lambert for the single barrel.' (Phil was his bosom chum.)

'All right,' I said. 'Make the best bargain you can.'

He got his own breakfast and made an early start next morning, to get clear of any instructions or messages that Mary might have forgotten to give him overnight. He took his gun with him.

I'd always thought that a man was a fool who couldn't keep a secret from his wife—that there was something womanish about him. I found out. Those three days waiting for the buggy were about the longest I ever spent in my life. It made me scotty with every one and everything; and poor Mary had to suffer for it. I put in the time patching up the harness and mending the stockyard and the roof, and, the third morning, I rode up the ridges to look for trees for fencing-timber. I remember I hurried home that afternoon because I thought the buggy might get there before me.

At tea-time I got Mary on to the buggy business.

'What's the good of a single buggy to you, Mary?' I asked. 'There's only room for two, and what are you going to do with the children when we go out together?'

'We can put them on the floor at our feet, like other people do. I can always fold up a blanket or 'possum rug for them to sit on.'

But she didn't take half so much interest in buggy talk as she would have taken at any other time, when I didn't want her to. Women are aggravating that way. But the poor girl was tired and not very well, and both the children were cross. She did look knocked up.

'We'll give the buggy a rest, Joe,' she said. (I thought I heard it coming then.) 'It seems as far off as ever. I don't know why you want to harp on it to-day. Now, don't look so cross, Joe—I didn't mean to hurt you. We'll wait until we can get a double buggy, since you're so set on it. There'll be plenty of time when we're better off.'

After tea, when the youngsters were in bed, and she'd washed up, we sat outside on the edge of the verandah floor, Mary sewing, and I smoking and watching the track up the creek.

'Why don't you talk, Joe?' asked Mary. 'You scarcely ever speak to me now: it's like drawing blood out of a stone to get a word from you. What makes you so cross, Joe?'

'Well, I've got nothing to say.'

'But you should find something. Think of me—it's very miserable for me. Have you anything on your mind? Is there any new trouble? Better tell me, no matter what it is, and not go worrying and brooding and making both our lives miserable. If you never tell one anything, how can you expect me to understand?'

I said there was nothing the matter.

'But there must be, to make you so unbearable. Have you been drinking, Joe—or gambling?'

I asked her what she'd accuse me of next.

'And another thing I want to speak to you about,' she went on. 'Now, don't knit up your forehead like that, Joe, and get impatient—'

'Well, what is it?'

'I wish you wouldn't swear in the hearing of the children. Now, little Jim to-day, he was trying to fix his little go-cart and it wouldn't run right, and—and—'

'Well, what did he say?'

'He—he' (she seemed a little hysterical, trying not to laugh)—'he said "damn it!"'

I had to laugh. Mary tried to keep serious, but it was no use.

'Never mind, old woman,' I said, putting an arm round her, for her mouth was trembling, and she was crying more than laughing. 'It won't be always like this. Just wait till we're a bit better off.'

Just then a black boy we had (I must tell you about him some other time) came sidling along by the wall, as if he were afraid somebody was going to hit him—poor little devil! I never did.

'What is it, Harry?' said Mary.

'Buggy comin', I bin thinkit.'

'Where?'

He pointed up the creek.

'Sure it's a buggy?'

'Yes, missus.'

'How many horses?'

'One—two.'

We knew that he could hear and see things long before we could. Mary went and perched on the wood-heap, and shaded her eyes—though the sun had gone—and peered through between the eternal grey trunks of the stunted trees on the flat across the creek. Presently she jumped down and came running in.

'There's some one coming in a buggy, Joe!' she cried, excitedly. 'And both my white table-cloths are rough dry. Harry! put two flat-irons down to the fire, quick, and put on some more wood. It's lucky I kept those new sheets packed away. Get up out of that, Joe! What are you sitting grinning like that for? Go and get on another shirt. Hurry—Why! It's only James—by himself.'

She stared at me, and I sat there, grinning like a fool.

'Joe!' she said, 'whose buggy is that?'

'Well, I suppose it's yours,' I said.

She caught her breath, and stared at the buggy and then at me again. James drove down out of sight into the crossing, and came up close to the house.

'Oh, Joe! what have you done?' cried Mary. 'Why, it's a new double buggy!' Then she rushed at me and hugged my head. 'Why didn't you tell me, Joe? You poor old boy!—and I've been nagging at you all day!' and she hugged me again.

James got down and started taking the horses out—as if it was an everyday occurrence. I saw the double-barrel gun sticking out from under the seat. He'd stopped to wash the buggy, and I suppose that's what made him grumpy. Mary stood on the verandah, with her eyes twice as big as usual, and breathing hard—taking the buggy in.

James skimmed the harness off, and the horses shook themselves and went down to the dam for a drink. 'You'd better look under the seats,' growled James, as he took his gun out with great care.

Mary dived for the buggy. There was a dozen of lemonade and ginger-beer in a candle-box from Galletly—James said that Galletly's men had a gallon of beer, and they cheered him, James (I suppose he meant they cheered the buggy), as he drove off; there was a 'little bit of a ham' from Pat Murphy, the storekeeper at Home Rule, that he'd 'cured himself'—it was the biggest I ever saw; there were three loaves of baker's bread, a cake, and a dozen yards of something 'to make up for the children', from Aunt Gertrude at Gulgong; there was a fresh-water cod, that long Dave Regan had caught the night before in the Macquarie river, and sent out packed in salt in a box; there was a holland suit for the black boy, with red braid to trim it; and there was a jar of preserved ginger, and some lollies (sweets) ['for the lil' boy'), and a rum-looking Chinese doll and a rattle ['for lil' girl'] from Sun Tong Lee, our storekeeper at Gulgong—James was chummy with Sun Tong Lee, and got his powder and shot and caps there on tick when he was short of money. And James said that the people would have loaded the buggy with 'rubbish' if he'd waited. They all seemed glad to see Joe Wilson getting on—and these things did me good.

We got the things inside, and I don't think either of us knew what we were saying or doing for the next half-hour. Then James put his head in and said, in a very injured tone,—

'What about my tea? I ain't had anything to speak of since I left Cudgeegong. I want some grub.'

Then Mary pulled herself together.

'You'll have your tea directly,' she said. 'Pick up that harness at once, and hang it on the pegs in the skillion; and you, Joe, back that buggy under the end of the verandah, the dew will be on it presently—and we'll put wet bags up in front of it to-morrow, to keep the sun off. And James will have to go back to Cudgeegong for the cart,—we can't have that buggy to knock about in.'

'All right,' said James—'anything! Only get me some grub.'

Mary fried the fish, in case it wouldn't keep till the morning, and rubbed over the tablecloths, now the irons were hot—James growling all the time—and got out some crockery she had packed away that had belonged to her mother, and set the table in a style that made James uncomfortable.

'I want some grub—not a blooming banquet!' he said. And he growled a lot because Mary wanted him to eat his fish without a knife, 'and that sort of Tommy-rot.' When he'd finished he took his gun, and the black boy, and the dogs, and went out 'possum-shooting.

When we were alone Mary climbed into the buggy to try the seat, and made me get up alongside her. We hadn't had such a comfortable seat for years; but we soon got down, in case any one came by, for we began to feel like a pair of fools up there.

Then we sat, side by side, on the edge of the verandah, and talked more than we'd done for years—and there was a good deal of 'Do you remember?' in it—and I think we got to understand each other better that night.

And at last Mary said, 'Do you know, Joe, why, I feel to-night just—just like I did the day we were married.'

And somehow I had that strange, shy sort of feeling too.

Part II

The Golden Graveyard

Mother Middleton was an awful woman, an 'old hand' (transported convict) some said. The prefix 'mother' in Australia mostly means 'old hag', and is applied in that sense. In early boyhood we understood, from old diggers, that Mother Middleton—in common with most other 'old hands'—had been sent out for 'knocking a donkey off a hen-roost.' We had never seen a donkey. She drank like a fish and swore like a trooper when the spirit moved her; she went on periodical sprees, and swore on most occasions. There was a fearsome yarn, which impressed us greatly as boys, to the effect that once, in her best (or worst) days, she had pulled a mounted policeman off his horse, and half-killed him with a heavy pick-handle, which she used for poking down clothes in her boiler. She said that he had insulted her.

She could still knock down a tree and cut a load of firewood with any Bushman; she was square and muscular, with arms like a navvy's; she had often worked shifts, below and on top, with her husband, when he'd be putting down a prospecting shaft without a mate, as he often had to do—because of her mainly. Old diggers said that it was lovely to see how she'd spin up a heavy green-hide bucket full of clay and 'tailings', and land and empty it with a twist of her wrist. Most men were afraid of her, and few diggers' wives were strong-minded enough to seek a second row with Mother Middleton. Her voice could be heard right across Golden Gully and Specimen Flat, whether raised in argument or in friendly greeting. She came to the old Pipeclay diggings with the 'rough crowd' (mostly Irish), and when the old and new Pipeclays were worked out, she went with the rush to Gulgong (about the last of the great alluvial or 'poor-man's' goldfields) and came back to Pipeclay when the Log Paddock goldfield 'broke out', adjacent to the old fields, and so helped prove the truth of the old digger's saying, that no matter how thoroughly ground has been worked, there is always room for a new Ballarat.

Jimmy Middleton died at Log Paddock, and was buried, about the last, in the little old cemetery—appertaining to the old farming town on the river, about four miles away—which adjoined the district racecourse, in the Bush, on the far edge of Specimen Flat. She conducted the funeral. Some said she made the coffin, and there were alleged jokes to the effect that her tongue had provided the corpse; but this, I think, was unfair and cruel, for she loved Jimmy Middleton in her awful way, and was, for all I ever heard to the contrary, a good wife to him. She then lived in a hut in Log Paddock, on a little money in the bank, and did sewing and washing for single diggers.

I remember hearing her one morning in neighbourly conversation, carried on across the gully, with a selector, Peter Olsen, who was hopelessly slaving to farm a dusty patch in the scrub.

'Why don't you chuck up that dust-hole and go up country and settle on good land, Peter Olsen? You're only slaving your stomach out here.' (She didn't say stomach.)

Peter Olsen (mild-whiskered little man, afraid of his wife). 'But then you know my wife is so delicate, Mrs Middleton. I wouldn't like to take her out in the Bush.'

Mrs Middleton. 'Delicate, be damned! she's only shamming!' (at her loudest.) 'Why don't you kick her off the bed and the book out of her hand, and make her go to work? She's as delicate as I am. Are you a man, Peter Olsen, or a—?'

This for the edification of the wife and of all within half a mile.

Long Paddock was 'petering'. There were a few claims still being worked down at the lowest end, where big, red-and-white waste-heaps of clay and gravel, rising above the blue-grey gum-bushes, advertised deep sinking; and little, yellow, clay-stained streams, running towards the creek over the drought-parched surface, told of trouble with the water below—time lost in baling and extra expense in timbering. And diggers came up with their flannels and moleskins yellow and heavy, and dripping with wet 'mullock'.

Most of the diggers had gone to other fields, but there were a few prospecting, in parties and singly, out on the flats and amongst the ridges round Pipeclay. Sinking holes in search of a new Ballarat.

Dave Regan—lanky, easy-going Bush native; Jim Bently—a bit of a 'Flash Jack'; and Andy Page—a character like what 'Kit' (in the 'Old Curiosity Shop') might have been after a voyage to Australia and some Colonial experience. These three were mates from habit and not necessity, for it was all shallow sinking where they worked. They were poking down pot-holes in the scrub in the vicinity of the racecourse, where the sinking was from ten to fifteen feet.

Dave had theories—'ideers' or 'notions' he called them; Jim Bently laid claim to none—he ran by sight, not scent, like a kangaroo-dog. Andy Page—by the way, great admirer and faithful retainer of Dave

Regan—was simple and trusting, but, on critical occasions, he was apt to be obstinately, uncomfortably, exasperatingly truthful, honest, and he had reverence for higher things.

Dave thought hard all one quiet drowsy Sunday afternoon, and next morning he, as head of the party, started to sink a hole as close to the cemetery fence as he dared. It was a nice quiet spot in the thick scrub, about three panels along the fence from the farthest corner post from the road. They bottomed here at nine feet, and found encouraging indications. They 'drove' (tunnelled) inwards at right angles to the fence, and at a point immediately beneath it they were 'making tucker'; a few feet farther and they were making wages. The old alluvial bottom sloped gently that way. The bottom here, by the way, was shelving, brownish, rotten rock.

Just inside the cemetery fence, and at right angles to Dave's drive, lay the shell containing all that was left of the late fiercely lamented James Middleton, with older graves close at each end. A grave was supposed to be six feet deep, and local gravediggers had been conscientious. The old alluvial bottom sloped from nine to fifteen feet here.

Dave worked the ground all round from the bottom of his shaft, timbering—i.e., putting in a sapling prop—here and there where he worked wide; but the 'payable dirt' ran in under the cemetery, and in no other direction.

Dave, Jim, and Andy held a consultation in camp over their pipes after tea, as a result of which Andy next morning rolled up his swag, sorrowfully but firmly shook hands with Dave and Jim, and started to tramp Out-Back to look for work on a sheep-station.

This was Dave's theory—drawn from a little experience and many long yarns with old diggers:—

He had bottomed on a slope to an old original water-course, covered with clay and gravel from the hills by centuries of rains to the depth of from nine or ten to twenty feet; he had bottomed on a gutter running into the bed of the old buried creek, and carrying patches and streaks of 'wash' or gold-bearing dirt. If he went on he might strike it rich at any stroke of his pick; he might strike the rich 'lead' which was supposed to exist round there. (There was always supposed to be a rich lead round there somewhere. 'There's gold in them ridges yet—if a man can only git at it,' says the toothless old relic of the Roaring Days.)

Dave might strike a ledge, 'pocket', or 'pot-hole' holding wash rich with gold. He had prospected on the opposite side of the cemetery, found no gold, and the bottom sloping upwards towards the graveyard. He had prospected at the back of the cemetery, found a few 'colours', and the bottom sloping downwards towards the point under the cemetery towards which all indications were now leading him. He had sunk shafts across the road opposite the cemetery frontage and found the sinking twenty feet and not a colour of gold. Probably the whole of the ground under the cemetery was rich—maybe the richest in the district. The old gravediggers had not been gold-diggers—besides, the graves, being six feet, would, none of them, have touched the alluvial bottom. There was nothing strange in the fact that none of the crowd of experienced diggers who rushed the district had thought of the cemetery and racecourse. Old brick chimneys and houses, the clay for the bricks of which had been taken from sites of subsequent goldfields, had been put through the crushing-mill in subsequent years and had yielded 'payable gold'. Fossicking Chinamen were said to have been the first to detect a case of this kind.

Dave reckoned to strike the 'lead', or a shelf or ledge with a good streak of wash lying along it, at a point about forty feet within the cemetery. But a theory in alluvial gold-mining was much like a theory in gambling, in some respects. The theory might be right enough, but old volcanic disturbances—'the shrinkage of the earth's surface,' and that sort of old thing—upset everything. You might follow good gold along a ledge, just under the grass, till it suddenly broke off and the continuation might be a hundred feet or so under your nose.

Had the 'ground' in the cemetery been 'open' Dave would have gone to the point under which he expected the gold to lie, sunk a shaft there, and worked the ground. It would have been the quickest and easiest way—it would have saved the labour and the time lost in dragging heavy buckets of dirt along a low lengthy drive to the shaft outside the fence. But it was very doubtful if the Government could have been moved to open the cemetery even on the strongest evidence of the existence of a rich goldfield under it, and backed by the influence of a number of diggers and their backers—which last was what Dave wished for least of all. He wanted, above all things, to keep the thing shady. Then, again, the old clannish local spirit of the old farming town, rooted in years way back of the goldfields, would have been too strong for the Government, or even a rush of wild diggers.

'We'll work this thing on the strict Q.T.,' said Dave.

He and Jim had a consultation by the camp fire outside their tent. Jim grumbled, in conclusion,—

'Well, then, best go under Jimmy Middleton. It's the shortest and straightest, and Jimmy's the freshest, anyway.'

Then there was another trouble. How were they to account for the size of the waste-heap of clay on the surface which would be the result of such an extraordinary length of drive or tunnel for shallow sinkings? Dave had an idea of carrying some of the dirt away by night and putting it down a deserted shaft close by; but that would double the labour, and might lead to detection sooner than anything else. There were boys 'possum-hunting on those flats every night. Then Dave got an idea.

There was supposed to exist—and it has since been proved—another, a second gold-bearing alluvial bottom on that field, and several had tried for it. One, the town watchmaker, had sunk all his money in 'duffers', trying for the second bottom. It was supposed to exist at a depth of from eighty to a hundred feet—on solid rock, I suppose. This watchmaker, an Italian, would put men on to sink, and superintend in person, and whenever he came to a little 'colour'-showing shelf, or false bottom, thirty or forty feet down—he'd go rooting round and spoil the shaft, and then start to sink another. It was extraordinary that he hadn't the sense to sink straight down, thoroughly test the second bottom, and if he found no gold there, to fill the shaft up to the other bottoms, or build platforms at the proper level and then explore them. He was living in a lunatic asylum the last time I heard of him. And the last time I heard from that field, they were boring the ground like a sieve, with the latest machinery, to find the best place to put down a deep shaft, and finding gold from the second bottom on the bore. But I'm right off the line again.

'Old Pinter', Ballarat digger—his theory on second and other bottoms ran as follows:—

'Ye see, THIS here grass surface—this here surface with trees an' grass on it, that we're livin' on, has got nothin' to do with us. This here bottom in the shaller sinkin's that we're workin' on is the slope to the bed of the NEW crick that was on the surface about the time that men was missin' links. The false bottoms, thirty or forty feet down, kin be said to have been on the surface about the time that men was monkeys. The SECON' bottom—eighty or a hundred feet down—was on the surface about the time when men was frogs. Now—'

But it's with the missing-link surface we have to do, and had the friends of the local departed known what Dave and Jim were up to they would have regarded them as something lower than missing-links.

'We'll give out we're tryin' for the second bottom,' said Dave Regan. 'We'll have to rig a fan for air, anyhow, and you don't want air in shallow sinkings.'

'And some one will come poking round, and look down the hole and see the bottom,' said Jim Bently.

'We must keep 'em away,' said Dave. 'Tar the bottom, or cover it with tarred canvas, to make it black. Then they won't see it. There's not many diggers left, and the rest are going; they're chucking up the claims in Log Paddock. Besides, I could get drunk and pick rows with the rest and they wouldn't come near me. The farmers ain't in love with us diggers, so they won't bother us. No man has a right to come poking round another man's claim: it ain't ettykit—I'll root up that old ettykit and stand to it—it's rather worn out now, but that's no matter. We'll shift the tent down near the claim and see that no one comes nosing round on Sunday. They'll think we're only some more second-bottom lunatics, like Francea [the mining watchmaker]. We're going to get our fortune out from under that old graveyard, Jim. You leave it all to me till you're born again with brains.'

Dave's schemes were always elaborate, and that was why they so often came to the ground. He logged up his windlass platform a little higher, bent about eighty feet of rope to the bole of the windlass, which was a new one, and thereafter, whenever a suspicious-looking party (that is to say, a digger) hove in sight, Dave would let down about forty feet of rope and then wind, with simulated exertion, until the slack was taken up and the rope lifted the bucket from the shallow bottom.

'It would look better to have a whip-pole and a horse, but we can't afford them just yet,' said Dave.

But I'm a little behind. They drove straight in under the cemetery, finding good wash all the way. The edge of Jimmy Middleton's box appeared in the top corner of the 'face' (the working end) of the drive. They went under the butt-end of the grave. They shoved up the end of the shell with a prop, to prevent the possibility of an accident which might disturb the mound above; they puddled—i.e., rammed—stiff clay up round the edges to keep the loose earth from dribbling down; and having given the bottom of the coffin a good coat of tar, they got over, or rather under, an unpleasant matter.

Jim Bently smoked and burnt paper during his shift below, and grumbled a good deal. 'Blowed if I ever thought I'd be rooting for gold down among the blanky dead men,' he said. But the dirt panned out better every dish they washed, and Dave worked the 'wash' out right and left as they drove.

But, one fine morning, who should come along but the very last man whom Dave wished to see round there—'Old Pinter' (James Poynton), Californian and Victorian digger of the old school. He'd been prospecting down the creek, carried his pick over his shoulder—threaded through the eye in the heft of his big-bladed, short-handled shovel that hung behind—and his gold-dish under his arm.

I mightn't get a chance again to explain what a gold-dish and what gold-washing is. A gold washing-dish is a flat dish—nearer the shape of a bedroom bath-tub than anything else I have seen in England, or the dish we used for setting milk—I don't know whether the same is used here: the gold-dish measures, say, eighteen inches across the top. You get it full of wash dirt, squat down at a convenient place at the edge of the water-hole, where there is a rest for the dish in the water just below its own depth. You sink the dish and let the clay and gravel soak a while, then you work and rub it up with your hands, and as the clay dissolves, dish it off as muddy water or mullock. You are careful to wash the pebbles in case there is any gold sticking to them. And so till all the muddy or clayey matter is gone, and there is nothing but clean gravel in the bottom of the dish. You work this off carefully, turning the dish about this way and that and swishing the water round in it. It requires some practice. The gold keeps to the bottom of the dish, by its own weight. At last there is only a little half-moon of sand or fine gravel in the bottom lower edge of the dish—you work the dish slanting from you. Presently the gold, if there was any in the dirt, appears in 'colours', grains, or little nuggets along the base of the half-moon of sand. The more gold there is in the dirt, or the coarser the gold is, the sooner it appears. A practised digger can work off the last speck of gravel, without losing a 'colour', by just working the water round and off in the dish. Also a careful digger could throw a handful of gold in a tub of dirt, and, washing it off in dishfuls, recover practically every colour.

The gold-washing 'cradle' is a box, shaped something like a boot, and the size of a travelling trunk, with rockers on, like a baby's cradle, and a stick up behind for a handle; on top, where you'll put your foot into the boot, is a tray with a perforated iron bottom; the clay and gravel is thrown on the tray, water thrown on it, and the cradle rocked smartly. The finer gravel and the mullock goes through and down over a sloping board covered with blanket, and with ledges on it to catch the gold. The dish was mostly used for prospecting; large quantities of wash dirt was put through the horse-power 'puddling-machine', which there isn't room to describe here.

"Ello, Dave!' said Pinter, after looking with mild surprise at the size of Dave's waste-heap. 'Tryin' for the second bottom?'

'Yes,' said Dave, guttural.

Pinter dropped his tools with a clatter at the foot of the waste-heap and scratched under his ear like an old cockatoo, which bird he resembled. Then he went to the windlass, and resting his hands on his knees, he peered down, while Dave stood by helpless and hopeless.

Pinter straightened himself, blinking like an owl, and looked carelessly over the graveyard.

'Tryin' for a secon' bottom,' he reflected absently. 'Eh, Dave?'

Dave only stood and looked black.

Pinter tilted back his head and scratched the roots of his chin-feathers, which stuck out all round like a dirty, ragged fan held horizontally.

'Kullers is safe,' reflected Pinter.

'All right?' snapped Dave. 'I suppose we must let him into it.'

'Kullers' was a big American buck nigger, and had been Pinter's mate for some time—Pinter was a man of odd mates; and what Pinter meant was that Kullers was safe to hold his tongue.

Next morning Pinter and his coloured mate appeared on the ground early, Pinter with some tools and the nigger with a windlass-bole on his shoulders. Pinter chose a spot about three panels or thirty feet along the other fence, the back fence of the cemetery, and started his hole. He lost no time for the sake of appearances, he sunk his shaft and started to drive straight for the point under the cemetery for which Dave was making; he gave out that he had bottomed on good 'indications' running in the other direction, and would work the ground outside the fence. Meanwhile Dave rigged a fan—partly for the sake of appearances, but mainly because his and Jim's lively imaginations made the air in the drive worse than it really was. A 'fan' is a thing like a paddle-wheel rigged in a box, about the size of a cradle, and something the shape of a shoe, but rounded over the top. There is a small grooved wheel on the axle of the fan outside, and an endless line, like a clothes-line, is carried over this wheel and a groove in the edge of a high light wooden driving-wheel rigged between two uprights in the rear and with a handle to turn. That's how the thing is driven. A wind-chute, like an endless pillow-slip, made of calico, with the mouth tacked over the open toe of the fan-box, and the end taken down the shaft and along the drive—this carries the fresh air into the workings.

Dave was working the ground on each side as he went, when one morning a thought struck him that should have struck him the day Pinter went to work. He felt mad that it hadn't struck him sooner.

Pinter and Kullers had also shifted their tent down into a nice quiet place in the Bush close handy; so, early next Sunday morning, while Pinter and Kullers were asleep, Dave posted Jim Bently to watch their tent, and whistle an alarm if they stirred, and then dropped down into Pinter's hole and saw at a glance what he was up to.

After that Dave lost no time: he drove straight on, encouraged by the thuds of Pinter's and Kullers' picks drawing nearer. They would strike his tunnel at right angles. Both parties worked long hours, only knocking off to fry a bit of steak in the pan, boil the billy, and throw themselves dressed on their bunks to get a few hours' sleep. Pinter had practical experience and a line clear of graves, and he made good time. The two parties now found it more comfortable to be not on speaking terms. Individually they grew furtive, and began to feel criminal like—at least Dave and Jim did. They'd start if a horse stumbled through the Bush, and expected to see a mounted policeman ride up at any moment and hear him ask questions. They had driven about thirty-five feet when, one Saturday afternoon, the strain became too great, and Dave and Jim got drunk. The spree lasted over Sunday, and on Monday morning they felt too shaky to come to work and had more drink. On Monday afternoon, Kullers, whose shift it was below, stuck his pick through the face of his drive into the wall of Dave's, about four feet from the end of it: the clay flaked away, leaving a hole as big as a wash-hand basin. They knocked off for the day and decided to let the other party take the offensive.

Tuesday morning Dave and Jim came to work, still feeling shaky. Jim went below, crawled along the drive, lit his candle, and stuck it in the spiked iron socket and the spike in the wall of the drive, quite close to the hole, without noticing either the hole or the increased freshness in the air. He started picking away at the 'face' and scraping the clay back from under his feet, and didn't hear Kullers come to work. Kullers came in softly and decided to try a bit of cheerful bluff. He stuck his great round black face through the hole, the whites of his eyes rolling horribly in the candle-light, and said, with a deep guffaw—

"Ullo! you dar'?'

No bandicoot ever went into his hole with the dogs after him quicker than Jim came out of his. He scrambled up the shaft by the foot-holes, and sat on the edge of the waste-heap, looking very pale.

'What's the matter?' asked Dave. 'Have you seen a ghost?'

'I've seen the—the devil!' gasped Jim. 'I'm—I'm done with this here ghoul business.'

The parties got on speaking terms again. Dave was very warm, but Jim's language was worse. Pinter scratched his chin-feathers reflectively till the other party cooled. There was no appealing to the Commissioner for goldfields; they were outside all law, whether of the goldfields or otherwise—so they did the only thing possible and sensible, they joined forces and became 'Poynton, Regan, & Party'. They agreed to work the ground from the separate shafts, and decided to go ahead, irrespective of appearances, and get as much dirt out and cradled as possible before the inevitable exposure came along. They found plenty of 'payable dirt', and soon the drive ended in a cluster of roomy chambers. They timbered up many coffins of various ages, burnt tarred canvas and brown paper, and kept the fan going. Outside they paid the storekeeper with difficulty and talked of hard times.

But one fine sunny morning, after about a week of partnership, they got a bad scare. Jim and Kullers were below, getting out dirt for all they were worth, and Pinter and Dave at their windlasses, when who should march down from the cemetery gate but Mother Middleton herself. She was a hard woman to look at. She still wore the old-fashioned crinoline and her hair in a greasy net; and on this as on most other sober occasions, she wore the expression of a rough Irish navvy who has just enough drink to make him nasty and is looking out for an excuse for a row. She had a stride like a grenadier. A digger had once measured her step by her footprints in the mud where she had stepped across a gutter: it measured three feet from toe to heel.

She marched to the grave of Jimmy Middleton, laid a dingy bunch of flowers thereon, with the gesture of an angry man banging his fist down on the table, turned on her heel, and marched out. The diggers were dirt beneath her feet. Presently they heard her drive on in her spring-cart on her way into town, and they drew breaths of relief.

It was afternoon. Dave and Pinter were feeling tired, and were just deciding to knock off work for that day when they heard a scuffling in the direction of the different shafts, and both Jim and Kullers dropped down and bundled in in a great hurry. Jim chuckled in a silly way, as if there was something funny, and Kullers guffawed in sympathy.

'What's up now?' demanded Dave apprehensively.

'Mother Middleton,' said Jim; 'she's blind mad drunk, and she's got a bottle in one hand and a new pitchfork in the other, that she's bringing out for some one.'

'How the hell did she drop to it?' exclaimed Pinter.

'Dunno,' said Jim. 'Anyway she's coming for us. Listen to her!'

They didn't have to listen hard. The language which came down the shaft—they weren't sure which one—and along the drives was enough to scare up the dead and make them take to the Bush.

'Why didn't you fools make off into the Bush and give us a chance, instead of giving her a lead here?' asked Dave.

Jim and Kullers began to wish they had done so.

Mrs Middleton began to throw stones down the shaft—it was Pinter's—and they, even the oldest and most anxious, began to grin in spite of themselves, for they knew she couldn't hurt them from the surface, and that, though she had been a working digger herself, she couldn't fill both shafts before the fumes of liquor overtook her.

'I wonder which shaf' she'll come down,' asked Kullers in a tone befitting the place and occasion.

'You'd better go and watch your shaft, Pinter,' said Dave, 'and Jim and I'll watch mine.'

'I—I won't,' said Pinter hurriedly. 'I'm—I'm a modest man.'

Then they heard a clang in the direction of Pinter's shaft.

'She's thrown her bottle down,' said Dave.

Jim crawled along the drive a piece, urged by curiosity, and returned hurriedly.

'She's broke the pitchfork off short, to use in the drive, and I believe she's coming down.'

'Her crinoline'll handicap her,' said Pinter vacantly, 'that's a comfort.'

'She's took it off!' said Dave excitedly; and peering along Pinter's drive, they saw first an elastic-sided boot, then a red-striped stocking, then a section of scarlet petticoat.

'Lemme out!' roared Pinter, lurching forward and making a swimming motion with his hands in the direction of Dave's drive. Kullers was already gone, and Jim well on the way. Dave, lanky and awkward, scrambled up the shaft last. Mrs Middleton made good time, considering she had the darkness to face and didn't know the workings, and when Dave reached the top he had a tear in the leg of his moleskins, and the blood ran from a nasty scratch. But he didn't wait to argue over the price of a new pair of trousers. He made off through the Bush in the direction of an encouraging whistle thrown back by Jim.

'She's too drunk to get her story listened to to-night,' said Dave. 'But to-morrow she'll bring the neighbourhood down on us.'

'And she's enough, without the neighbourhood,' reflected Pinter.

Some time after dark they returned cautiously, reconnoitred their camp, and after hiding in a hollow log such things as they couldn't carry, they rolled up their tents like the Arabs, and silently stole away.

The Chinaman's Ghost

'Simple as striking matches,' said Dave Regan, Bushman; 'but it gave me the biggest scare I ever had—except, perhaps, the time I stumbled in the dark into a six-feet digger's hole, which might have been eighty feet deep for all I knew when I was falling. (There was an eighty-feet shaft left open close by.)

'It was the night of the day after the Queen's birthday. I was sinking a shaft with Jim Bently and Andy Page on the old Redclay goldfield, and we camped in a tent on the creek. Jim and me went to some races that was held at Peter Anderson's pub., about four miles across the ridges, on Queen's birthday. Andy was a quiet sort of chap, a teetotaller, and we'd disgusted him the last time he was out for a holiday with us, so he stayed at home and washed and mended his clothes, and read an arithmetic book. (He used to keep the accounts, and it took him most of his spare time.)

'Jim and me had a pretty high time. We all got pretty tight after the races, and I wanted to fight Jim, or Jim wanted to fight me—I don't remember which. We were old chums, and we nearly always wanted to fight each other when we got a bit on, and we'd fight if we weren't stopped. I remember once Jim got maudlin drunk and begged and prayed of me to fight him, as if he was praying for his life. Tom Tarrant, the coach-driver, used to say that Jim and me must be related, else we wouldn't hate each other so much when we were tight and truthful.

'Anyway, this day, Jim got the sulks, and caught his horse and went home early in the evening. My dog went home with him too; I must have been carrying on pretty bad to disgust the dog.

'Next evening I got disgusted with myself, and started to walk home. I'd lost my hat, so Peter Anderson lent me an old one of his, that he'd worn on Ballarat he said: it was a hard, straw, flat, broad-brimmed affair, and fitted my headache pretty tight. Peter gave me a small flask of whisky to help me home. I had to go across some flats and up a long dark gully called Murderer's Gully, and over a gap called Dead Man's Gap, and down the ridge and gullies to Redclay Creek. The lonely flats were covered with blue-grey gum bush, and looked ghostly enough in the moonlight, and I was pretty shaky, but I had a pull at the flask and a mouthful of water at a creek and felt right enough. I began to whistle, and then to sing: I never used to sing unless I thought I was a couple of miles out of earshot of any one.

'Murderer's Gully was deep and pretty dark most times, and of course it was haunted. Women and children wouldn't go through it after dark; and even me, when I'd grown up, I'd hold my back pretty holler, and whistle, and walk quick going along there at night-time. We're all afraid of ghosts, but we won't let on.

'Some one had skinned a dead calf during the day and left it on the track, and it gave me a jump, I promise you. It looked like two corpses laid out naked. I finished the whisky and started up over the gap. All of a sudden a great 'old man' kangaroo went across the track with a thud-thud, and up the siding, and that startled me. Then the naked, white glistening trunk of a stringy-bark tree, where some one had stripped off a sheet of bark, started out from a bend in the track in a shaft of moonlight, and that gave me a jerk. I was pretty shaky before I started. There was a Chinaman's grave close by the track on the top of the gap. An old chow had lived in a hut there for many years, and fossicked on the old diggings, and one day he was found dead in the hut, and the Government gave some one a pound to bury him. When I was a nipper we reckoned that his ghost haunted the gap, and cursed in Chinese because the bones hadn't been sent home to China. It was a lonely, ghostly place enough.

'It had been a smotheringly hot day and very close coming across the flats and up the gully—not a breath of air; but now as I got higher I saw signs of the thunderstorm we'd expected all day, and felt the breath of a warm breeze on my face. When I got into the top of the gap the first thing I saw was something white amongst the dark bushes over the spot where the Chinaman's grave was, and I stood staring at it with both eyes. It moved out of the shadow presently, and I saw that it was a white bullock, and I felt relieved. I'd hardly felt relieved when, all at once, there came a "pat-pat-pat" of running feet close behind me! I jumped round quick, but there was nothing there, and while I stood staring all ways for Sunday, there came a "pat-pat", then a pause, and then "pat-pat-pat-pat" behind me again: it was like some one dodging and running off that time. I started to walk down the track pretty fast, but hadn't gone a dozen yards when "pat-pat-pat", it was close behind me again. I jerked my eyes over my shoulder but kept my legs going. There was nothing behind, but I fancied I saw something slip into the Bush to the right. It must have been the moonlight on the moving boughs; there was a good breeze blowing now. I got down to a more level track, and was making across a spur to the main road, when "pat-pat!" "pat-pat-pat, pat-pat-pat!" it was after me again. Then I began to run—and it began to run too! "pat-pat-pat" after me all the time. I hadn't time to look round. Over the spur and down the siding and across the flat to the road I went as fast as I could split my legs apart. I had a scared idea that I was getting a touch of the "jim-jams", and that frightened me more than any outside ghost could have done. I stumbled a few times, and saved myself, but, just before I reached the road, I fell slithering on to my hands on the grass and gravel. I thought I'd broken both my wrists. I stayed for a moment on my hands and knees, quaking and listening, squinting round like a great gohana; I couldn't hear nor see anything. I picked myself up, and had hardly got on one end, when "pat-pat!" it was after me again. I must have run a mile and a half altogether that night. It was still about three-quarters of a mile to the camp, and I ran till my heart beat in my head and my lungs choked up in my throat. I saw our tent-fire and took off my hat to run faster. The footsteps stopped, then something about the hat touched my fingers, and I stared at it—and the thing dawned on me. I hadn't noticed at Peter Anderson's—my head was too swimmy to notice anything. It was an old hat of the style that the first diggers used to wear, with a couple of loose ribbon ends, three or four inches long, from the band behind. As long as I walked quietly through the gully, and there was no wind, the tails didn't flap, but when I got up into the breeze, they flapped or were still according to how the wind lifted them or pressed them down flat on the brim. And when I ran they tapped all the time; and the hat being tight on my head, the tapping of the ribbon ends against the straw sounded loud of course.

'I sat down on a log for a while to get some of my wind back and cool down, and then I went to the camp as quietly as I could, and had a long drink of water.

'"You seem to be a bit winded, Dave," said Jim Bently, "and mighty thirsty. Did the Chinaman's ghost chase you?"

'I told him not to talk rot, and went into the tent, and lay down on my bunk, and had a good rest.'

The Loaded Dog

Dave Regan, Jim Bently, and Andy Page were sinking a shaft at Stony Creek in search of a rich gold quartz reef which was supposed to exist in the vicinity. There is always a rich reef supposed to exist in the vicinity; the only questions are whether it is ten feet or hundreds beneath the surface, and in which direction. They had struck some pretty solid rock, also water which kept them baling. They used the old-fashioned blasting-powder and time-fuse. They'd make a sausage or cartridge of blasting-powder in a skin of strong calico or canvas, the mouth sewn and bound round the end of the fuse; they'd dip the cartridge in melted tallow to make it water-tight, get the drill-hole as dry as possible, drop in the cartridge with some dry dust, and wad and ram with stiff clay and broken brick. Then they'd light the fuse and get out of the hole and wait. The result was usually an ugly pot-hole in the bottom of the shaft and half a barrow-load of broken rock.

There was plenty of fish in the creek, fresh-water bream, cod, cat-fish, and tailers. The party were fond of fish, and Andy and Dave of fishing. Andy would fish for three hours at a stretch if encouraged by a 'nibble' or a 'bite' now and then—say once in twenty minutes. The butcher was always willing to give meat in exchange for fish when they caught more than they could eat; but now it was winter, and these fish wouldn't bite. However, the creek was low, just a chain of muddy water-holes, from the hole with a few bucketfuls in it to the sizable pool with an average depth of six or seven feet, and they could get fish by baling out the smaller holes or muddying up the water in the larger ones till the fish rose to the surface. There was the cat-fish, with spikes growing out of the sides of its head, and if you got pricked you'd know it, as Dave said. Andy took off his boots, tucked up his trousers, and went into a hole one day to stir up the mud with his feet, and he knew it. Dave scooped one out with his hand and got pricked, and he knew it too; his arm swelled, and the pain throbbed up into his shoulder, and down into his stomach too, he said, like a toothache he had once, and kept him awake for two nights—only the toothache pain had a 'burred edge', Dave said.

Dave got an idea.

'Why not blow the fish up in the big water-hole with a cartridge?' he said. 'I'll try it.'

He thought the thing out and Andy Page worked it out. Andy usually put Dave's theories into practice if they were practicable, or bore the blame for the failure and the chaffing of his mates if they weren't.

He made a cartridge about three times the size of those they used in the rock. Jim Bently said it was big enough to blow the bottom out of the river. The inner skin was of stout calico; Andy stuck the end of a six-foot piece of fuse well down in the powder and bound the mouth of the bag firmly to it with whipcord. The idea was to sink the cartridge in the water with the open end of the fuse attached to a float on the surface, ready for lighting. Andy dipped the cartridge in melted bees'-wax to make it water-tight. 'We'll have to leave it some time before we light it,' said Dave, 'to give the fish time to get over their scare when we put it in, and come nosing round again; so we'll want it well water-tight.'

Round the cartridge Andy, at Dave's suggestion, bound a strip of sail canvas—that they used for making water-bags—to increase the force of the explosion, and round that he pasted layers of stiff brown paper—on the plan of the sort of fireworks we called 'gun-crackers'. He let the paper dry in the sun, then he sewed a covering of two thicknesses of canvas over it, and bound the thing from end to end with stout fishing-line. Dave's schemes were elaborate, and he often worked his inventions out to nothing. The cartridge was rigid and solid enough now—a formidable bomb; but Andy and Dave wanted to be sure. Andy sewed on another layer of canvas, dipped the cartridge in melted tallow, twisted a length of fencing-wire round it as an afterthought, dipped it in tallow again, and stood it carefully against a tent-peg, where he'd know where to find it, and wound the fuse loosely round it. Then he went to the camp-fire to try some potatoes which were boiling in their jackets in a billy, and to see about frying some chops for dinner. Dave and Jim were at work in the claim that morning.

They had a big black young retriever dog—or rather an overgrown pup, a big, foolish, four-footed mate, who was always slobbering round them and lashing their legs with his heavy tail that swung round like a stock-whip. Most of his head was usually a red, idiotic, slobbering grin of appreciation of his own silliness. He seemed to take life, the world, his two-legged mates, and his own instinct as a huge joke. He'd retrieve anything: he carted back most of the camp rubbish that Andy threw away. They had a cat that died in hot weather, and Andy threw it a good distance away in the scrub; and early one morning the dog found the cat, after it had been dead a week or so, and carried it back to camp, and laid it just inside the tent-flaps, where it could best make its presence known when the mates should rise and begin to sniff suspiciously in the sickly smothering atmosphere of the summer sunrise. He used to retrieve them when they went in swimming; he'd jump in after them, and take their hands in his mouth, and try to swim out with them, and scratch their naked bodies with his paws. They loved him for his good-heartedness and his foolishness, but when they wished to enjoy a swim they had to tie him up in camp.

He watched Andy with great interest all the morning making the cartridge, and hindered him considerably, trying to help; but about noon he went off to the claim to see how Dave and Jim were getting on, and to come home to dinner with them. Andy saw them coming, and put a panful of mutton-chops on the fire. Andy was cook to-day; Dave and Jim stood with their backs to the fire, as Bushmen do in all weathers, waiting till dinner should be ready. The retriever went nosing round after something he seemed to have missed.

Andy's brain still worked on the cartridge; his eye was caught by the glare of an empty kerosene-tin lying in the bushes, and it struck him that it wouldn't be a bad idea to sink the cartridge packed with clay, sand, or stones in the tin, to increase the force of the explosion. He may have been all out, from a scientific point of view, but the notion looked all right to him. Jim Bently, by the way, wasn't interested in their 'damned silliness'. Andy noticed an empty treacle-tin—the sort with the little tin neck or spout soldered on to the top for the convenience of pouring out the treacle—and it struck him that this would have made the best kind of cartridge-case: he would only have had to pour in the powder, stick the fuse in through the neck, and cork and seal it with bees'-wax. He was turning to suggest this to Dave, when Dave glanced over his shoulder to see how the chops were doing—and bolted. He explained afterwards that he thought he heard the pan spluttering extra, and looked to see if the chops were burning. Jim Bently looked behind and bolted after Dave. Andy stood stock-still, staring after them.

'Run, Andy! run!' they shouted back at him. 'Run!!! Look behind you, you fool!' Andy turned slowly and looked, and there, close behind him, was the retriever with the cartridge in his mouth—wedged into his broadest and silliest grin. And that wasn't all. The dog had come round the fire to Andy, and the loose end of the fuse had trailed and waggled over the burning sticks into the blaze; Andy had slit and nicked the firing end of the fuse well, and now it was hissing and spitting properly.

Andy's legs started with a jolt; his legs started before his brain did, and he made after Dave and Jim. And the dog followed Andy.

Dave and Jim were good runners—Jim the best—for a short distance; Andy was slow and heavy, but he had the strength and the wind and could last. The dog leapt and capered round him, delighted as a dog could be to find his mates, as he thought, on for a frolic. Dave and Jim kept shouting back, 'Don't foller us! don't foller us, you coloured fool!' but Andy kept on, no matter how they dodged. They could never explain, any more than the dog, why they followed each other, but so they ran, Dave keeping in Jim's track in all its turnings, Andy after Dave, and the dog circling round Andy—the live fuse swishing in all directions and hissing and spluttering and stinking. Jim yelling to Dave not to follow him, Dave shouting to Andy to go in another direction—to 'spread out', and Andy roaring at the dog to go home. Then

Andy's brain began to work, stimulated by the crisis: he tried to get a running kick at the dog, but the dog dodged; he snatched up sticks and stones and threw them at the dog and ran on again. The retriever saw that he'd made a mistake about Andy, and left him and bounded after Dave. Dave, who had the presence of mind to think that the fuse's time wasn't up yet, made a dive and a grab for the dog, caught him by the tail, and as he swung round snatched the cartridge out of his mouth and flung it as far as he could: the dog immediately bounded after it and retrieved it. Dave roared and cursed at the dog, who seeing that Dave was offended, left him and went after Jim, who was well ahead. Jim swung to a sapling and went up it like a native bear; it was a young sapling, and Jim couldn't safely get more than ten or twelve feet from the ground. The dog laid the cartridge, as carefully as if it was a kitten, at the foot of the sapling, and capered and leaped and whooped joyously round under Jim. The big pup reckoned that this was part of the lark—he was all right now—it was Jim who was out for a spree. The fuse sounded as if it were going a mile a minute. Jim tried to climb higher and the sapling bent and cracked. Jim fell on his feet and ran. The dog swooped on the cartridge and followed. It all took but a very few moments. Jim ran to a digger's hole, about ten feet deep, and dropped down into it—landing on soft mud—and was safe. The dog grinned sardonically down on him, over the edge, for a moment, as if he thought it would be a good lark to drop the cartridge down on Jim.

'Go away, Tommy,' said Jim feebly, 'go away.'

The dog bounded off after Dave, who was the only one in sight now; Andy had dropped behind a log, where he lay flat on his face, having suddenly remembered a picture of the Russo-Turkish war with a circle of Turks lying flat on their faces (as if they were ashamed) round a newly-arrived shell.

There was a small hotel or shanty on the creek, on the main road, not far from the claim. Dave was desperate, the time flew much faster in his stimulated imagination than it did in reality, so he made for the shanty. There were several casual Bushmen on the verandah and in the bar; Dave rushed into the bar, banging the door to behind him. 'My dog!' he gasped, in reply to the astonished stare of the publican, 'the blanky retriever—he's got a live cartridge in his mouth—'

The retriever, finding the front door shut against him, had bounded round and in by the back way, and now stood smiling in the doorway leading from the passage, the cartridge still in his mouth and the fuse spluttering. They burst out of that bar. Tommy bounded first after one and then after another, for, being a young dog, he tried to make friends with everybody.

The Bushmen ran round corners, and some shut themselves in the stable. There was a new weather-board and corrugated-iron kitchen and wash-house on piles in the back-yard, with some women washing clothes inside. Dave and the publican bundled in there and shut the door—the publican cursing Dave and calling him a crimson fool, in hurried tones, and wanting to know what the hell he came here for.

The retriever went in under the kitchen, amongst the piles, but, luckily for those inside, there was a vicious yellow mongrel cattle-dog sulking and nursing his nastiness under there—a sneaking, fighting, thieving canine, whom neighbours had tried for years to shoot or poison. Tommy saw his danger—he'd had experience from this dog—and started out and across the yard, still sticking to the cartridge. Half-way across the yard the yellow dog caught him and nipped him. Tommy dropped the cartridge, gave one terrified yell, and took to the Bush. The yellow dog followed him to the fence and then ran back to see what he had dropped.

Nearly a dozen other dogs came from round all the corners and under the buildings—spidery, thievish, cold-blooded kangaroo-dogs, mongrel sheep- and cattle-dogs, vicious black and yellow dogs—that slip after you in the dark, nip your heels, and vanish without explaining—and yapping, yelping small fry. They kept at a respectable distance round the nasty yellow dog, for it was dangerous to go near him when he thought he had found something which might be good for a dog to eat. He sniffed at the cartridge twice, and was just taking a third cautious sniff when—

It was very good blasting powder—a new brand that Dave had recently got up from Sydney; and the cartridge had been excellently well made. Andy was very patient and painstaking in all he did, and nearly as handy as the average sailor with needles, twine, canvas, and rope.

Bushmen say that that kitchen jumped off its piles and on again. When the smoke and dust cleared away, the remains of the nasty yellow dog were lying against the paling fence of the yard looking as if he had been kicked into a fire by a horse and afterwards rolled in the dust under a barrow, and finally thrown against the fence from a distance. Several saddle-horses, which had been 'hanging-up' round the verandah, were galloping wildly down the road in clouds of dust, with broken bridle-reins flying; and from a circle round the outskirts, from every point of the compass in the scrub, came the yelping of dogs. Two of them went home, to the place where they were born, thirty miles away, and reached it the same night and stayed there; it was not till towards evening that the rest came back cautiously to make inquiries. One was trying to walk on two legs, and most of 'em looked more or less singed; and a little, singed, stumpy-tailed dog, who had been in the habit of hopping the back half of him along on one leg, had reason to be glad that he'd saved up the other leg all those years, for he needed it now. There was one old one-eyed cattle-dog round that shanty for years afterwards, who couldn't stand the smell of a gun being cleaned. He it was who had taken an interest, only second to that of the yellow dog, in the cartridge. Bushmen said that it was amusing to slip up on his blind side and stick a dirty ramrod under his nose: he wouldn't wait to bring his solitary eye to bear—he'd take to the Bush and stay out all night.

For half an hour or so after the explosion there were several Bushmen round behind the stable who crouched, doubled up, against the wall, or rolled gently on the dust, trying to laugh without shrieking. There were two white women in hysterics at the house, and a half-caste rushing aimlessly round with a dipper of cold water. The publican was holding his wife tight and begging her between her squawks, to 'hold up for my sake, Mary, or I'll lam the life out of ye.'

Dave decided to apologise later on, 'when things had settled a bit,' and went back to camp. And the dog that had done it all, 'Tommy', the great, idiotic mongrel retriever, came slobbering round Dave and lashing his legs with his tail, and trotted home after him, smiling his broadest, longest, and reddest smile of amiability, and apparently satisfied for one afternoon with the fun he'd had.

Andy chained the dog up securely, and cooked some more chops, while Dave went to help Jim out of the hole.

And most of this is why, for years afterwards, lanky, easy-going Bushmen, riding lazily past Dave's camp, would cry, in a lazy drawl and with just a hint of the nasal twang—

"El-lo, Da-a-ve! How's the fishin' getting on, Da-a-ve?'

Poisonous Jimmy Gets Left

I

Dave Regan's Yarn

'When we got tired of digging about Mudgee-Budgee, and getting no gold,' said Dave Regan, Bushman, 'me and my mate, Jim Bently, decided to take a turn at droving; so we went with Bob Baker, the drover, overland with a big mob of cattle, way up into Northern Queensland.

'We couldn't get a job on the home track, and we spent most of our money, like a pair of fools, at a pub. at a town way up over the border, where they had a flash barmaid from Brisbane. We sold our pack-horses and pack-saddles, and rode out of that town with our swags on our riding-horses in front of us. We had another spree at another place, and by the time we got near New South Wales we were pretty well stumped.

'Just the other side of Mulgatown, near the border, we came on a big mob of cattle in a paddock, and a party of drovers camped on the creek. They had brought the cattle down from the north and were going no farther with them; their boss had ridden on into Mulgatown to get the cheques to pay them off, and they were waiting for him.

'"And Poisonous Jimmy is waiting for us," said one of them.

'Poisonous Jimmy kept a shanty a piece along the road from their camp towards Mulgatown. He was called "Poisonous Jimmy" perhaps on account of his liquor, or perhaps because he had a job of poisoning dingoes on a station in the Bogan scrubs at one time. He was a sharp publican. He had a girl, and they said that whenever a shearing-shed cut-out on his side and he saw the shearers coming along the road, he'd say to the girl, "Run and get your best frock on, Mary! Here's the shearers comin'." And if a chequeman wouldn't drink he'd try to get him into his bar and shout for him till he was too drunk to keep his hands out of his pockets.

'"But he won't get us," said another of the drovers. "I'm going to ride straight into Mulgatown and send my money home by the post as soon as I get it."

'"You've always said that, Jack," said the first drover.

'We yarned a while, and had some tea, and then me and Jim got on our horses and rode on. We were burned to bricks and ragged and dusty and parched up enough, and so were our horses. We only had a few shillings to carry us four or five hundred miles home, but it was mighty hot and dusty, and we felt that we must have a drink at the shanty. This was west of the sixpenny-line at that time—all drinks were a shilling along here.

'Just before we reached the shanty I got an idea.

'"We'll plant our swags in the scrub," I said to Jim.

'"What for?" said Jim.

'"Never mind—you'll see," I said.

'So we unstrapped our swags and hid them in the mulga scrub by the side of the road; then we rode on to the shanty, got down, and hung our horses to the verandah posts.

'"Poisonous" came out at once, with a smile on him that would have made anybody home-sick.

'He was a short nuggety man, and could use his hands, they said; he looked as if he'd be a nasty, vicious, cool customer in a fight—he wasn't the sort of man you'd care to try and swindle a second time. He had a monkey shave when he shaved, but now it was all frill and stubble—like a bush fence round a stubble-field. He had a broken nose, and a cunning, sharp, suspicious eye that squinted, and a cold stony eye that seemed fixed. If you didn't know him well you might talk to him for five minutes, looking at him in the cold stony eye, and then discover that it was the sharp cunning little eye that was watching you all the time. It was awful embarrassing. It must have made him awkward to deal with in a fight.

'"Good day, mates," he said.

'"Good day," we said.

'"It's hot."

'"It's hot."

'We went into the bar, and Poisonous got behind the counter.

'"What are you going to have?" he asked, rubbing up his glasses with a rag.

'We had two long-beers.

'"Never mind that," said Poisonous, seeing me put my hand in my pocket; "it's my shout. I don't suppose your boss is back yet? I saw him go in to Mulgatown this morning."

'"No, he ain't back," I said; "I wish he was. We're getting tired of waiting for him. We'll give him another hour, and then some of us will have to ride in to see whether he's got on the boose, and get hold of him if he has."

'"I suppose you're waiting for your cheques?" he said, turning to fix some bottles on the shelf.

'"Yes," I said, "we are;" and I winked at Jim, and Jim winked back as solemn as an owl.

'Poisonous asked us all about the trip, and how long we'd been on the track, and what sort of a boss we had, dropping the questions offhand now an' then, as for the sake of conversation. We could see that he was trying to get at the size of our supposed cheques, so we answered accordingly.

'"Have another drink," he said, and he filled the pewters up again. "It's up to me," and he set to work boring out the glasses with his rag, as if he was short-handed and the bar was crowded with customers, and screwing up his face into what I suppose he considered an innocent or unconscious expression. The girl began to sidle in and out with a smart frock and a see-you-after-dark smirk on.

'"Have you had dinner?" she asked. We could have done with a good meal, but it was too risky—the drovers' boss might come along while we were at dinner and get into conversation with Poisonous. So we said we'd had dinner.

'Poisonous filled our pewters again in an offhand way.

'"I wish the boss would come," said Jim with a yawn. "I want to get into Mulgatown to-night, and I want to get some shirts and things before I go in. I ain't got a decent rag to me back. I don't suppose there's ten bob amongst the lot of us."

'There was a general store back on the creek, near the drovers' camp.

'"Oh, go to the store and get what you want," said Poisonous, taking a sovereign from the till and tossing it on to the counter. "You can fix it up with me when your boss comes. Bring your mates along."

'"Thank you," said Jim, taking up the sovereign carelessly and dropping it into his pocket.

'"Well, Jim," I said, "suppose we get back to camp and see how the chaps are getting on?"

'"All right," said Jim.

'"Tell them to come down and get a drink," said Poisonous; "or, wait, you can take some beer along to them if you like," and he gave us half a gallon of beer in a billy-can. He knew what the first drink meant with Bushmen back from a long dry trip.

'We got on our horses, I holding the billy very carefully, and rode back to where our swags were.

'"I say," said Jim, when we'd strapped the swags to the saddles, "suppose we take the beer back to those chaps: it's meant for them, and it's only a fair thing, anyway—we've got as much as we can hold till we get into Mulgatown."

'"It might get them into a row," I said, "and they seem decent chaps. Let's hang the billy on a twig, and that old swagman that's coming along will think there's angels in the Bush."

'"Oh! what's a row?" said Jim. "They can take care of themselves; they'll have the beer anyway and a lark with Poisonous when they take the can back and it comes to explanations. I'll ride back to them."

'So Jim rode back to the drovers' camp with the beer, and when he came back to me he said that the drovers seemed surprised, but they drank good luck to him.

'We rode round through the mulga behind the shanty and came out on the road again on the Mulgatown side: we only stayed at Mulgatown to buy some tucker and tobacco, then we pushed on and camped for the night about seven miles on the safe side of the town.'

II

'Talkin' o' Poisonous Jimmy, I can tell you a yarn about him. We'd brought a mob of cattle down for a squatter the other side of Mulgatown. We camped about seven miles the other side of the town, waitin' for the station hands to come and take charge of the stock, while the boss rode on into town to draw our money. Some of us was goin' back, though in the end we all went into Mulgatown and had a boose up with the boss. But while we was waitin' there come along two fellers that had been drovin' up north. They yarned a while, an' then went on to Poisonous Jimmy's place, an' in about an hour one on 'em come ridin' back with a can of beer that he said Poisonous had sent for us. We all knew Jimmy's little games—the beer was a bait to get us on the drunk at his place; but we drunk the beer, and reckoned to have a lark with him afterwards. When the boss come back, an' the station hands to take the bullocks, we started into Mulgatown. We stopped outside Poisonous's place an' handed the can to the girl that was grinnin' on the verandah. Poisonous come out with a grin on him like a parson with a broken nose.

'"Good day, boys!" he says.

'"Good day, Poisonous," we says.

'"It's hot," he says.

'"It's blanky hot," I says.

'He seemed to expect us to get down. "Where are you off to?" he says.

'"Mulgatown," I says. "It will be cooler there," and we sung out, "So-long, Poisonous!" and rode on.

'He stood starin' for a minute; then he started shoutin', "Hi! hi there!" after us, but we took no notice, an' rode on. When we looked back last he was runnin' into the scrub with a bridle in his hand.

'We jogged along easily till we got within a mile of Mulgatown, when we heard somebody gallopin' after us, an' lookin' back we saw it was Poisonous.

'He was too mad and too winded to speak at first, so he rode along with us a bit gasping: then he burst out.

'"Where's them other two carnal blanks?" he shouted.

'"What other two?" I asked. "We're all here. What's the matter with you anyway?"

'"All here!" he yelled. "You're a lurid liar! What the flamin' sheol do you mean by swiggin' my beer an' flingin' the coloured can in me face? without as much as thank yer! D'yer think I'm a flamin'—!"

'Oh, but Poisonous Jimmy was wild.

'"Well, we'll pay for your dirty beer," says one of the chaps, puttin' his hand in his pocket. "We didn't want yer slush. It tasted as if it had been used before."

'"Pay for it!" yelled Jimmy. "I'll—well take it out of one of yer bleedin' hides!"

'We stopped at once, and I got down an' obliged Jimmy for a few rounds. He was a nasty customer to fight; he could use his hands, and was cool as a cucumber as soon as he took his coat off: besides, he had one squirmy little business eye, and a big wall-eye, an', even if you knowed him well, you couldn't help watchin' the stony eye—it was no good watchin' his eyes, you had to watch his hands, and he might have managed me if the boss hadn't stopped the fight. The boss was a big, quiet-voiced man, that didn't swear.

'"Now, look here, Myles," said the boss (Jimmy's name was Myles)—"Now, look here, Myles," sez the boss, "what's all this about?"

'"What's all this about?" says Jimmy, gettin' excited agen. "Why, two fellers that belonged to your party come along to my place an' put up half-a-dozen drinks, an' borrered a sovereign, an' got a can o' beer on the strength of their cheques. They sez they was waitin' for you—an' I want my crimson money out o' some one!"

'"What was they like?" asks the boss.

'"Like?" shouted Poisonous, swearin' all the time. "One was a blanky long, sandy, sawny feller, and the other was a short, slim feller with black hair. Your blanky men knows all about them because they had the blanky billy o' beer."

'"Now, what's this all about, you chaps?" sez the boss to us.

'So we told him as much as we knowed about them two fellers.

'I've heard men swear that could swear in a rough shearin'-shed, but I never heard a man swear like Poisonous Jimmy when he saw how he'd been left. It was enough to split stumps. He said he wanted to see those fellers, just once, before he died.

'He rode with us into Mulgatown, got mad drunk, an' started out along the road with a tomahawk after the long sandy feller and the slim dark feller; but two mounted police went after him an' fetched him back. He said he only wanted justice; he said he only wanted to stun them two fellers till he could give 'em in charge.

'They fined him ten bob.'

The Ghostly Door

Told by one of Dave's mates.

Dave and I were tramping on a lonely Bush track in New Zealand, making for a sawmill where we expected to get work, and we were caught in one of those three-days' gales, with rain and hail in it and cold enough to cut off a man's legs. Camping out was not to be thought of, so we just tramped on in silence, with the stinging pain coming between our shoulder-blades—from cold, weariness, and the weight of our swags—and our boots, full of water, going splosh, splosh, splosh along the track. We were settled to it—to drag on like wet, weary, muddy working bullocks till we came to somewhere—when, just before darkness settled down, we saw the loom of a humpy of some sort on the slope of a tussock hill, back from the road, and we made for it, without holding a consultation.

It was a two-roomed hut built of waste timber from a sawmill, and was either a deserted settler's home or a hut attached to an abandoned sawmill round there somewhere. The windows were boarded up. We dumped our swags under the little verandah and banged at the door, to make sure; then Dave pulled a couple of boards off a window and looked in: there was light enough to see that the place was empty. Dave pulled off some more boards, put his arm in through a broken pane, clicked the catch back, and then pushed up the window and got in. I handed in the swags to him. The room was very draughty; the wind came in through the broken window and the cracks between the slabs, so we tried the partitioned-off room—the bedroom—and that was better. It had been lined with chaff-bags, and there were two stretchers left by some timber-getters or other Bush contractors who'd camped there last; and there were a box and a couple of three-legged stools.

We carried the remnant of the wood-heap inside, made a fire, and put the billy on. We unrolled our swags and spread the blankets on the stretchers; and then we stripped and hung our clothes about the fire to dry. There was plenty in our tucker-bags, so we had a good feed. I hadn't shaved for days, and Dave had a coarse red beard with a twist in it like an ill-used fibre brush—a beard that got redder the longer it grew; he had a hooked nose, and his hair stood straight up (I never saw a man so easy-going about the expression and so scared about the head), and he was very tall, with long, thin, hairy legs. We must have looked a weird pair as we sat there, naked, on the low three-legged stools, with the billy and the tucker on the box between us, and ate our bread and meat with clasp-knives.

'I shouldn't wonder,' says Dave, 'but this is the "whare"* where the murder was that we heard about along the road. I suppose if any one was to come along now and look in he'd get scared.' Then after a while he looked down at the flooring-boards close to my feet, and scratched his ear, and said, 'That looks very much like a blood-stain under your stool, doesn't it, Jim?'

* 'Whare', 'whorrie', Maori name for house.

I shifted my feet and presently moved the stool farther away from the fire—it was too hot.

I wouldn't have liked to camp there by myself, but I don't think Dave would have minded—he'd knocked round too much in the Australian Bush to mind anything much, or to be surprised at anything; besides, he was more than half murdered once by a man who said afterwards that he'd mistook him for some one else: he must have been a very short-sighted murderer.

Presently we put tobacco, matches, and bits of candle we had, on the two stools by the heads of our bunks, turned in, and filled up and smoked comfortably, dropping in a lazy word now and again about nothing in particular. Once I happened to look across at Dave, and saw him sitting up a bit and watching the door. The door opened very slowly, wide, and a black cat walked in, looked first at me, then at Dave, and walked out again; and the door closed behind it.

Dave scratched his ear. 'That's rum,' he said. 'I could have sworn I fastened that door. They must have left the cat behind.'

'It looks like it,' I said. 'Neither of us has been on the boose lately.'

He got out of bed and up on his long hairy spindle-shanks.

The door had the ordinary, common black oblong lock with a brass knob. Dave tried the latch and found it fast; he turned the knob, opened the door, and called, 'Puss—puss—puss!' but the cat wouldn't come. He shut the door, tried the knob to see that the catch had caught, and got into bed again.

He'd scarcely settled down when the door opened slowly, the black cat walked in, stared hard at Dave, and suddenly turned and darted out as the door closed smartly.

I looked at Dave and he looked at me—hard; then he scratched the back of his head. I never saw a man look so puzzled in the face and scared about the head.

He got out of bed very cautiously, took a stick of firewood in his hand, sneaked up to the door, and snatched it open. There was no one there. Dave took the candle and went into the next room, but couldn't see the cat. He came back and sat down by the fire and meowed, and presently the cat answered him and came in from somewhere—she'd been outside the window, I suppose; he kept on meowing and she sidled up and rubbed against his hairy shin. Dave could generally bring a cat that way. He had a weakness for cats. I'd seen him kick a dog, and hammer a horse—brutally, I thought—but I never saw him hurt a cat or let any one else do it. Dave was good to cats: if a cat had a family where Dave was round, he'd see her all right and comfortable, and only drown a fair surplus. He said once to me, 'I can understand a man kicking a dog, or hammering a horse when it plays up, but I can't understand a man hurting a cat.'

He gave this cat something to eat. Then he went and held the light close to the lock of the door, but could see nothing wrong with it. He found a key on the mantel-shelf and locked the door. He got into bed again, and the cat jumped up and curled down at the foot and started her old drum going, like shot in a sieve. Dave bent down and patted her, to tell her he'd meant no harm when he stretched out his legs, and then he settled down again.

We had some books of the 'Deadwood Dick' school. Dave was reading 'The Grisly Ghost of the Haunted Gulch', and I had 'The Dismembered Hand', or 'The Disembowelled Corpse', or some such names. They were first-class preparation for a ghost.

I was reading away, and getting drowsy, when I noticed a movement and saw Dave's frightened head rising, with the terrified shadow of it on the wall. He was staring at the door, over his book, with both eyes. And that door was opening again—slowly—and Dave had locked it! I never felt anything so creepy: the foot of my bunk was behind the door, and I drew up my feet as it came open; it opened wide, and stood so. We waited, for five minutes it seemed, hearing each other breathe, watching for the door to close; then Dave got out, very gingerly, and up on one end, and went to the door like a cat on wet bricks.

'You shot the bolt OUTSIDE the catch,' I said, as he caught hold of the door—like one grabs a craw-fish.

'I'll swear I didn't,' said Dave. But he'd already turned the key a couple of times, so he couldn't be sure. He shut and locked the door again. 'Now, get out and see for yourself,' he said.

I got out, and tried the door a couple of times and found it all right. Then we both tried, and agreed that it was locked.

I got back into bed, and Dave was about half in when a thought struck him. He got the heaviest piece of firewood and stood it against the door.

'What are you doing that for?' I asked.

'If there's a broken-down burglar camped round here, and trying any of his funny business, we'll hear him if he tries to come in while we're asleep,' says Dave. Then he got back into bed. We composed our nerves with the 'Haunted Gulch' and 'The Disembowelled Corpse', and after a while I heard Dave snore, and was just dropping off when the stick fell from the door against my big toe and then to the ground with tremendous clatter. I snatched up my feet and sat up with a jerk, and so did Dave—the cat went over the partition. That door opened, only a little way this time, paused, and shut suddenly. Dave got out, grabbed a stick, skipped to the door, and clutched at the knob as if it were a nettle, and the door wouldn't come!—it was fast and locked! Then Dave's face began to look as frightened as his hair. He lit his candle at the fire, and asked me to come with him; he unlocked the door and we went into the other room, Dave shading his candle very carefully and feeling his way slow with his feet. The room was empty; we tried the outer door and found it locked.

'It muster gone by the winder,' whispered Dave. I noticed that he said 'it' instead of 'he'. I saw that he himself was shook up, and it only needed that to scare me bad.

We went back to the bedroom, had a drink of cold tea, and lit our pipes. Then Dave took the waterproof cover off his bunk, spread it on the floor, laid his blankets on top of it, his spare clothes, &c., on top of them, and started to roll up his swag.

'What are you going to do, Dave?' I asked.

'I'm going to take the track,' says Dave, 'and camp somewhere farther on. You can stay here, if you like, and come on in the morning.'

I started to roll up my swag at once. We dressed and fastened on the tucker-bags, took up the billies, and got outside without making any noise. We held our backs pretty hollow till we got down on to the road.

'That comes of camping in a deserted house,' said Dave, when we were safe on the track. No Australian Bushman cares to camp in an abandoned homestead, or even near it—probably because a deserted home looks ghostlier in the Australian Bush than anywhere else in the world.

It was blowing hard, but not raining so much.

We went on along the track for a couple of miles and camped on the sheltered side of a round tussock hill, in a hole where there had been a landslip. We used all our candle-ends to get a fire alight, but once we got it started we knocked the wet bark off 'manuka' sticks and logs and piled them on, and soon had a roaring fire. When the ground got a little drier we rigged a bit of shelter from the showers with some sticks and the oil-cloth swag-covers; then we made some coffee and got through the night pretty comfortably. In the morning Dave said, 'I'm going back to that house.'

'What for?' I said.

'I'm going to find out what's the matter with that crimson door. If I don't I'll never be able to sleep easy within a mile of a door so long as I live.'

So we went back. It was still blowing. The thing was simple enough by daylight—after a little watching and experimenting. The house was built of odds and ends and badly fitted. It 'gave' in the wind in almost any direction—not much, not more than an inch or so, but just enough to throw the door-frame out of plumb and out of square in such a way as to bring the latch and bolt of the lock clear of the catch (the door-frame was of scraps joined). Then the door swung open according to the hang of it; and when the gust was over the house gave back, and the door swung to—the frame easing just a little in another direction. I suppose it would take Edison to invent a thing like that, that came about by accident. The different strengths and directions of the gusts of wind must have accounted for the variations of the door's movements—and maybe the draught of our big fire had helped.

Dave scratched his head a good bit.

'I never lived in a house yet,' he said, as we came away—'I never lived in a house yet without there was something wrong with it. Gimme a good tent.'

A Wild Irishman

About seven years ago I drifted from Out-Back in Australia to Wellington, the capital of New Zealand, and up country to a little town called Pahiatua, which meaneth the 'home of the gods', and is situated in the Wairarappa (rippling or sparkling water) district. They have a pretty little legend to the effect that the name of the district was not originally suggested by its rivers, streams, and lakes, but by the tears alleged to have been noticed, by a dusky squire, in the eyes of a warrior chief who was looking his first, or last—I don't remember which—upon the scene. He was the discoverer, I suppose, now I come to think of it, else the place would have been already named. Maybe the scene reminded the old cannibal of the home of his childhood.

Pahiatua was not the home of my god; and it rained for five weeks. While waiting for a remittance, from an Australian newspaper—which I anxiously hoped, would arrive in time for enough of it to be left (after paying board) to take me away somewhere—I spent many hours in the little shop of a shoemaker who had been a digger; and he told me yarns of the old days on the West Coast of Middle Island. And, ever and anon, he returned to one, a hard-case from the West Coast, called 'The Flour of Wheat', and his cousin, and his mate, Dinny Murphy, dead. And ever and again the shoemaker (he was large, humorous, and good-natured) made me promise that, when I dropped across an old West Coast digger—no matter who or what he was, or whether he was drunk or sober—I'd ask him if he knew the 'Flour of Wheat', and hear what he had to say.

I make no attempt to give any one shade of the Irish brogue—it can't be done in writing.

'There's the little red Irishman,' said the shoemaker, who was Irish himself, 'who always wants to fight when he has a glass in him; and there's the big sarcastic dark Irishman who makes more trouble and fights at a spree than half-a-dozen little red ones put together; and there's the cheerful easy-going Irishman. Now the Flour was a combination of all three and several other sorts. He was known from the first amongst the boys at Th' Canary as the Flour o' Wheat, but no one knew exactly why. Some said that the right name was the F-l-o-w-e-r, not F-l-o-u-r, and that he was called that because there was no flower on wheat. The name might have been a compliment paid to the man's character by some one who understood and appreciated it—or appreciated it without understanding it. Or it might have come of some chance saying of the Flour himself, or his mates—or an accident with bags of flour. He might have worked in a mill. But we've had enough of that. It's the man—not the name. He was just a big, dark, blue-eyed Irish digger. He worked hard, drank hard, fought hard—and didn't swear. No man had ever heard him swear (except once); all things were 'lovely' with him. He was always lucky. He got gold and threw it away.

'The Flour was sent out to Australia (by his friends) in connection with some trouble in Ireland in eighteen-something. The date doesn't matter: there was mostly trouble in Ireland in those days; and nobody, that knew the man, could have the slightest doubt that he helped the trouble—provided he was there at the time. I heard all this from a man who knew him in Australia. The relatives that he was sent out to were soon very anxious to see the end of him. He was as wild as they made them in Ireland. When he had a few drinks, he'd walk restlessly to and fro outside the shanty, swinging his right arm across in front of him with elbow bent and hand closed, as if he had a head in chancery, and muttering, as though in explanation to himself—

'"Oi must be walkin' or foightin'!—Oi must be walkin' or foightin'!—Oi must be walkin' or foightin'!"

'They say that he wanted to eat his Australian relatives before he was done; and the story goes that one night, while he was on the spree, they put their belongings into a cart and took to the Bush.

'There's no floury record for several years; then the Flour turned up on the west coast of New Zealand and was never very far from a pub. kept by a cousin (that he had tracked, unearthed, or discovered somehow) at a place called "Th' Canary". I remember the first time I saw the Flour.

'I was on a bit of a spree myself, at Th' Canary, and one evening I was standing outside Brady's (the Flour's cousin's place) with Tom Lyons and Dinny Murphy, when I saw a big man coming across the flat with a swag on his back.

'"B' God, there's the Flour o' Wheat comin' this minute," says Dinny Murphy to Tom, "an' no one else."

'"B' God, ye're right!" says Tom.

'There were a lot of new chums in the big room at the back, drinking and dancing and singing, and Tom says to Dinny—

'"Dinny, I'll bet you a quid an' the Flour'll run against some of those new chums before he's an hour on the spot."

'But Dinny wouldn't take him up. He knew the Flour.

'"Good day, Tom! Good day, Dinny!"

'"Good day to you, Flour!"

'I was introduced.

'"Well, boys, come along," says the Flour.

'And so we went inside with him. The Flour had a few drinks, and then he went into the back-room where the new chums were. One of them was dancing a jig, and so the Flour stood up in front of him and commenced to dance too. And presently the new chum made a step that didn't please the Flour, so he hit him between the eyes, and knocked him down—fair an' flat on his back.

'"Take that," he says. "Take that, me lovely whipper-snapper, an' lay there! You can't dance. How dare ye stand up in front of me face to dance when ye can't dance?"

'He shouted, and drank, and gambled, and danced, and sang, and fought the new chums all night, and in the morning he said—

'"Well, boys, we had a grand time last night. Come and have a drink with me."

'And of course they went in and had a drink with him.

'Next morning the Flour was walking along the street, when he met a drunken, disreputable old hag, known among the boys as the "Nipper".

'"Good MORNING, me lovely Flour o' Wheat!" says she.

'"Good MORNING, me lovely Nipper!" says the Flour.

'And with that she outs with a bottle she had in her dress, and smashed him across the face with it. Broke the bottle to smithereens!

'A policeman saw her do it, and took her up; and they had the Flour as a witness, whether he liked it or not. And a lovely sight he looked, with his face all done up in bloody bandages, and only one damaged eye and a corner of his mouth on duty.

'"It's nothing at all, your Honour," he said to the S.M.; "only a pin-scratch—it's nothing at all. Let it pass. I had no right to speak to the lovely woman at all."

'But they didn't let it pass,—they fined her a quid.

'And the Flour paid the fine.

'But, alas for human nature! It was pretty much the same even in those days, and amongst those men, as it is now. A man couldn't do a woman a good turn without the dirty-minded blackguards taking it for granted there was something between them. It was a great joke amongst the boys who knew the Flour, and who also knew the Nipper; but as it was carried too far in some quarters, it got to be no joke to the Flour—nor to those who laughed too loud or grinned too long.

'The Flour's cousin thought he was a sharp man. The Flour got "stiff". He hadn't any money, and his credit had run out, so he went and got a blank summons from one of the police he knew. He pretended that he wanted to frighten a man who owed him some money. Then he filled it up and took it to his cousin.

'"What d'ye think of that?" he says, handing the summons across the bar. "What d'ye think of me lovely Dinny Murphy now?"

'"Why, what's this all about?"

'"That's what I want to know. I borrowed a five-pound-note off of him a fortnight ago when I was drunk, an' now he sends me that."

'"Well, I never would have dream'd that of Dinny," says the cousin, scratching his head and blinking. "What's come over him at all?"

'"That's what I want to know."

'"What have you been doing to the man?"

'"Divil a thing that I'm aware of."

'The cousin rubbed his chin-tuft between his forefinger and thumb.

'"Well, what am I to do about it?" asked the Flour impatiently.

'"Do? Pay the man, of course?"

'"How can I pay the lovely man when I haven't got the price of a drink about me?"

'The cousin scratched his chin.

'"Well—here, I'll lend you a five-pound-note for a month or two. Go and pay the man, and get back to work."

'And the Flour went and found Dinny Murphy, and the pair of them had a howling spree together up at Brady's, the opposition pub. And the cousin said he thought all the time he was being had.

'He was nasty sometimes, when he was about half drunk. For instance, he'd come on the ground when the Orewell sports were in full swing and walk round, soliloquising just loud enough for you to hear; and just when a big event was coming off he'd pass within earshot of some committee men—who had been bursting themselves for weeks to work the thing up and make it a success—saying to himself—

'"Where's the Orewell sports that I hear so much about? I don't see them! Can any one direct me to the Orewell sports?"

'Or he'd pass a raffle, lottery, lucky-bag, or golden-barrel business of some sort,—

'"No gamblin' for the Flour. I don't believe in their little shwindles. It ought to be shtopped. Leadin' young people ashtray."

'Or he'd pass an Englishman he didn't like,—

'"Look at Jinneral Roberts! He's a man! He's an Irishman! England has to come to Ireland for its Jinnerals! Luk at Jinneral Roberts in the marshes of Candyhar!"

'They always had sports at Orewell Creek on New Year's Day—except once—and old Duncan was always there,—never missed it till the day he died. He was a digger, a humorous and good-hearted "hard-case". They all knew "old Duncan".

'But one New Year's Eve he didn't turn up, and was missed at once. "Where's old Duncan? Any one seen old Duncan?" "Oh, he'll turn up alright." They inquired, and argued, and waited, but Duncan didn't come.

'Duncan was working at Duffers. The boys inquired of fellows who came from Duffers, but they hadn't seen him for two days. They had fully expected to find him at the creek. He wasn't at Aliaura nor Notown. They inquired of men who came from Nelson Creek, but Duncan wasn't there.

'"There's something happened to the lovely man," said the Flour of Wheat at last. "Some of us had better see about it."

'Pretty soon this was the general opinion, and so a party started out over the hills to Duffers before daylight in the morning, headed by the Flour.

'The door of Duncan's "whare" was closed—BUT NOT PADLOCKED. The Flour noticed this, gave his head a jerk, opened the door, and went in. The hut was tidied up and swept out—even the fireplace. Duncan had "lifted the boxes" and "cleaned up", and his little bag of gold stood on a shelf by his side—all ready for his spree. On the table lay a clean neckerchief folded ready to tie on. The blankets had been folded neatly and laid on the bunk, and on them was stretched Old Duncan, with his arms lying crossed on his chest, and one foot—with a boot on—resting on the ground. He had his "clean things" on, and was dressed except for one boot, the necktie, and his hat. Heart disease.

'"Take your hats off and come in quietly, lads," said the Flour. "Here's the lovely man lying dead in his bunk."

'There were no sports at Orewell that New Year. Some one said that the crowd from Nelson Creek might object to the sports being postponed on old Duncan's account, but the Flour said he'd see to that.

'One or two did object, but the Flour reasoned with them and there were no sports.

'And the Flour used to say, afterwards, "Ah, but it was a grand time we had at the funeral when Duncan died at Duffers."

'The Flour of Wheat carried his mate, Dinny Murphy, all the way in from Th' Canary to the hospital on his back. Dinny was very bad—the man was dying of the dysentery or something. The Flour laid him down on a spare bunk in the reception-room, and hailed the staff.

'"Inside there—come out!"

'The doctor and some of the hospital people came to see what was the matter. The doctor was a heavy swell, with a big cigar, held up in front of him between two fat, soft, yellow-white fingers, and a dandy little pair of gold-rimmed eye-glasses nipped onto his nose with a spring.

'"There's me lovely mate lying there dying of the dysentry," says the Flour, "and you've got to fix him up and bring him round."

'Then he shook his fist in the doctor's face and said—

'"If you let that lovely man die—look out!"

'The doctor was startled. He backed off at first; then he took a puff at his cigar, stepped forward, had a careless look at Dinny, and gave some order to the attendants. The Flour went to the door, turned half round as he went out, and shook his fist at them again, and said—

'"If you let that lovely man die—mind!"

'In about twenty minutes he came back, wheeling a case of whisky in a barrow. He carried the case inside, and dumped it down on the floor.

'"There," he said, "pour that into the lovely man."

'Then he shook his fist at such members of the staff as were visible, and said—

'"If you let that lovely man die—look out!"

'They were used to hard-cases, and didn't take much notice of him, but he had the hospital in an awful mess; he was there all hours of the day and night; he would go down town, have a few drinks and a fight maybe, and then he'd say, "Ah, well, I'll have to go up and see how me lovely mate's getting on."

'And every time he'd go up he'd shake his fist at the hospital in general and threaten to murder 'em all if they let Dinny Murphy die.

'Well, Dinny Murphy died one night. The next morning the Flour met the doctor in the street, and hauled off and hit him between the eyes, and knocked him down before he had time to see who it was.

'"Stay there, ye little whipper-snapper," said the Flour of Wheat; "you let that lovely man die!"

'The police happened to be out of town that day, and while they were waiting for them the Flour got a coffin and carried it up to the hospital, and stood it on end by the doorway.

'"I've come for me lovely mate!" he said to the scared staff—or as much of it as he baled up and couldn't escape him. "Hand him over. He's going back to be buried with his friends at Th' Canary. Now, don't be sneaking round and sidling off, you there; you needn't be frightened; I've settled with the doctor."

'But they called in a man who had some influence with the Flour, and between them—and with the assistance of the prettiest nurse on the premises—they persuaded him to wait. Dinny wasn't ready yet; there were papers to sign; it wouldn't be decent to the dead; he had to be prayed over; he had to be washed and shaved, and fixed up decent and comfortable. Anyway, they'd have him ready in an hour, or take the consequences.

'The Flour objected on the ground that all this could be done equally as well and better by the boys at Th' Canary. "However," he said, "I'll be round in an hour, and if you haven't got me lovely mate ready—look out!" Then he shook his fist sternly at them once more and said—

'"I know yer dirty tricks and dodges, and if there's e'er a pin-scratch on me mate's body—look out! If there's a pairin' of Dinny's toe-nail missin'—look out!"

'Then he went out—taking the coffin with him.

'And when the police came to his lodgings to arrest him, they found the coffin on the floor by the side of the bed, and the Flour lying in it on his back, with his arms folded peacefully on his bosom. He was as dead drunk as any man could get to be and still be alive. They knocked air-holes in the coffin-lid, screwed it on, and carried the coffin, the Flour, and all to the local lock-up. They laid their burden down on the bare, cold floor of the prison-cell, and then went out, locked the door, and departed several ways to put the "boys" up to it. And about midnight the "boys" gathered round with a supply of liquor, and waited, and somewhere along in the small hours there was a howl, as of a strong Irishman in Purgatory, and presently the voice of the Flour was heard to plead in changed and awful tones—

'"Pray for me soul, boys—pray for me soul! Let bygones be bygones between us, boys, and pray for me lovely soul! The lovely Flour's in Purgatory!"

'Then silence for a while; and then a sound like a dray-wheel passing over a packing-case.... That was the only time on record that the Flour was heard to swear. And he swore then.

'They didn't pray for him—they gave him a month. And, when he came out, he went half-way across the road to meet the doctor, and he—to his credit, perhaps—came the other half. They had a drink together, and the Flour presented the doctor with a fine specimen of coarse gold for a pin.

'"It was the will o' God, after all, doctor," said the Flour. "It was the will o' God. Let bygones be bygones between us; gimme your hand, doctor.... Good-bye."

'Then he left for Th' Canary.'

The Babies in the Bush

'Oh, tell her a tale of the fairies bright—
That only the Bushmen know—
Who guide the feet of the lost aright,
Or carry them up through the starry night,
Where the Bush-lost babies go.'

He was one of those men who seldom smile. There are many in the Australian Bush, where drift wrecks and failures of all stations and professions (and of none), and from all the world. Or, if they do smile, the smile is either mechanical or bitter as a rule—cynical. They seldom talk. The sort of men who, as bosses, are set down by the majority—and without reason or evidence—as being proud, hard, and selfish,—'too mean to live, and too big for their boots.'

But when the Boss did smile his expression was very, very gentle, and very sad. I have seen him smile down on a little child who persisted in sitting on his knee and prattling to him, in spite of his silence and gloom. He was tall and gaunt, with haggard grey eyes—haunted grey eyes sometimes—and hair and beard thick and strong, but grey. He was not above forty-five. He was of the type of men who die in harness, with their hair thick and strong, but grey or white when it should be brown. The opposite type, I fancy, would be the soft, dark-haired, blue-eyed men who grow bald sooner than they grow grey, and fat and contented, and die respectably in their beds.

His name was Head—Walter Head. He was a boss drover on the overland routes. I engaged with him at a place north of the Queensland border to travel down to Bathurst, on the Great Western Line in New South Wales, with something over a thousand head of store bullocks for the Sydney market. I am an Australian Bushman (with city experience)—a rover, of course, and a ne'er-do-well, I suppose. I was born with brains and a thin skin—worse luck! It was in the days before I was married, and I went by the name of 'Jack Ellis' this trip,—not because the police were after me, but because I used to tell yarns about a man named Jack Ellis—and so the chaps nicknamed me.

The Boss spoke little to the men: he'd sit at tucker or with his pipe by the camp-fire nearly as silently as he rode his night-watch round the big, restless, weird-looking mob of bullocks camped on the dusky starlit plain. I believe that from the first he spoke oftener and more confidentially to me than to any other of the droving party. There was a something of sympathy between us—I can't explain what it was. It seemed as though it were an understood thing between us that we understood each other. He sometimes said things to me which would have needed a deal of explanation—so I thought—had he said them to any other of the party. He'd often, after brooding a long while, start a sentence, and break off with 'You know, Jack.' And somehow I understood, without being able to explain why. We had never met before I engaged with him for this trip. His men respected him, but he was not a popular boss: he was too gloomy, and never drank a glass nor 'shouted' on the trip: he was reckoned a 'mean boss', and rather a nigger-driver.

He was full of Adam Lindsay Gordon, the English-Australian poet who shot himself, and so was I. I lost an old copy of Gordon's poems on the route, and the Boss overheard me inquiring about it; later on he asked me if I liked Gordon. We got to it rather sheepishly at first, but by-and-by we'd quote Gordon freely in turn when we were alone in camp. 'Those are grand lines about Burke and Wills, the explorers, aren't they, Jack?' he'd say, after chewing his cud, or rather the stem of his briar, for a long while without a word. (He had his pipe in his mouth as often as any of us, but somehow I fancied he didn't enjoy it: an empty pipe or a stick would have suited him just as well, it seemed to me.) 'Those are great lines,' he'd say—

'"In Collins Street standeth a statue tall—
A statue tall on a pillar of stone—
Telling its story to great and small
Of the dust reclaimed from the sand-waste lone.

Weary and wasted, worn and wan,
Feeble and faint, and languid and low,
He lay on the desert a dying man,
Who has gone, my friends, where we all must go."

That's a grand thing, Jack. How does it go?—
"With a pistol clenched in his failing hand,
And the film of death o'er his fading eyes,
He saw the sun go down on the sand,"'—

The Boss would straighten up with a sigh that might have been half a yawn—
'"And he slept and never saw it rise,"'—speaking with a sort of quiet force all the time.
Then maybe he'd stand with his back to the fire roasting his dusty leggings,
with his hands behind his back and looking out over the dusky plain.

'"What mattered the sand or the whit'ning chalk,
The blighted herbage or blackened log,
The crooked beak of the eagle-hawk,
Or the hot red tongue of the native dog?"

They don't matter much, do they, Jack?'

'Damned if I think they do, Boss!' I'd say.

'"The couch was rugged, those sextons rude,
But, in spite of a leaden shroud, we know
That the bravest and fairest are earth-worms' food
Where once they have gone where we all must go."'

Once he repeated the poem containing the lines—

'"Love, when we wandered here together,
Hand in hand through the sparkling weather—
God surely loved us a little then."

Beautiful lines those, Jack.

"Then skies were fairer and shores were firmer,
And the blue sea over the white sand rolled—
Babble and prattle, and prattle and murmur'—

How does it go, Jack?' He stood up and turned his face to the light, but not before I had a glimpse of it. I think that the saddest eyes on earth are mostly women's eyes, but I've seen few so sad as the Boss's were just then.

It seemed strange that he, a Bushman, preferred Gordon's sea poems to his horsey and bushy rhymes; but so he did. I fancy his favourite poem was that one of Gordon's with the lines—

'I would that with sleepy soft embraces
The sea would fold me, would find me rest
In the luminous depths of its secret places,
Where the wealth of God's marvels is manifest!'

He usually spoke quietly, in a tone as though death were in camp; but after we'd been on Gordon's poetry for a while he'd end it abruptly with, 'Well, it's time to turn in,' or, 'It's time to turn out,' or he'd give me an order in connection with the cattle. He had been a well-to-do squatter on the Lachlan riverside, in New South Wales, and had been ruined by the drought, they said. One night in camp, and after smoking in silence for nearly an hour, he asked—

'Do you know Fisher, Jack—the man that owns these bullocks?'

'I've heard of him,' I said. Fisher was a big squatter, with stations both in New South Wales and in Queensland.

'Well, he came to my station on the Lachlan years ago without a penny in his pocket, or decent rag to his back, or a crust in his tucker-bag, and I gave him a job. He's my boss now. Ah, well! it's the way of Australia, you know, Jack.'

The Boss had one man who went on every droving trip with him; he was 'bred' on the Boss's station, they said, and had been with him practically all his life. His name was 'Andy'. I forget his other name, if he really had one. Andy had charge of the 'droving-plant' (a tilted two-horse waggonette, in which we carried the rations and horse-feed), and he did the cooking and kept accounts. The Boss had no head for figures. Andy might have been twenty-five or thirty-five, or anything in between. His hair stuck up like a well-made brush all round, and his big grey eyes also had an inquiring expression. His weakness was girls, or he theirs, I don't know which (half-castes not barred). He was, I think, the most innocent, good-natured, and open-hearted scamp I ever met. Towards the middle of the trip Andy spoke to me one night alone in camp about the Boss.

'The Boss seems to have taken to you, Jack, all right.'

'Think so?' I said. I thought I smelt jealousy and detected a sneer.

'I'm sure of it. It's very seldom HE takes to any one.'

I said nothing.

Then after a while Andy said suddenly—

'Look here, Jack, I'm glad of it. I'd like to see him make a chum of some one, if only for one trip. And don't you make any mistake about the Boss. He's a white man. There's precious few that know him—precious few now; but I do, and it'll do him a lot of good to have some one to yarn with.' And Andy said no more on the subject for that trip.

The long, hot, dusty miles dragged by across the blazing plains—big clearings rather—and through the sweltering hot scrubs, and we reached Bathurst at last; and then the hot dusty days and weeks and months that we'd left behind us to the Great North-West seemed as nothing,—as I suppose life will seem when we come to the end of it.

The bullocks were going by rail from Bathurst to Sydney. We were all one long afternoon getting them into the trucks, and when we'd finished the boss said to me—

'Look here, Jack, you're going on to Sydney, aren't you?'

'Yes; I'm going down to have a fly round.'

'Well, why not wait and go down with Andy in the morning? He's going down in charge of the cattle. The cattle-train starts about daylight. It won't be so comfortable as the passenger; but you'll save your fare, and you can give Andy a hand with the cattle. You've only got to have a look at 'em every other station, and poke up any that fall down in the trucks. You and Andy are mates, aren't you?'

I said it would just suit me. Somehow I fancied that the Boss seemed anxious to have my company for one more evening, and, to tell the truth, I felt really sorry to part with him. I'd had to work as hard as any of the other chaps; but I liked him, and I believed he liked me. He'd struck me as a man who'd been quietened down by some heavy trouble, and I felt sorry for him without knowing what the trouble was.

'Come and have a drink, Boss,' I said. The agent had paid us off during the day.

He turned into a hotel with me.

'I don't drink, Jack,' he said; 'but I'll take a glass with you.'

'I didn't know you were a teetotaller, Boss,' I said. I had not been surprised at his keeping so strictly from the drink on the trip; but now that it was over it was a different thing.

'I'm not a teetotaller, Jack,' he said. 'I can take a glass or leave it.' And he called for a long beer, and we drank 'Here's luck!' to each other.

'Well,' I said, 'I wish I could take a glass or leave it.' And I meant it.

Then the Boss spoke as I'd never heard him speak before. I thought for the moment that the one drink had affected him; but I understood before the night was over. He laid his hand on my shoulder with a grip like a man who has suddenly made up his mind to lend you five pounds. 'Jack!' he said, 'there's worse things than drinking, and there's worse things than heavy smoking. When a man who smokes gets such a load of trouble on him that he can find no comfort in his pipe, then it's a heavy load. And when a man who drinks gets so deep into trouble that he can find no comfort in liquor, then it's deep trouble. Take my tip for it, Jack.'

He broke off, and half turned away with a jerk of his head, as if impatient with himself; then presently he spoke in his usual quiet tone—

'But you're only a boy yet, Jack. Never mind me. I won't ask you to take the second drink. You don't want it; and, besides, I know the signs.'

He paused, leaning with both hands on the edge of the counter, and looking down between his arms at the floor. He stood that way thinking for a while; then he suddenly straightened up, like a man who'd made up his mind to something.

'I want you to come along home with me, Jack,' he said; 'we'll fix you a shake-down.'

I forgot to tell you that he was married and lived in Bathurst.

'But won't it put Mrs Head about?'

'Not at all. She's expecting you. Come along; there's nothing to see in Bathurst, and you'll have plenty of knocking round in Sydney. Come on, we'll just be in time for tea.'

He lived in a brick cottage on the outskirts of the town—an old-fashioned cottage, with ivy and climbing roses, like you see in some of those old settled districts. There was, I remember, the stump of a tree in front, covered with ivy till it looked like a giant's club with the thick end up.

When we got to the house the Boss paused a minute with his hand on the gate. He'd been home a couple of days, having ridden in ahead of the bullocks.

'Jack,' he said, 'I must tell you that Mrs Head had a great trouble at one time. We—we lost our two children. It does her good to talk to a stranger now and again—she's always better afterwards; but there's very few I care to bring. You—you needn't notice anything strange. And agree with her, Jack. You know, Jack.'

'That's all right, Boss,' I said. I'd knocked about the Bush too long, and run against too many strange characters and things, to be surprised at anything much.

The door opened, and he took a little woman in his arms. I saw by the light of a lamp in the room behind that the woman's hair was grey, and I reckoned that he had his mother living with him. And—we do have odd thoughts at odd times in a flash—and I wondered how Mrs Head and her mother-in-law got on together. But the next minute I was in the room, and introduced to 'My wife, Mrs Head,' and staring at her with both eyes.

It was his wife. I don't think I can describe her. For the first minute or two, coming in out of the dark and before my eyes got used to the lamp-light, I had an impression as of a little old woman—one of those fresh-faced, well-preserved, little old ladies—who dressed young, wore false teeth, and aped the giddy girl. But this was because of Mrs Head's impulsive welcome of me, and her grey hair. The hair was not so grey as I thought at first, seeing it with the lamp-light behind it: it was like dull-brown hair lightly dusted with flour. She wore it short, and it became her that way. There was something aristocratic about her face—her nose and chin—I fancied, and something that you couldn't describe. She had big dark eyes—dark-brown, I thought, though they might have been hazel: they were a bit too big and bright for me, and now and again, when she got excited, the white showed all round the pupils—just a little, but a little was enough.

She seemed extra glad to see me. I thought at first that she was a bit of a gusher.

'Oh, I'm so glad you've come, Mr Ellis,' she said, giving my hand a grip. 'Walter—Mr Head—has been speaking to me about you. I've been expecting you. Sit down by the fire, Mr Ellis; tea will be ready presently. Don't you find it a bit chilly?' She shivered. It was a bit chilly now at night on the Bathurst plains. The table was set for tea, and set rather in swell style. The cottage was too well furnished even for a lucky boss drover's home; the furniture looked as if it had belonged to a tony homestead at one time. I felt a bit strange at first, sitting down to tea, and almost wished that I was having a comfortable tuck-in at a restaurant or in a pub. dining-room. But she knew a lot about the Bush, and chatted away, and asked questions about the trip, and soon put me at my ease. You see, for the last year or two I'd taken my tucker in my hands,—hunk of damper and meat and a clasp-knife mostly,—sitting on my heel in the dust, or on a log or a tucker-box.

There was a hard, brown, wrinkled old woman that the Heads called 'Auntie'. She waited at the table; but Mrs Head kept bustling round herself most of the time, helping us. Andy came in to tea.

Mrs Head bustled round like a girl of twenty instead of a woman of thirty-seven, as Andy afterwards told me she was. She had the figure and movements of a girl, and the impulsiveness and expression too—a womanly girl; but sometimes I fancied there was something very childish about her face and talk. After tea she and the Boss sat on one side of the fire and Andy and I on the other—Andy a little behind me at the corner of the table.

'Walter—Mr Head—tells me you've been out on the Lachlan river, Mr Ellis?' she said as soon as she'd settled down, and she leaned forward, as if eager to hear that I'd been there.

'Yes, Mrs Head. I've knocked round all about out there.'

She sat up straight, and put the tips of her fingers to the side of her forehead and knitted her brows. This was a trick she had—she often did it during the evening. And when she did that she seemed to forget what she'd said last.

She smoothed her forehead, and clasped her hands in her lap.

'Oh, I'm so glad to meet somebody from the back country, Mr Ellis,' she said. 'Walter so seldom brings a stranger here, and I get tired of talking to the same people about the same things, and seeing the same faces. You don't know what a relief it is, Mr Ellis, to see a new face and talk to a stranger.'

'I can quite understand that, Mrs Head,' I said. And so I could. I never stayed more than three months in one place if I could help it.

She looked into the fire and seemed to try to think. The Boss straightened up and stroked her head with his big sun-browned hand, and then put his arm round her shoulders. This brought her back.

'You know we had a station out on the Lachlan, Mr Ellis. Did Walter ever tell you about the time we lived there?'

'No,' I said, glancing at the Boss. 'I know you had a station there; but, you know, the Boss doesn't talk much.'

'Tell Jack, Maggie,' said the Boss; 'I don't mind.'

She smiled. 'You know Walter, Mr Ellis,' she said. 'You won't mind him. He doesn't like me to talk about the children; he thinks it upsets me, but that's foolish: it always relieves me to talk to a stranger.' She leaned forward, eagerly it seemed, and went on quickly: 'I've been wanting to tell you about the children ever since Walter spoke to me about you. I knew you would understand directly I saw your face. These town people don't understand. I like to talk to a Bushman. You know we lost our children out on the station. The fairies took them. Did Walter ever tell you about the fairies taking the children away?'

This was a facer. 'I—I beg pardon,' I commenced, when Andy gave me a dig in the back. Then I saw it all.

'No, Mrs Head. The Boss didn't tell me about that.'

'You surely know about the Bush Fairies, Mr Ellis,' she said, her big eyes fixed on my face—'the Bush Fairies that look after the little ones that are lost in the Bush, and take them away from the Bush if they are not found? You've surely heard of them, Mr Ellis? Most Bushmen have that I've spoken to. Maybe you've seen them? Andy there has?' Andy gave me another dig.

'Of course I've heard of them, Mrs Head,' I said; 'but I can't swear that I've seen one.'

'Andy has. Haven't you, Andy?'

'Of course I have, Mrs Head. Didn't I tell you all about it the last time we were home?'

'And didn't you ever tell Mr Ellis, Andy?'

'Of course he did!' I said, coming to Andy's rescue; 'I remember it now. You told me that night we camped on the Bogan river, Andy.'

'Of course!' said Andy.

'Did he tell you about finding a lost child and the fairy with it?'

'Yes,' said Andy; 'I told him all about that.'

'And the fairy was just going to take the child away when Andy found it, and when the fairy saw Andy she flew away.'

'Yes,' I said; 'that's what Andy told me.'

'And what did you say the fairy was like, Andy?' asked Mrs Head, fixing her eyes on his face.

'Like. It was like one of them angels you see in Bible pictures, Mrs Head,' said Andy promptly, sitting bolt upright, and keeping his big innocent grey eyes fixed on hers lest she might think he was telling lies. 'It was just like the angel in that Christ-in-the-stable picture we had at home on the station—the right-hand one in blue.'

She smiled. You couldn't call it an idiotic smile, nor the foolish smile you see sometimes in melancholy mad people. It was more of a happy childish smile.

'I was so foolish at first, and gave poor Walter and the doctors a lot of trouble,' she said. 'Of course it never struck me, until afterwards, that the fairies had taken the children.'

She pressed the tips of the fingers of both hands to her forehead, and sat so for a while; then she roused herself again—

'But what am I thinking about? I haven't started to tell you about the children at all yet. Auntie! bring the children's portraits, will you, please? You'll find them on my dressing-table.'

The old woman seemed to hesitate.

'Go on, Auntie, and do what I ask you,' said Mrs Head. 'Don't be foolish. You know I'm all right now.'

'You mustn't take any notice of Auntie, Mr Ellis,' she said with a smile, while the old woman's back was turned. 'Poor old body, she's a bit crotchety at times, as old women are. She doesn't like me to get talking about the children. She's got an idea that if I do I'll start talking nonsense, as I used to do the first year after the children were lost. I was very foolish then, wasn't I, Walter?'

'You were, Maggie,' said the Boss. 'But that's all past. You mustn't think of that time any more.'

'You see,' said Mrs Head, in explanation to me, 'at first nothing would drive it out of my head that the children had wandered about until they perished of hunger and thirst in the Bush. As if the Bush Fairies would let them do that.'

'You were very foolish, Maggie,' said the Boss; 'but don't think about that.'

The old woman brought the portraits, a little boy and a little girl: they must have been very pretty children.

'You see,' said Mrs Head, taking the portraits eagerly, and giving them to me one by one, 'we had these taken in Sydney some years before the children were lost; they were much younger then. Wally's is not a good portrait; he was teething then, and very thin. That's him standing on the chair. Isn't the pose good? See, he's got one hand and one little foot forward, and an eager look in his eyes. The portrait is very dark, and you've got to look close to see the foot. He wants a toy rabbit that the photographer is tossing up to make him laugh. In the next portrait he's sitting on the chair—he's just settled himself to enjoy the fun. But see how happy little Maggie looks! You can see my arm where I was holding her in the chair. She was six months old then, and little Wally had just turned two.'

She put the portraits up on the mantel-shelf.

'Let me see; Wally (that's little Walter, you know)—Wally was five and little Maggie three and a half when we lost them. Weren't they, Walter?'

'Yes, Maggie,' said the Boss.

'You were away, Walter, when it happened.'

'Yes, Maggie,' said the Boss—cheerfully, it seemed to me—'I was away.'

'And we couldn't find you, Walter. You see,' she said to me, 'Walter—Mr Head—was away in Sydney on business, and we couldn't find his address. It was a beautiful morning, though rather warm, and just after the break-up of the drought. The grass was knee-high all over the run. It was a lonely place; there wasn't much bush cleared round the homestead, just a hundred yards or so, and the great awful scrubs ran back from the edges of the clearing all round for miles and miles—fifty or a hundred miles in some directions without a break; didn't they, Walter?'

'Yes, Maggie.'

'I was alone at the house except for Mary, a half-caste girl we had, who used to help me with the housework and the children. Andy was out on the run with the men, mustering sheep; weren't you, Andy?'

'Yes, Mrs Head.'

'I used to watch the children close as they got to run about, because if they once got into the edge of the scrub they'd be lost; but this morning little Wally begged hard to be let take his little sister down under a clump of blue-gums in a corner of the home paddock to gather buttercups. You remember that clump of gums, Walter?'

'I remember, Maggie.'

'"I won't go through the fence a step, mumma," little Wally said. I could see Old Peter—an old shepherd and station-hand we had—I could see him working on a dam we were making across a creek that ran down there. You remember Old Peter, Walter?'

'Of course I do, Maggie.'

'I knew that Old Peter would keep an eye to the children; so I told little Wally to keep tight hold of his sister's hand and go straight down to Old Peter and tell him I sent them.'

She was leaning forward with her hands clasping her knee, and telling me all this with a strange sort of eagerness.

'The little ones toddled off hand in hand, with their other hands holding fast their straw hats. "In case a bad wind blowed," as little Maggie said. I saw them stoop under the first fence, and that was the last that any one saw of them.'

'Except the fairies, Maggie,' said the Boss quickly.

'Of course, Walter, except the fairies.'

She pressed her fingers to her temples again for a minute.

'It seems that Old Peter was going to ride out to the musterers' camp that morning with bread for the men, and he left his work at the dam and started into the Bush after his horse just as I turned back into the house, and before the children got near him. They either followed him for some distance or wandered into the Bush after flowers or butterflies—' She broke off, and then suddenly asked me, 'Do you think the Bush Fairies would entice children away, Mr Ellis?'

The Boss caught my eye, and frowned and shook his head slightly.

'No. I'm sure they wouldn't, Mrs Head,' I said—'at least not from what I know of them.'

She thought, or tried to think, again for a while, in her helpless puzzled way. Then she went on, speaking rapidly, and rather mechanically, it seemed to me—

'The first I knew of it was when Peter came to the house about an hour afterwards, leading his horse, and without the children. I said—I said, "O my God! where's the children?"' Her fingers fluttered up to her temples.

'Don't mind about that, Maggie,' said the Boss, hurriedly, stroking her head. 'Tell Jack about the fairies.'

'You were away at the time, Walter?'

'Yes, Maggie.'

'And we couldn't find you, Walter?'

'No, Maggie,' very gently. He rested his elbow on his knee and his chin on his hand, and looked into the fire.

'It wasn't your fault, Walter; but if you had been at home do you think the fairies would have taken the children?'

'Of course they would, Maggie. They had to: the children were lost.'

'And they're bringing the children home next year?'

'Yes, Maggie—next year.'

She lifted her hands to her head in a startled way, and it was some time before she went on again. There was no need to tell me about the lost children. I could see it all. She and the half-caste rushing towards where the children were seen last, with Old Peter after them. The hurried search in the nearer scrub. The mother calling all the time for Maggie and Wally, and growing wilder as the minutes flew past. Old Peter's ride to the musterers' camp. Horsemen seeming to turn up in no time and from nowhere, as they do in a case like this, and no matter how lonely the district. Bushmen galloping through the scrub in all directions. The hurried search the first day, and the mother mad with anxiety as night came on. Her long, hopeless, wild-eyed watch through the night; starting up at every sound of a horse's hoof, and reading the worst in one glance at the rider's face. The systematic work of the search-parties next day and the days following. How those days do fly past. The women from the next run or selection, and some from the town, driving from ten or twenty miles, perhaps, to stay with and try to comfort the mother. ['Put the horse to the cart, Jim: I must go to that poor woman!'] Comforting her with improbable stories of children who had been lost for days, and were none the worse for it when they were found. The mounted policemen out with the black trackers. Search-parties cooeeing to each other about the Bush, and lighting signal-fires. The reckless break-neck rides for news or more help. And the Boss himself, wild-eyed and haggard, riding about the Bush with Andy and one or two others perhaps, and searching hopelessly, days after the rest had given up all hope of finding the children alive. All this passed before me as Mrs Head talked, her voice sounding the while as if she were in another room; and when I roused myself to listen, she was on to the fairies again.

'It was very foolish of me, Mr Ellis. Weeks after—months after, I think—I'd insist on going out on the verandah at dusk and calling for the children. I'd stand there and call "Maggie!" and "Wally!" until Walter took me inside; sometimes he had to force me inside. Poor Walter! But of course I didn't know about the fairies then, Mr Ellis. I was really out of my mind for a time.'

'No wonder you were, Mrs Head,' I said. 'It was terrible trouble.'

'Yes, and I made it worse. I was so selfish in my trouble. But it's all right now, Walter,' she said, rumpling the Boss's hair. 'I'll never be so foolish again.'

'Of course you won't, Maggie.'

'We're very happy now, aren't we, Walter?'

'Of course we are, Maggie.'

'And the children are coming back next year.'

'Next year, Maggie.'

He leaned over the fire and stirred it up.

'You mustn't take any notice of us, Mr Ellis,' she went on. 'Poor Walter is away so much that I'm afraid I make a little too much of him when he does come home.'

She paused and pressed her fingers to her temples again. Then she said quickly—

'They used to tell me that it was all nonsense about the fairies, but they were no friends of mine. I shouldn't have listened to them, Walter. You told me not to. But then I was really not in my right mind.'

'Who used to tell you that, Mrs Head?' I asked.

'The Voices,' she said; 'you know about the Voices, Walter?'

'Yes, Maggie. But you don't hear the Voices now, Maggie?' he asked anxiously. 'You haven't heard them since I've been away this time, have you, Maggie?'

'No, Walter. They've gone away a long time. I hear voices now sometimes, but they're the Bush Fairies' voices. I hear them calling Maggie and Wally to come with them.' She paused again. 'And sometimes I think I hear them call me. But of course I couldn't go away without you, Walter. But I'm foolish again. I was going to ask you about the other voices, Mr Ellis. They used to say that it was madness about the fairies; but then, if the fairies hadn't taken the children, Black Jimmy, or the black trackers with the police, could have tracked and found them at once.'

'Of course they could, Mrs Head,' I said.

'They said that the trackers couldn't track them because there was rain a few hours after the children were lost. But that was ridiculous. It was only a thunderstorm.'

'Why!' I said, 'I've known the blacks to track a man after a week's heavy rain.'

She had her head between her fingers again, and when she looked up it was in a scared way.

'Oh, Walter!' she said, clutching the Boss's arm; 'whatever have I been talking about? What must Mr Ellis think of me? Oh! why did you let me talk like that?'

He put his arm round her. Andy nudged me and got up.

'Where are you going, Mr Ellis?' she asked hurriedly. 'You're not going to-night. Auntie's made a bed for you in Andy's room. You mustn't mind me.'

'Jack and Andy are going out for a little while,' said the Boss. 'They'll be in to supper. We'll have a yarn, Maggie.'

'Be sure you come back to supper, Mr Ellis,' she said. 'I really don't know what you must think of me,—I've been talking all the time.'

'Oh, I've enjoyed myself, Mrs Head,' I said; and Andy hooked me out.

'She'll have a good cry and be better now,' said Andy when we got away from the house. 'She might be better for months. She has been fairly reasonable for over a year, but the Boss found her pretty bad when he came back this time. It upset him a lot, I can tell you. She has turns now and again, and always ends up like she did just now. She gets a longing to talk about it to a Bushman and a stranger; it seems to do her good. The doctor's against it, but doctors don't know everything.'

'It's all true about the children, then?' I asked.

'It's cruel true,' said Andy.

'And were the bodies never found?'

'Yes;' then, after a long pause, 'I found them.'

'You did!'

'Yes; in the scrub, and not so very far from home either—and in a fairly clear space. It's a wonder the search-parties missed it; but it often happens that way. Perhaps the little ones wandered a long way and came round in a circle. I found them about two months after they were lost. They had to be found, if only for the Boss's sake. You see, in a case like this, and when the bodies aren't found, the parents never quite lose the idea that the little ones are wandering about the Bush to-night (it might be years after) and perishing from hunger, thirst, or cold. That mad idea haunts 'em all their lives. It's the same, I believe, with friends drowned at sea. Friends ashore are haunted for a long while with the idea of the white sodden corpse tossing about and drifting round in the water.'

'And you never told Mrs Head about the children being found?'

'Not for a long time. It wouldn't have done any good. She was raving mad for months. He took her to Sydney and then to Melbourne—to the best doctors he could find in Australia. They could do no good, so he sold the station—sacrificed everything, and took her to England.'

'To England?'

'Yes; and then to Germany to a big German doctor there. He'd offer a thousand pounds where they only wanted fifty. It was no good. She got worse in England, and raved to go back to Australia and find the children. The doctors advised him to take her back, and he did. He spent all his money, travelling saloon, and with reserved cabins, and a nurse, and trying to get her cured; that's why he's droving now. She was restless in Sydney. She wanted to go back to the station and wait there till the fairies brought the children home. She'd been getting the fairy idea into her head slowly all the time. The Boss encouraged it. But the station was sold, and he couldn't have lived there anyway without going mad himself. He'd married her from Bathurst. Both of them have got friends and relations here, so he thought best to bring her here. He persuaded her that the fairies were going to bring the children here. Everybody's very kind to them. I think it's a mistake to run away from a town where you're known, in a case like this, though most people do it. It was years before he gave up hope. I think he has hopes yet—after she's been fairly well for a longish time.'

'And you never tried telling her that the children were found?'

'Yes; the Boss did. The little ones were buried on the Lachlan river at first; but the Boss got a horror of having them buried in the Bush, so he had them brought to Sydney and buried in the Waverley Cemetery near the sea. He bought the ground, and room for himself and Maggie when they go out. It's all the ground he owns in wide Australia, and once he had thousands of acres. He took her to the grave one day. The doctors were against it; but he couldn't rest till he tried it. He took her out, and explained it all to her. She scarcely seemed interested. She read the names on the stone, and said it was a nice stone, and asked questions about how the children were found and brought here. She seemed quite sensible, and very cool about it. But when he got her home she was back on the fairy idea again. He tried another day, but it was no use; so then he let it be. I think it's better as it is. Now and again, at her best, she seems to understand that the children were found dead, and buried, and she'll talk sensibly about it, and ask questions in a quiet way, and make him promise to take her to Sydney to see the grave next time he's down. But it doesn't last long, and she's always worse afterwards.'

We turned into a bar and had a beer. It was a very quiet drink. Andy 'shouted' in his turn, and while I was drinking the second beer a thought struck me.

'The Boss was away when the children were lost?'

'Yes,' said Andy.

'Strange you couldn't find him.'

'Yes, it was strange; but HE'LL have to tell you about that. Very likely he will; it's either all or nothing with him.'

'I feel damned sorry for the Boss,' I said.

'You'd be sorrier if you knew all,' said Andy. 'It's the worst trouble that can happen to a man. It's like living with the dead. It's—it's like a man living with his dead wife.'

When we went home supper was ready. We found Mrs Head, bright and cheerful, bustling round. You'd have thought her one of the happiest and brightest little women in Australia. Not a word about children or the fairies. She knew the Bush, and asked me all about my trips. She told some good Bush stories too. It was the pleasantest hour I'd spent for a long time.

'Good night, Mr Ellis,' she said brightly, shaking hands with me when Andy and I were going to turn in. 'And don't forget your pipe. Here it is! I know that Bushmen like to have a whiff or two when they turn in. Walter smokes in bed. I don't mind. You can smoke all night if you like.'

'She seems all right,' I said to Andy when we were in our room.

He shook his head mournfully. We'd left the door ajar, and we could hear the Boss talking to her quietly. Then we heard her speak; she had a very clear voice.

'Yes, I'll tell you the truth, Walter. I've been deceiving you, Walter, all the time, but I did it for the best. Don't be angry with me, Walter! The Voices did come back while you were away. Oh, how I longed for you to come back! They haven't come since you've been home, Walter. You must stay with me a while now. Those awful Voices kept calling me, and telling me lies about the children, Walter! They told me to kill myself; they told me it was all my own fault—that I killed the children. They said I was a drag on you, and they'd laugh—Ha! ha! ha!—like that. They'd say, "Come on, Maggie; come on, Maggie." They told me to come to the river, Walter.'

Andy closed the door. His face was very miserable.

We turned in, and I can tell you I enjoyed a soft white bed after months and months of sleeping out at night, between watches, on the hard ground or the sand, or at best on a few boughs when I wasn't too tired to pull them down, and my saddle for a pillow.

But the story of the children haunted me for an hour or two. I've never since quite made up my mind as to why the Boss took me home. Probably he really did think it would do his wife good to talk to a stranger; perhaps he wanted me to understand—maybe he was weakening as he grew older, and craved for a new word or hand-grip of sympathy now and then.

When I did get to sleep I could have slept for three or four days, but Andy roused me out about four o'clock. The old woman that they called Auntie was up and had a good breakfast of eggs and bacon and coffee ready in the detached kitchen at the back. We moved about on tiptoe and had our breakfast quietly.

'The wife made me promise to wake her to see to our breakfast and say Good-bye to you; but I want her to sleep this morning, Jack,' said the Boss. 'I'm going to walk down as far as the station with you. She made up a parcel of fruit and sandwiches for you and Andy. Don't forget it.'

Andy went on ahead. The Boss and I walked down the wide silent street, which was also the main road; and we walked two or three hundred yards without speaking. He didn't seem sociable this morning, or any way sentimental; when he did speak it was something about the cattle.

But I had to speak; I felt a swelling and rising up in my chest, and at last I made a swallow and blurted out—

'Look here, Boss, old chap! I'm damned sorry!'

Our hands came together and gripped. The ghostly Australian daybreak was over the Bathurst plains.

We went on another hundred yards or so, and then the Boss said quietly—

'I was away when the children were lost, Jack. I used to go on a howling spree every six or nine months. Maggie never knew. I'd tell her I had to go to Sydney on business, or Out-Back to look after some stock. When the children were lost, and for nearly a fortnight after, I was beastly drunk in an out-of-the-way shanty in the Bush—a sly grog-shop. The old brute that kept it was too true to me. He thought that the story of the lost children was a trick to get me home, and he swore that he hadn't seen me. He never told me. I could have found those children, Jack. They were mostly new chums and fools about the run, and not one of the three policemen was a Bushman. I knew those scrubs better than any man in the country.'

I reached for his hand again, and gave it a grip. That was all I could do for him.

'Good-bye, Jack!' he said at the door of the brake-van. 'Good-bye, Andy!—keep those bullocks on their feet.'

The cattle-train went on towards the Blue Mountains. Andy and I sat silent for a while, watching the guard fry three eggs on a plate over a coal-stove in the centre of the van.

'Does the boss never go to Sydney?' I asked.

'Very seldom,' said Andy, 'and then only when he has to, on business. When he finishes his business with the stock agents, he takes a run out to Waverley Cemetery perhaps, and comes home by the next train.'

After a while I said, 'He told me about the drink, Andy—about his being on the spree when the children were lost.'

'Well, Jack,' said Andy, 'that's the thing that's been killing him ever since, and it happened over ten years ago.'

A Bush Dance

'Tap, tap, tap, tap.'

The little schoolhouse and residence in the scrub was lighted brightly in the midst of the 'close', solid blackness of that moonless December night, when the sky and stars were smothered and suffocated by drought haze.

It was the evening of the school children's 'Feast'. That is to say that the children had been sent, and 'let go', and the younger ones 'fetched' through the blazing heat to the school, one day early in the holidays, and raced—sometimes in couples tied together by the legs—and caked, and bunned, and finally improved upon by the local Chadband, and got rid of. The schoolroom had been cleared for dancing, the maps rolled and tied, the desks and blackboards stacked against the wall outside. Tea was over, and the trestles and boards, whereon had been spread better things than had been provided for the unfortunate youngsters, had been taken outside to keep the desks and blackboards company.

On stools running end to end along one side of the room sat about twenty more or less blooming country girls of from fifteen to twenty odd.

On the rest of the stools, running end to end along the other wall, sat about twenty more or less blooming chaps.

It was evident that something was seriously wrong. None of the girls spoke above a hushed whisper. None of the men spoke above a hushed oath. Now and again two or three sidled out, and if you had followed them you would have found that they went outside to listen hard into the darkness and to swear.

'Tap, tap, tap.'

The rows moved uneasily, and some of the girls turned pale faces nervously towards the side-door, in the direction of the sound.

'Tap—tap.'

The tapping came from the kitchen at the rear of the teacher's residence, and was uncomfortably suggestive of a coffin being made: it was also accompanied by a sickly, indescribable odour—more like that of warm cheap glue than anything else.

In the schoolroom was a painful scene of strained listening. Whenever one of the men returned from outside, or put his head in at the door, all eyes were fastened on him in the flash of a single eye, and then withdrawn hopelessly. At the sound of a horse's step all eyes and ears were on the door, till some one muttered, 'It's only the horses in the paddock.'

Some of the girls' eyes began to glisten suspiciously, and at last the belle of the party—a great, dark-haired, pink-and-white Blue Mountain girl, who had been sitting for a full minute staring before her, with blue eyes unnaturally bright, suddenly covered her face with her hands, rose, and started blindly from the room, from which she was steered in a hurry by two sympathetic and rather 'upset' girl friends, and as she passed out she was heard sobbing hysterically—

'Oh, I can't help it! I did want to dance! It's a sh-shame! I can't help it! I—I want to dance! I rode twenty miles to dance—and—and I want to dance!'

A tall, strapping young Bushman rose, without disguise, and followed the girl out. The rest began to talk loudly of stock, dogs, and horses, and other Bush things; but above their voices rang out that of the girl from the outside—being man comforted—

'I can't help it, Jack! I did want to dance! I—I had such—such—a job—to get mother—and—and father to let me come—and—and now!'

The two girl friends came back. 'He sez to leave her to him,' they whispered, in reply to an interrogatory glance from the schoolmistress.

'It's—it's no use, Jack!' came the voice of grief. 'You don't know what—what father and mother—is. I—I won't—be able—to ge-get away—again—for—for—not till I'm married, perhaps.'

The schoolmistress glanced uneasily along the row of girls. 'I'll take her into my room and make her lie down,' she whispered to her sister, who was staying with her. 'She'll start some of the other girls presently—it's just the weather for it,' and she passed out quietly. That schoolmistress was a woman of penetration.

A final 'tap-tap' from the kitchen; then a sound like the squawk of a hurt or frightened child, and the faces in the room turned quickly in that direction and brightened. But there came a bang and a sound like 'damn!' and hopelessness settled down.

A shout from the outer darkness, and most of the men and some of the girls rose and hurried out. Fragments of conversation heard in the darkness—

'It's two horses, I tell you!'

'It's three, you—!'

'Lay you—!'

'Put the stuff up!'

A clack of gate thrown open.

'Who is it, Tom?'

Voices from gatewards, yelling, 'Johnny Mears! They've got Johnny Mears!'

Then rose yells, and a cheer such as is seldom heard in scrub-lands.

Out in the kitchen long Dave Regan grabbed, from the far side of the table, where he had thrown it, a burst and battered concertina, which he had been for the last hour vainly trying to patch and make air-tight; and, holding it out towards the back-door, between his palms, as a football is held, he let it drop, and fetched it neatly on the toe of his riding-boot. It was a beautiful kick, the concertina shot out into the blackness, from which was projected, in return, first a short, sudden howl, then a face with one eye glaring and the other covered by an enormous brick-coloured hand, and a voice that wanted to know who shot 'that lurid loaf of bread?'

But from the schoolroom was heard the loud, free voice of Joe Matthews, M.C.,—

'Take yer partners! Hurry up! Take yer partners! They've got Johnny Mears with his fiddle!'

The Buck-Jumper

Saturday afternoon.

There were about a dozen Bush natives, from anywhere, most of them lanky and easy-going, hanging about the little slab-and-bark hotel on the edge of the scrub at Capertee Camp (a teamster's camp) when Cob & Co.'s mail-coach and six came dashing down the siding from round Crown Ridge, in all its glory, to the end of the twelve-mile stage. Some wiry, ill-used hacks were hanging to the fence and to saplings about the place. The fresh coach-horses stood ready in a stock-yard close to the shanty. As the coach climbed the nearer bank of the creek at the foot of the ridge, six of the Bushmen detached themselves from verandah posts, from their heels, from the clay floor of the verandah and the rough slab wall against which they'd been resting, and joined a group of four or five who stood round one. He stood with his back to the corner post of the stock-yard, his feet well braced out in front of him, and contemplated the toes of his tight new 'lastic-side boots and whistled softly. He was a clean-limbed, handsome fellow, with riding-cords, leggings, and a blue sash; he was Graeco-Roman-nosed, blue-eyed, and his glossy, curly black hair bunched up in front of the brim of a new cabbage-tree hat, set well back on his head.

'Do it for a quid, Jack?' asked one.

'Damned if I will, Jim!' said the young man at the post. 'I'll do it for a fiver—not a blanky sprat less.'

Jim took off his hat and 'shoved' it round, and 'bobs' were 'chucked' into it. The result was about thirty shillings.

Jack glanced contemptuously into the crown of the hat.

'Not me!' he said, showing some emotion for the first time. 'D'yer think I'm going to risk me blanky neck for your blanky amusement for thirty blanky bob. I'll ride the blanky horse for a fiver, and I'll feel the blanky quids in my pocket before I get on.'

Meanwhile the coach had dashed up to the door of the shanty. There were about twenty passengers aboard—inside, on the box-seat, on the tail-board, and hanging on to the roof—most of them Sydney men going up to the Mudgee races. They got down and went inside with the driver for a drink, while the stablemen changed horses. The Bushmen raised their voices a little and argued.

One of the passengers was a big, stout, hearty man—a good-hearted, sporting man and a racehorse-owner, according to his brands. He had a round red face and a white cork hat. 'What's those chaps got on outside?' he asked the publican.

'Oh, it's a bet they've got on about riding a horse,' replied the publican. 'The flash-looking chap with the sash is Flash Jack, the horse-breaker; and they reckon they've got the champion outlaw in the district out there—that chestnut horse in the yard.'

The sporting man was interested at once, and went out and joined the Bushmen.

'Well, chaps! what have you got on here?' he asked cheerily.

'Oh,' said Jim carelessly, 'it's only a bit of a bet about ridin' that blanky chestnut in the corner of the yard there.' He indicated an ungroomed chestnut horse, fenced off by a couple of long sapling poles in a corner of the stock-yard. 'Flash Jack there—he reckons he's the champion horse-breaker round here—Flash Jack reckons he can take it out of that horse first try.'

'What's up with the horse?' inquired the big, red-faced man. 'It looks quiet enough. Why, I'd ride it myself.'

'Would yer?' said Jim, who had hair that stood straight up, and an innocent, inquiring expression. 'Looks quiet, does he? YOU ought to know more about horses than to go by the looks of 'em. He's quiet enough just now, when there's no one near him; but you should have been here an hour ago. That horse has killed two men and put another chap's shoulder out—besides breaking a cove's leg. It took six of us all the morning to run him in and get the saddle on him; and now Flash Jack wants to back out of it.'

'Euraliar!' remarked Flash Jack cheerfully. 'I said I'd ride that blanky horse out of the yard for a fiver. I ain't goin' to risk my blanky neck for nothing and only to amuse you blanks.'

'He said he'd ride the horse inside the yard for a quid,' said Jim.

'And get smashed against the rails!' said Flash Jack. 'I would be a fool. I'd rather take my chance outside in the scrub—and it's rough country round here.'

'Well, how much do you want?' asked the man in the mushroom hat.

'A fiver, I said,' replied Jack indifferently. 'And the blanky stuff in my pocket before I get on the blanky horse.'

'Are you frightened of us running away without paying you?' inquired one of the passengers who had gathered round.

'I'm frightened of the horse bolting with me without me being paid,' said Flash Jack. 'I know that horse; he's got a mouth like iron. I might be at the bottom of the cliff on Crown Ridge road in twenty minutes with my head caved in, and then what chance for the quids?'

'You wouldn't want 'em then,' suggested a passenger. 'Or, say!—we'd leave the fiver with the publican to bury you.'

Flash Jack ignored that passenger. He eyed his boots and softly whistled a tune.

'All right!' said the man in the cork hat, putting his hand in his pocket. 'I'll start with a quid; stump up, you chaps.'

The five pounds were got together.

'I'll lay a quid to half a quid he don't stick on ten minutes!' shouted Jim to his mates as soon as he saw that the event was to come off. The passengers also betted amongst themselves. Flash Jack, after putting the money in his breeches-pocket, let down the rails and led the horse into the middle of the yard.

'Quiet as an old cow!' snorted a passenger in disgust. 'I believe it's a sell!'

'Wait a bit,' said Jim to the passenger, 'wait a bit and you'll see.'

They waited and saw.

Flash Jack leisurely mounted the horse, rode slowly out of the yard, and trotted briskly round the corner of the shanty and into the scrub, which swallowed him more completely than the sea might have done.

Most of the other Bushmen mounted their horses and followed Flash Jack to a clearing in the scrub, at a safe distance from the shanty; then they dismounted and hung on to saplings, or leaned against their horses, while they laughed.

At the hotel there was just time for another drink. The driver climbed to his seat and shouted, 'All aboard!' in his usual tone. The passengers climbed to their places, thinking hard. A mile or so along the road the man with the cork hat remarked, with much truth—

'Those blanky Bushmen have got too much time to think.'

The Bushmen returned to the shanty as soon as the coach was out of sight, and proceeded to 'knock down' the fiver.

Jimmy Grimshaw's Wooing

The Half-way House at Tinned Dog (Out-Back in Australia) kept Daniel Myers—licensed to retail spirituous and fermented liquors—in drink and the horrors for upward of five years, at the end of which time he lay hidden for weeks in a back skillion, an object which no decent man would care to see—or hear when it gave forth sound. 'Good accommodation for man and beast'; but few shanties save his own might, for a consideration, have accommodated the sort of beast which the man Myers had become towards the end of his career. But at last the eccentric Bush doctor, 'Doc' Wild' (who perhaps could drink as much as Myers without its having any further effect upon his temperament than to keep him awake and cynical), pronounced the publican dead enough to be buried legally; so the widow buried him, had the skillion cleaned out, and the sign altered to read, 'Margaret Myers, licensed, &c.', and continued to conduct the pub. just as she had run it for over five years, with the joyful and blessed exception that there was no longer a human pig and pigstye attached, and that the atmosphere was calm. Most of the regular patrons of the Half-way House could have their horrors decently, and, comparatively, quietly—or otherwise have them privately—in the Big Scrub adjacent; but Myers had not been one of that sort.

Mrs Myers settled herself to enjoy life comfortably and happily, at the fixed age of thirty-nine, for the next seven years or so. She was a pleasant-faced dumpling, who had been baked solid in the droughts of Out-Back without losing her good looks, and had put up with a hard life, and Myers, all those years without losing her good humour and nature. Probably, had her husband been the opposite kind of man, she would have been different—haggard, bad-tempered, and altogether impossible—for of such is woman. But then it might be taken into consideration that she had been practically a widow during at least the last five years of her husband's alleged life.

Mrs Myers was reckoned a good catch in the district, but it soon seemed that she was not to be caught.

'It would be a grand thing,' one of the periodical boozers of Tinned Dog would say to his mates, 'for one of us to have his name up on a pub.; it would save a lot of money.'

'It wouldn't save you anything, Bill, if I got it,' was the retort. 'You needn't come round chewing my lug then. I'd give you one drink and no more.'

The publican at Dead Camel, station managers, professional shearers, even one or two solvent squatters and promising cockatoos, tried their luck in vain. In answer to the suggestion that she ought to have a man to knock round and look after things, she retorted that she had had one, and was perfectly satisfied. Few trav'lers on those tracks but tried 'a bit of bear-up' in that direction, but all to no purpose. Chequemen knocked down their cheques manfully at the Half-way House—to get courage and goodwill and 'put it off' till, at the last moment, they offered themselves abjectly to the landlady; which was worse than bad judgment on their part—it was very silly, and she told them so.

One or two swore off, and swore to keep straight; but she had no faith in them, and when they found that out, it hurt their feelings so much that they 'broke out' and went on record-breaking sprees.

About the end of each shearing the sign was touched up, with an extra coat of paint on the 'Margaret', whereat suitors looked hopeless.

One or two of the rejected died of love in the horrors in the Big Scrub—anyway, the verdict was that they died of love aggravated by the horrors. But the climax was reached when a Queensland shearer, seizing the opportunity when the mate, whose turn it was to watch him, fell asleep, went down to the yard and hanged himself on the butcher's gallows—having first removed his clothes, with some drink-lurid idea of leaving the world as naked as he came into it. He climbed the pole, sat astride on top, fixed the rope to neck and bar, but gave a yell—a yell of drunken triumph—before he dropped, and woke his mates.

They cut him down and brought him to. Next day he apologised to Mrs Myers, said, 'Ah, well! So long!' to the rest, and departed—cured of drink and love apparently. The verdict was that the blanky fool should have dropped before he yelled; but she was upset and annoyed, and it began to look as though, if she wished to continue to live on happily and comfortably for a few years longer at the fixed age of thirty-nine, she would either have to give up the pub. or get married.

Her fame was carried far and wide, and she became a woman whose name was mentioned with respect in rough shearing-sheds and huts, and round the camp-fire.

About thirty miles south of Tinned Dog one James Grimshaw, widower—otherwise known as 'Old Jimmy', though he was little past middle age—had a small selection which he had worked, let, given up, and tackled afresh (with sinews of war drawn from fencing contracts) ever since the death of his young wife some fifteen years agone. He was a practical, square-faced, clean-shaven, clean, and tidy man, with a certain 'cleanness' about the shape of his limbs which suggested the old jockey or hostler. There were two strong theories in connection with Jimmy—one was that he had had a university education, and the other that he couldn't write his own name. Not nearly such a ridiculous nor simple case Out-Back as it might seem.

Jimmy smoked and listened without comment to the 'heard tells' in connection with Mrs Myers, till at last one night, at the end of his contract and over a last pipe, he said quietly, 'I'll go up to Tinned Dog next week and try my luck.'

His mates and the casual Jims and Bills were taken too suddenly to laugh, and the laugh having been lost, as Bland Holt, the Australian actor would put it in a professional sense, the audience had time to think, with the result that the joker swung his hand down through an imaginary table and exclaimed—

'By God! Jimmy'll do it.' (Applause.)

So one drowsy afternoon at the time of the year when the breathless day runs on past 7 P.M., Mrs Myers sat sewing in the bar parlour, when a clean-shaved, clean-shirted, clean-neckerchiefed, clean-moleskinned, greased-bluchered—altogether a model or stage swagman came up, was served in the bar by the half-caste female cook, and took his way to the river-bank, where he rigged a small tent and made a model camp.

A couple of hours later he sat on a stool on the verandah, smoking a clean clay pipe. Just before the sunset meal Mrs Myers asked, 'Is that trav'ler there yet, Mary?'

'Yes, missus. Clean pfellar that.'

The landlady knitted her forehead over her sewing, as women do when limited for 'stuff' or wondering whether a section has been cut wrong—or perhaps she thought of that other who hadn't been a 'clean pfellar'. She put her work aside, and stood in the doorway, looking out across the clearing.

'Good-day, mister,' she said, seeming to become aware of him for the first time.

'Good-day, missus!'

'Hot!'

'Hot!'

Pause.

'Trav'lin'?'

'No, not particular!'

She waited for him to explain. Myers was always explaining when he wasn't raving. But the swagman smoked on.

'Have a drink?' she suggested, to keep her end up.

'No, thank you, missus. I had one an hour or so ago. I never take more than two a-day—one before breakfast, if I can get it, and a night-cap.'

What a contrast to Myers! she thought.

'Come and have some tea; it's ready.'

'Thank you. I don't mind if I do.'

They got on very slowly, but comfortably. She got little out of him except the facts that he had a selection, had finished a contract, and was 'just having a look at the country.' He politely declined a 'shake-down', saying he had a comfortable camp, and preferred being out this weather. She got his name with a 'by-the-way', as he rose to leave, and he went back to camp.

He caught a cod, and they had it for breakfast next morning, and got along so comfortable over breakfast that he put in the forenoon pottering about the gates and stable with a hammer, a saw, and a box of nails.

And, well—to make it short—when the big Tinned Dog shed had cut-out, and the shearers struck the Half-way House, they were greatly impressed by a brand-new sign whereon glistened the words—

HALF-WAY HOUSE HOTEL, BY JAMES GRIMSHAW.

Good Stabling.

The last time I saw Mrs Grimshaw she looked about thirty-five.

At Dead Dingo

It was blazing hot outside and smothering hot inside the weather-board and iron shanty at Dead Dingo, a place on the Cleared Road, where there was a pub. and a police-station, and which was sometimes called 'Roasted', and other times 'Potted Dingo'—nicknames suggested by the everlasting drought and the vicinity of the one-pub. township of Tinned Dog.

From the front verandah the scene was straight-cleared road, running right and left to Out-Back, and to Bourke (and ankle-deep in the red sand dust for perhaps a hundred miles); the rest blue-grey bush, dust, and the heat-wave blazing across every object.

There were only four in the bar-room, though it was New Year's Day. There weren't many more in the county. The girl sat behind the bar—the coolest place in the shanty—reading 'Deadwood Dick'. On a worn and torn and battered horse-hair sofa, which had seen cooler places and better days, lay an awful and healthy example, a bearded swagman, with his arms twisted over his head and his face to the wall, sleeping off the death of the dead drunk. Bill and Jim—shearer and rouseabout—sat at a table playing cards. It was about three o'clock in the afternoon, and they had been gambling since nine—and the greater part of the night before—so they were, probably, in a worse condition morally (and perhaps physically) than the drunken swagman on the sofa.

Close under the bar, in a dangerous place for his legs and tail, lay a sheep-dog with a chain attached to his collar and wound round his neck.

Presently a thump on the table, and Bill, unlucky gambler, rose with an oath that would have been savage if it hadn't been drawled.

'Stumped?' inquired Jim.

'Not a blanky, lurid deener!' drawled Bill.

Jim drew his reluctant hands from the cards, his eyes went slowly and hopelessly round the room and out the door. There was something in the eyes of both, except when on the card-table, of the look of a man waking in a strange place.

'Got anything?' asked Jim, fingering the cards again.

Bill sucked in his cheeks, collecting the saliva with difficulty, and spat out on to the verandah floor.

'That's all I got,' he drawled. 'It's gone now.'

Jim leaned back in his chair, twisted, yawned, and caught sight of the dog.

'That there dog yours?' he asked, brightening.

They had evidently been strangers the day before, or as strange to each other as Bushmen can be.

Bill scratched behind his ear, and blinked at the dog. The dog woke suddenly to a flea fact.

'Yes,' drawled Bill, 'he's mine.'

'Well, I'm going Out-Back, and I want a dog,' said Jim, gathering the cards briskly. 'Half a quid agin the dog?'

'Half a quid be—!' drawled Bill. 'Call it a quid?'

'Half a blanky quid!'

'A gory, lurid quid!' drawled Bill desperately, and he stooped over his swag.

But Jim's hands were itching in a ghastly way over the cards.

'Alright. Call it a— quid.'

The drunkard on the sofa stirred, showed signs of waking, but died again. Remember this, it might come in useful.

Bill sat down to the table once more.

Jim rose first, winner of the dog. He stretched, yawned 'Ah, well!' and shouted drinks. Then he shouldered his swag, stirred the dog up with his foot, unwound the chain, said 'Ah, well—so long!' and drifted out and along the road toward Out-Back, the dog following with head and tail down.

Bill scored another drink on account of girl-pity for bad luck, shouldered his swag, said, 'So long, Mary!' and drifted out and along the road towards Tinned Dog, on the Bourke side.

A long, drowsy, half hour passed—the sort of half hour that is as long as an hour in the places where days are as long as years, and years hold about as much as days do in other places.

The man on the sofa woke with a start, and looked scared and wild for a moment; then he brought his dusty broken boots to the floor, rested his elbows on his knees, took his unfortunate head between his hands, and came back to life gradually.

He lifted his head, looked at the girl across the top of the bar, and formed with his lips, rather than spoke, the words—

'Put up a drink?'*

* 'Put up a drink'—i.e., 'Give me a drink on credit', or 'Chalk it up'.

She shook her head tightly and went on reading.

He staggered up, and, leaning on the bar, made desperate distress signals with hand, eyes, and mouth.

'No!' she snapped. 'I means no when I says no! You've had too many last drinks already, and the boss says you ain't to have another. If you swear again, or bother me, I'll call him.'

He hung sullenly on the counter for a while, then lurched to his swag, and shouldered it hopelessly and wearily. Then he blinked round, whistled, waited a moment, went on to the front verandah, peered round, through the heat, with bloodshot eyes, and whistled again. He turned and started through to the back-door.

'What the devil do you want now?' demanded the girl, interrupted in her reading for the third time by him. 'Stampin' all over the house. You can't go through there! It's privit! I do wish to goodness you'd git!'

'Where the blazes is that there dog o' mine got to?' he muttered. 'Did you see a dog?'

'No! What do I want with your dog?'

He whistled out in front again, and round each corner. Then he came back with a decided step and tone.

'Look here! that there dog was lyin' there agin the wall when I went to sleep. He wouldn't stir from me, or my swag, in a year, if he wasn't dragged. He's been blanky well touched [stolen], and I wouldn'ter lost him for a fiver. Are you sure you ain't seen a dog?' then suddenly, as the thought struck him: 'Where's them two chaps that was playin' cards when I wenter sleep?'

'Why!' exclaimed the girl, without thinking, 'there was a dog, now I come to think of it, but I thought it belonged to one of them chaps. Anyway, they played for it, and the other chap won it and took it away.'

He stared at her blankly, with thunder gathering in the blankness.

'What sort of a dog was it?'

Dog described; the chain round the neck settled it.

He scowled at her darkly.

'Now, look here,' he said; 'you've allowed gamblin' in this bar—your boss has. You've got no right to let spielers gamble away a man's dog. Is a customer to lose his dog every time he has a doze to suit your boss? I'll go straight across to the police camp and put you away, and I don't care if you lose your licence. I ain't goin' to lose my dog. I wouldn'ter taken a ten-pound note for that blanky dog! I—'

She was filling a pewter hastily.

'Here! for God's sake have a drink an' stop yer row.'

He drank with satisfaction. Then he hung on the bar with one elbow and scowled out the door.

'Which blanky way did them chaps go?' he growled.

'The one that took the dog went towards Tinned Dog.'

'And I'll haveter go all the blanky way back after him, and most likely lose me shed! Here!' jerking the empty pewter across the bar, 'fill that up again; I'm narked properly, I am, and I'll take twenty-four blanky hours to cool down now. I wouldn'ter lost that dog for twenty quid.'

He drank again with deeper satisfaction, then he shuffled out, muttering, swearing, and threatening louder every step, and took the track to Tinned Dog.

Now the man, girl, or woman, who told me this yarn has never quite settled it in his or her mind as to who really owned the dog. I leave it to you.

Telling Mrs Baker

Most Bushmen who hadn't 'known Bob Baker to speak to', had 'heard tell of him'. He'd been a squatter, not many years before, on the Macquarie river in New South Wales, and had made money in the good seasons, and had gone in for horse-racing and racehorse-breeding, and long trips to Sydney, where he put up at swell hotels and went the pace. So after a pretty severe drought, when the sheep died by thousands on his runs, Bob Baker went under, and the bank took over his station and put a manager in charge.

He'd been a jolly, open-handed, popular man, which means that he'd been a selfish man as far as his wife and children were concerned, for they had to suffer for it in the end. Such generosity is often born of vanity, or moral cowardice, or both mixed. It's very nice to hear the chaps sing 'For he's a jolly good fellow', but you've mostly got to pay for it twice—first in company, and afterwards alone. I once heard the chaps singing that I was a jolly good fellow, when I was leaving a place and they were giving me a send-off. It thrilled me, and brought a warm gush to my eyes; but, all the same, I wished I had half the money I'd lent them, and spent on 'em, and I wished I'd used the time I'd wasted to be a jolly good fellow.

When I first met Bob Baker he was a boss-drover on the great north-western route, and his wife lived at the township of Solong on the Sydney side. He was going north to new country round by the Gulf of Carpentaria, with a big mob of cattle, on a two years' trip; and I and my mate, Andy M'Culloch, engaged to go with him. We wanted to have a look at the Gulf Country.

After we had crossed the Queensland border it seemed to me that the Boss was too fond of going into wayside shanties and town pubs. Andy had been with him on another trip, and he told me that the Boss was only going this way lately. Andy knew Mrs Baker well, and seemed to think a deal of her. 'She's a good little woman,' said Andy. 'One of the right stuff. I worked on their station for a while when I was a nipper, and I know. She was always a damned sight too good for the Boss, but she believed in him. When I was coming away this time she says to me, "Look here, Andy, I'm afraid Robert is drinking again. Now I want you to look after him for me, as much as you can—you seem to have as much influence with him as any one. I want you to promise me that you'll never have a drink with him."

'And I promised,' said Andy, 'and I'll keep my word.' Andy was a chap who could keep his word, and nothing else. And, no matter how the Boss persuaded, or sneered, or swore at him, Andy would never drink with him.

It got worse and worse: the Boss would ride on ahead and get drunk at a shanty, and sometimes he'd be days behind us; and when he'd catch up to us his temper would be just about as much as we could stand. At last he went on a howling spree at Mulgatown, about a hundred and fifty miles north of the border, and, what was worse, he got in tow with a flash barmaid there—one of those girls who are engaged, by the publicans up country, as baits for chequemen.

He went mad over that girl. He drew an advance cheque from the stock-owner's agent there, and knocked that down; then he raised some more money somehow, and spent that—mostly on the girl.

We did all we could. Andy got him along the track for a couple of stages, and just when we thought he was all right, he slipped us in the night and went back.

We had two other men with us, but had the devil's own bother on account of the cattle. It was a mixed-up job all round. You see it was all big runs round there, and we had to keep the bullocks moving along the route all the time, or else get into trouble for trespass. The agent wasn't going to go to the expense of putting the cattle in a paddock until the Boss sobered up; there was very little grass on the route or the travelling-stock reserves or camps, so we had to keep travelling for grass.

The world might wobble and all the banks go bung, but the cattle have to go through—that's the law of the stock-routes. So the agent wired to the owners, and, when he got their reply, he sacked the Boss and sent the cattle on in charge of another man. The new Boss was a drover coming south after a trip; he had his two brothers with him, so he didn't want me and Andy; but, anyway, we were full up of this trip, so we arranged, between the agent and the new Boss, to get most of the wages due to us—the Boss had drawn some of our stuff and spent it.

We could have started on the back track at once, but, drunk or sober, mad or sane, good or bad, it isn't Bush religion to desert a mate in a hole; and the Boss was a mate of ours; so we stuck to him.

We camped on the creek, outside the town, and kept him in the camp with us as much as possible, and did all we could for him.

'How could I face his wife if I went home without him?' asked Andy, 'or any of his old mates?'

The Boss got himself turned out of the pub. where the barmaid was, and then he'd hang round the other pubs., and get drink somehow, and fight, and get knocked about. He was an awful object by this time, wild-eyed and gaunt, and he hadn't washed or shaved for days.

Andy got the constable in charge of the police station to lock him up for a night, but it only made him worse: we took him back to the camp next morning and while our eyes were off him for a few minutes he slipped away into the scrub, stripped himself naked, and started to hang himself to a leaning tree with a piece of clothes-line rope. We got to him just in time.

Then Andy wired to the Boss's brother Ned, who was fighting the drought, the rabbit-pest, and the banks, on a small station back on the border. Andy reckoned it was about time to do something.

Perhaps the Boss hadn't been quite right in his head before he started drinking—he had acted queer some time, now we came to think of it; maybe he'd got a touch of sunstroke or got brooding over his troubles—anyway he died in the horrors within the week.

His brother Ned turned up on the last day, and Bob thought he was the devil, and grappled with him. It took the three of us to hold the Boss down sometimes.

Sometimes, towards the end, he'd be sensible for a few minutes and talk about his 'poor wife and children'; and immediately afterwards he'd fall a-cursing me, and Andy, and Ned, and calling us devils. He cursed everything; he cursed his wife and children, and yelled that they were dragging him down to hell. He died raving mad. It was the worst case of death in the horrors of drink that I ever saw or heard of in the Bush.

Ned saw to the funeral: it was very hot weather, and men have to be buried quick who die out there in the hot weather—especially men who die in the state the Boss was in. Then Ned went to the public-house where the barmaid was and called the landlord out. It was a desperate fight: the publican was a big man, and a bit of a fighting man; but Ned was one of those quiet, simple-minded chaps who will carry a thing through to death when they make up their minds. He gave that publican nearly as good a thrashing as he deserved. The constable in charge of the station backed Ned, while another policeman picked up the publican. Sounds queer to you city people, doesn't it?

Next morning we three started south. We stayed a couple of days at Ned Baker's station on the border, and then started on our three-hundred-mile ride down-country. The weather was still very hot, so we decided to travel at night for a while, and left Ned's place at dusk. He parted from us at the homestead gate. He gave Andy a small packet, done up in canvas, for Mrs Baker, which Andy told me contained Bob's pocket-book, letters, and papers. We looked back, after we'd gone a piece along the dusty road, and saw Ned still standing by the gate; and a very lonely figure he looked. Ned was a bachelor. 'Poor old Ned,' said Andy to me. 'He was in love with Mrs Bob Baker before she got married, but she picked the wrong man—girls mostly do. Ned and Bob were together on the Macquarie, but Ned left when his brother married, and he's been up in these God-forsaken scrubs ever since. Look, I want to tell you something, Jack: Ned has written to Mrs Bob to tell her that Bob died of fever, and everything was done for him that could be done, and that he died easy—and all that sort of thing. Ned sent her some money, and she is to think that it was the money due to Bob when he died. Now I'll have to go and see her when we get to Solong; there's no getting out of it, I'll have to face her—and you'll have to come with me.'

'Damned if I will!' I said.

'But you'll have to,' said Andy. 'You'll have to stick to me; you're surely not crawler enough to desert a mate in a case like this? I'll have to lie like hell—I'll have to lie as I never lied to a woman before; and you'll have to back me and corroborate every lie.'

I'd never seen Andy show so much emotion.

'There's plenty of time to fix up a good yarn,' said Andy. He said no more about Mrs Baker, and we only mentioned the Boss's name casually, until we were within about a day's ride of Solong; then Andy told me the yarn he'd made up about the Boss's death.

'And I want you to listen, Jack,' he said, 'and remember every word—and if you can fix up a better yarn you can tell me afterwards. Now it was like this: the Boss wasn't too well when he crossed the border. He complained of pains in his back and head and a stinging pain in the back of his neck, and he had dysentery bad,—but that doesn't matter; it's lucky I ain't supposed to tell a woman all the symptoms. The Boss stuck to the job as long as he could, but we managed the cattle and made it as easy as we could for him. He'd just take it easy, and ride on from camp to camp, and rest. One night I rode to a town off the route (or you did, if you like) and got some medicine for him; that made him better for a while, but at last, a day or two this side of Mulgatown, he had to give up. A squatter there drove him into town in his buggy and put him up at the best hotel. The publican knew the Boss and did all he could for him—put him in the best room and wired for another doctor. We wired for Ned as soon as we saw how bad the Boss was, and Ned rode night and day and got there three days before the Boss died. The Boss was a bit off his head some of the time with the fever, but was calm and quiet towards the end and died easy. He talked a lot about his wife and children, and told us to tell the wife not to fret but to cheer up for the children's sake. How does that sound?'

I'd been thinking while I listened, and an idea struck me.

'Why not let her know the truth?' I asked. 'She's sure to hear of it sooner or later; and if she knew he was only a selfish, drunken blackguard she might get over it all the sooner.'

'You don't know women, Jack,' said Andy quietly. 'And, anyway, even if she is a sensible woman, we've got a dead mate to consider as well as a living woman.'

'But she's sure to hear the truth sooner or later,' I said, 'the Boss was so well known.'

'And that's just the reason why the truth might be kept from her,' said Andy. 'If he wasn't well known—and nobody could help liking him, after all, when he was straight—if he wasn't so well known the truth might leak out unawares. She won't know if I can help it, or at least not yet a while. If I see any chaps that come from the North I'll put them up to it. I'll tell M'Grath, the publican at Solong, too: he's a straight man—he'll keep his ears open and warn chaps. One of Mrs Baker's sisters is staying with her, and I'll give her a hint so that she can warn off any women that might get hold of a yarn. Besides, Mrs Baker is sure to go and live in Sydney, where all her people are—she was a Sydney girl; and she's not likely to meet any one there that will tell her the truth. I can tell her that it was the last wish of the Boss that she should shift to Sydney.'

We smoked and thought a while, and by-and-by Andy had what he called a 'happy thought'. He went to his saddle-bags and got out the small canvas packet that Ned had given him: it was sewn up with packing-thread, and Andy ripped it open with his pocket-knife.

'What are you doing, Andy?' I asked.

'Ned's an innocent old fool, as far as sin is concerned,' said Andy. 'I guess he hasn't looked through the Boss's letters, and I'm just going to see that there's nothing here that will make liars of us.'

He looked through the letters and papers by the light of the fire. There were some letters from Mrs Baker to her husband, also a portrait of her and the children; these Andy put aside. But there were other letters from barmaids and women who were not fit to be seen in the same street with the Boss's wife; and there were portraits—one or two flash ones. There were two letters from other men's wives too.

'And one of those men, at least, was an old mate of his!' said Andy, in a tone of disgust.

He threw the lot into the fire; then he went through the Boss's pocket-book and tore out some leaves that had notes and addresses on them, and burnt them too. Then he sewed up the packet again and put it away in his saddle-bag.

'Such is life!' said Andy, with a yawn that might have been half a sigh.

We rode into Solong early in the day, turned our horses out in a paddock, and put up at M'Grath's pub. until such time as we made up our minds as to what we'd do or where we'd go. We had an idea of waiting until the shearing season started and then making Out-Back to the big sheds.

Neither of us was in a hurry to go and face Mrs Baker. 'We'll go after dinner,' said Andy at first; then after dinner we had a drink, and felt sleepy—we weren't used to big dinners of roast-beef and vegetables and pudding, and, besides, it was drowsy weather—so we decided to have a snooze and then go. When we woke up it was late in the afternoon, so we thought we'd put it off till after tea. 'It wouldn't be manners to walk in while they're at tea,' said Andy—'it would look as if we only came for some grub.'

But while we were at tea a little girl came with a message that Mrs Baker wanted to see us, and would be very much obliged if we'd call up as soon as possible. You see, in those small towns you can't move without the thing getting round inside of half an hour.

'We'll have to face the music now!' said Andy, 'and no get out of it.' He seemed to hang back more than I did. There was another pub. opposite where Mrs Baker lived, and when we got up the street a bit I said to Andy—

'Suppose we go and have another drink first, Andy? We might be kept in there an hour or two.'

'You don't want another drink,' said Andy, rather short. 'Why, you seem to be going the same way as the Boss!' But it was Andy that edged off towards the pub. when we got near Mrs Baker's place. 'All right!' he said. 'Come on! We'll have this other drink, since you want it so bad.'

We had the drink, then we buttoned up our coats and started across the road—we'd bought new shirts and collars, and spruced up a bit. Half-way across Andy grabbed my arm and asked—

'How do you feel now, Jack?'

'Oh, I'M all right,' I said.

'For God's sake!' said Andy, 'don't put your foot in it and make a mess of it.'

'I won't, if you don't.'

Mrs Baker's cottage was a little weather-board box affair back in a garden. When we went in through the gate Andy gripped my arm again and whispered—

'For God's sake stick to me now, Jack!'

'I'll stick all right,' I said—'you've been having too much beer, Andy.'

I had seen Mrs Baker before, and remembered her as a cheerful, contented sort of woman, bustling about the house and getting the Boss's shirts and things ready when we started North. Just the sort of woman that is contented with housework and the children, and with nothing particular about her in the way of brains. But now she sat by the fire looking like the ghost of herself. I wouldn't have recognised her at first. I never saw such a change in a woman, and it came like a shock to me.

Her sister let us in, and after a first glance at Mrs Baker I had eyes for the sister and no one else. She was a Sydney girl, about twenty-four or twenty-five, and fresh and fair—not like the sun-browned women we were used to see. She was a pretty, bright-eyed girl, and seemed quick to understand, and very sympathetic. She had been educated, Andy had told me, and wrote stories for the Sydney 'Bulletin' and other Sydney papers. She had her hair done and was dressed in the city style, and that took us back a bit at first.

'It's very good of you to come,' said Mrs Baker in a weak, weary voice, when we first went in. 'I heard you were in town.'

'We were just coming when we got your message,' said Andy. 'We'd have come before, only we had to see to the horses.'

'It's very kind of you, I'm sure,' said Mrs Baker.

They wanted us to have tea, but we said we'd just had it. Then Miss Standish (the sister) wanted us to have tea and cake; but we didn't feel as if we could handle cups and saucers and pieces of cake successfully just then.

There was something the matter with one of the children in a back-room, and the sister went to see to it. Mrs Baker cried a little quietly.

'You mustn't mind me,' she said. 'I'll be all right presently, and then I want you to tell me all about poor Bob. It's seeing you, that saw the last of him, that set me off.'

Andy and I sat stiff and straight, on two chairs against the wall, and held our hats tight, and stared at a picture of Wellington meeting Blucher on the opposite wall. I thought it was lucky that that picture was there.

The child was calling 'mumma', and Mrs Baker went in to it, and her sister came out. 'Best tell her all about it and get it over,' she whispered to Andy. 'She'll never be content until she hears all about poor Bob from some one who was with him when he died. Let me take your hats. Make yourselves comfortable.'

She took the hats and put them on the sewing-machine. I wished she'd let us keep them, for now we had nothing to hold on to, and nothing to do with our hands; and as for being comfortable, we were just about as comfortable as two cats on wet bricks.

When Mrs Baker came into the room she brought little Bobby Baker, about four years old; he wanted to see Andy. He ran to Andy at once, and Andy took him up on his knee. He was a pretty child, but he reminded me too much of his father.

'I'm so glad you've come, Andy!' said Bobby.

'Are you, Bobby?'

'Yes. I wants to ask you about daddy. You saw him go away, didn't you?' and he fixed his great wondering eyes on Andy's face.

'Yes,' said Andy.

'He went up among the stars, didn't he?'

'Yes,' said Andy.

'And he isn't coming back to Bobby any more?'

'No,' said Andy. 'But Bobby's going to him by-and-by.'

Mrs Baker had been leaning back in her chair, resting her head on her hand, tears glistening in her eyes; now she began to sob, and her sister took her out of the room.

Andy looked miserable. 'I wish to God I was off this job!' he whispered to me.

'Is that the girl that writes the stories?' I asked.

'Yes,' he said, staring at me in a hopeless sort of way, 'and poems too.'

'Is Bobby going up among the stars?' asked Bobby.

'Yes,' said Andy—'if Bobby's good.'

'And auntie?'

'Yes.'

'And mumma?'

'Yes.'

'Are you going, Andy?'

'Yes,' said Andy hopelessly.

'Did you see daddy go up amongst the stars, Andy?'

'Yes,' said Andy, 'I saw him go up.'

'And he isn't coming down again any more?'

'No,' said Andy.

'Why isn't he?'

'Because he's going to wait up there for you and mumma, Bobby.'

There was a long pause, and then Bobby asked—

'Are you going to give me a shilling, Andy?' with the same expression of innocent wonder in his eyes.

Andy slipped half-a-crown into his hand. 'Auntie' came in and told him he'd see Andy in the morning and took him away to bed, after he'd kissed us both solemnly; and presently she and Mrs Baker settled down to hear Andy's story.

'Brace up now, Jack, and keep your wits about you,' whispered Andy to me just before they came in.

'Poor Bob's brother Ned wrote to me,' said Mrs Baker, 'but he scarcely told me anything. Ned's a good fellow, but he's very simple, and never thinks of anything.'

Andy told her about the Boss not being well after he crossed the border.

'I knew he was not well,' said Mrs Baker, 'before he left. I didn't want him to go. I tried hard to persuade him not to go this trip. I had a feeling that I oughtn't to let him go. But he'd never think of anything but me and the children. He promised he'd give up droving after this trip, and get something to do near home. The life was too much for him—riding in all weathers and camping out in the rain, and living like a dog. But he was never content at home. It was all for the sake of me and the children. He wanted to make money and start on a station again. I shouldn't have let him go. He only thought of me and the children! Oh! my poor, dear, kind, dead husband!' She broke down again and sobbed, and her sister comforted her, while Andy and I stared at Wellington meeting Blucher on the field of Waterloo. I thought the artist had heaped up the dead a bit extra, and I thought that I wouldn't like to be trod on by horses, even if I was dead.

'Don't you mind,' said Miss Standish, 'she'll be all right presently,' and she handed us the 'Illustrated Sydney Journal'. This was a great relief,—we bumped our heads over the pictures.

Mrs Baker made Andy go on again, and he told her how the Boss broke down near Mulgatown. Mrs Baker was opposite him and Miss Standish opposite me. Both of them kept their eyes on Andy's face: he sat, with his hair straight up like a brush as usual, and kept his big innocent grey eyes fixed on Mrs Baker's face all the time he was speaking. I watched Miss Standish. I thought she was the prettiest girl I'd ever seen; it was a bad case of love at first sight, but she was far and away above me, and the case was hopeless. I began to feel pretty miserable, and to think back into the past: I just heard Andy droning away by my side.

'So we fixed him up comfortable in the waggonette with the blankets and coats and things,' Andy was saying, 'and the squatter started into Mulgatown.... It was about thirty miles, Jack, wasn't it?' he asked, turning suddenly to me. He always looked so innocent that there were times when I itched to knock him down.

'More like thirty-five,' I said, waking up.

Miss Standish fixed her eyes on me, and I had another look at Wellington and Blucher.

'They were all very good and kind to the Boss,' said Andy. 'They thought a lot of him up there. Everybody was fond of him.'

'I know it,' said Mrs Baker. 'Nobody could help liking him. He was one of the kindest men that ever lived.'

'Tanner, the publican, couldn't have been kinder to his own brother,' said Andy. 'The local doctor was a decent chap, but he was only a young fellow, and Tanner hadn't much faith in him, so he wired for an older doctor at Mackintyre, and he even sent out fresh horses to meet the doctor's buggy. Everything was done that could be done, I assure you, Mrs Baker.'

'I believe it,' said Mrs Baker. 'And you don't know how it relieves me to hear it. And did the publican do all this at his own expense?'

'He wouldn't take a penny, Mrs Baker.'

'He must have been a good true man. I wish I could thank him.'

'Oh, Ned thanked him for you,' said Andy, though without meaning more than he said.

'I wouldn't have fancied that Ned would have thought of that,' said Mrs Baker. 'When I first heard of my poor husband's death, I thought perhaps he'd been drinking again—that worried me a bit.'

'He never touched a drop after he left Solong, I can assure you, Mrs Baker,' said Andy quickly.

Now I noticed that Miss Standish seemed surprised or puzzled, once or twice, while Andy was speaking, and leaned forward to listen to him; then she leaned back in her chair and clasped her hands behind her head and looked at him, with half-shut eyes, in a way I didn't like. Once or twice she looked at me as if she was going to ask me a question, but I always looked away quick and stared at Blucher and Wellington, or into the empty fireplace, till I felt that her eyes were off me. Then she asked Andy a question or two, in all innocence I believe now, but it scared him, and at last he watched his chance and winked at her sharp. Then she gave a little gasp and shut up like a steel trap.

The sick child in the bedroom coughed and cried again. Mrs Baker went to it. We three sat like a deaf-and-dumb institution, Andy and I staring all over the place: presently Miss Standish excused herself, and went out of the room after her sister. She looked hard at Andy as she left the room, but he kept his eyes away.

'Brace up now, Jack,' whispered Andy to me, 'the worst is coming.'

When they came in again Mrs Baker made Andy go on with his story.

'He—he died very quietly,' said Andy, hitching round, and resting his elbows on his knees, and looking into the fireplace so as to have his face away from the light. Miss Standish put her arm round her sister. 'He died very easy,' said Andy. 'He was a bit off his head at times, but that was while the fever was on him. He didn't suffer much towards the end—I don't think he suffered at all.... He talked a lot about you and the children.' (Andy was speaking very softly now.) 'He said that you were not to fret, but to cheer up for the children's sake.... It was the biggest funeral ever seen round there.'

Mrs Baker was crying softly. Andy got the packet half out of his pocket, but shoved it back again.

'The only thing that hurts me now,' says Mrs Baker presently, 'is to think of my poor husband buried out there in the lonely Bush, so far from home. It's—cruel!' and she was sobbing again.

'Oh, that's all right, Mrs Baker,' said Andy, losing his head a little. 'Ned will see to that. Ned is going to arrange to have him brought down and buried in Sydney.' Which was about the first thing Andy had told her that evening that wasn't a lie. Ned had said he would do it as soon as he sold his wool.

'It's very kind indeed of Ned,' sobbed Mrs Baker. 'I'd never have dreamed he was so kind-hearted and thoughtful. I misjudged him all along. And that is all you have to tell me about poor Robert?'

'Yes,' said Andy—then one of his 'happy thoughts' struck him. 'Except that he hoped you'd shift to Sydney, Mrs Baker, where you've got friends and relations. He thought it would be better for you and the children. He told me to tell you that.'

'He was thoughtful up to the end,' said Mrs Baker. 'It was just like poor Robert—always thinking of me and the children. We are going to Sydney next week.'

Andy looked relieved. We talked a little more, and Miss Standish wanted to make coffee for us, but we had to go and see to our horses. We got up and bumped against each other, and got each other's hats, and promised Mrs Baker we'd come again.

'Thank you very much for coming,' she said, shaking hands with us. 'I feel much better now. You don't know how much you have relieved me. Now, mind, you have promised to come and see me again for the last time.'

Andy caught her sister's eye and jerked his head towards the door to let her know he wanted to speak to her outside.

'Good-bye, Mrs Baker,' he said, holding on to her hand. 'And don't you fret. You've—you've got the children yet. It's—it's all for the best; and, besides, the Boss said you wasn't to fret.' And he blundered out after me and Miss Standish.

She came out to the gate with us, and Andy gave her the packet.

'I want you to give that to her,' he said; 'it's his letters and papers. I hadn't the heart to give it to her, somehow.'

'Tell me, Mr M'Culloch,' she said. 'You've kept something back—you haven't told her the truth. It would be better and safer for me to know. Was it an accident—or the drink?'

'It was the drink,' said Andy. 'I was going to tell you—I thought it would be best to tell you. I had made up my mind to do it, but, somehow, I couldn't have done it if you hadn't asked me.'

'Tell me all,' she said. 'It would be better for me to know.'

'Come a little farther away from the house,' said Andy. She came along the fence a piece with us, and Andy told her as much of the truth as he could.

'I'll hurry her off to Sydney,' she said. 'We can get away this week as well as next.' Then she stood for a minute before us, breathing quickly, her hands behind her back and her eyes shining in the moonlight. She looked splendid.

'I want to thank you for her sake,' she said quickly. 'You are good men! I like the Bushmen! They are grand men—they are noble! I'll probably never see either of you again, so it doesn't matter,' and she put her white hand on Andy's shoulder and kissed him fair and square on the mouth. 'And you, too!' she said to me. I was taller than Andy, and had to stoop. 'Good-bye!' she said, and ran to the gate and in, waving her hand to us. We lifted our hats again and turned down the road.

I don't think it did either of us any harm.

A Hero in Dingo-Scrubs

This is a story—about the only one—of Job Falconer, Boss of the Talbragar sheep-station up country in New South Wales in the early Eighties—when there were still runs in the Dingo-Scrubs out of the hands of the banks, and yet squatters who lived on their stations.

Job would never tell the story himself, at least not complete, and as his family grew up he would become as angry as it was in his easy-going nature to become if reference were made to the incident in his presence. But his wife—little, plump, bright-eyed Gerty Falconer—often told the story (in the mysterious voice which women use in speaking of private matters amongst themselves—but with brightening eyes) to women friends over tea; and always to a new woman friend. And on such occasions she would be particularly tender towards the unconscious Job, and ruffle his thin, sandy hair in a way that embarrassed him in company—made him look as sheepish as an old big-horned ram that has just been shorn and turned amongst the ewes. And the woman friend on parting would give Job's hand a squeeze which would surprise him mildly, and look at him as if she could love him.

According to a theory of mine, Job, to fit the story, should have been tall, and dark, and stern, or gloomy and quick-tempered. But he wasn't. He was fairly tall, but he was fresh-complexioned and sandy (his skin was pink to scarlet in some weathers, with blotches of umber), and his eyes were pale-grey; his big forehead loomed babyishly, his arms were short, and his legs bowed to the saddle. Altogether he was an awkward, unlovely Bush bird—on foot; in the saddle it was different. He hadn't even a 'temper'.

The impression on Job's mind which many years afterwards brought about the incident was strong enough. When Job was a boy of fourteen he saw his father's horse come home riderless—circling and snorting up by the stockyard, head jerked down whenever the hoof trod on one of the snapped ends of the bridle-reins, and saddle twisted over the side with bruised pommel and knee-pad broken off.

Job's father wasn't hurt much, but Job's mother, an emotional woman, and then in a delicate state of health, survived the shock for three months only. 'She wasn't quite right in her head,' they said, 'from the day the horse came home till the last hour before she died.' And, strange to say, Job's father (from whom Job inherited his seemingly placid nature) died three months later. The doctor from the town was of the opinion that he must have 'sustained internal injuries' when the horse threw him. 'Doc. Wild' (eccentric Bush doctor) reckoned that Job's father was hurt inside when his wife died, and hurt so badly that he couldn't pull round. But doctors differ all over the world.

Well, the story of Job himself came about in this way. He had been married a year, and had lately started wool-raising on a pastoral lease he had taken up at Talbragar: it was a new run, with new slab-and-bark huts on the creek for a homestead, new shearing-shed, yards—wife and everything new, and he was expecting a baby. Job felt brand-new himself at the time, so he said. It was a lonely place for a young woman; but Gerty was a settler's daughter. The newness took away some of the loneliness, she said, and there was truth in that: a Bush home in the scrubs looks lonelier the older it gets, and ghostlier in the twilight, as the bark and slabs whiten, or rather grow grey, in fierce summers. And there's nothing under God's sky so weird, so aggressively lonely, as a deserted old home in the Bush.

Job's wife had a half-caste gin for company when Job was away on the run, and the nearest white woman (a hard but honest Lancashire woman from within the kicking radius in Lancashire—wife of a selector) was only seven miles away. She promised to be on hand, and came over two or three times a-week; but Job grew restless as Gerty's time drew near, and wished that he had insisted on sending her to the nearest town (thirty miles away), as originally proposed. Gerty's mother, who lived in town, was coming to see her over her trouble; Job had made arrangements with the town doctor, but prompt attendance could hardly be expected of a doctor who was very busy, who was too fat to ride, and who lived thirty miles away.

Job, in common with most Bushmen and their families round there, had more faith in Doc. Wild, a weird Yankee who made medicine in a saucepan, and worked more cures on Bushmen than did the other three doctors of the district together—maybe because the Bushmen had faith in him, or he knew the Bush and Bush constitutions—or, perhaps, because he'd do things which no 'respectable practitioner' dared do. I've described him in another story. Some said he was a quack, and some said he wasn't. There are scores of wrecks and mysteries like him in the Bush. He drank fearfully, and 'on his own', but was seldom incapable of performing an operation. Experienced Bushmen preferred him three-quarters drunk: when perfectly sober he was apt to be a bit shaky. He was tall, gaunt, had a pointed black moustache, bushy eyebrows, and piercing black eyes. His movements were eccentric. He lived where he happened to be—in a town hotel, in the best room of a homestead, in the skillion of a sly-grog shanty, in a shearer's, digger's, shepherd's, or boundary-rider's hut; in a surveyor's camp or a black-fellows' camp—or, when the horrors were on him, by a log in the lonely Bush. It seemed all one to him. He lost all his things sometimes—even his clothes; but he never lost a pigskin bag which contained his surgical instruments and papers. Except once; then he gave the blacks 5 Pounds to find it for him.

His patients included all, from the big squatter to Black Jimmy; and he rode as far and fast to a squatter's home as to a swagman's camp. When nothing was to be expected from a poor selector or a station hand, and the doctor was hard up, he went to the squatter for a few pounds. He had on occasions been offered cheques of 50 Pounds and 100 Pounds by squatters for 'pulling round' their wives or children; but such offers always angered him. When he asked for 5 Pounds he resented being offered a 10 Pound cheque. He once sued a doctor for alleging that he held no diploma; but the magistrate, on reading certain papers, suggested a settlement out of court, which both doctors agreed to—the other doctor apologising briefly in the local paper. It was noticed thereafter that the magistrate and town doctors treated Doc. Wild with great respect—even at his worst. The thing was never explained, and the case deepened the mystery which surrounded Doc. Wild.

As Job Falconer's crisis approached Doc. Wild was located at a shanty on the main road, about half-way between Job's station and the town. (Township of Come-by-Chance—expressive name; and the shanty was the 'Dead Dingo Hotel', kept by James Myles—known as 'Poisonous Jimmy', perhaps as a compliment to, or a libel on, the liquor he sold.) Job's brother Mac. was stationed at the Dead Dingo Hotel with instructions to hang round on some pretence, see that the doctor didn't either drink himself into the 'D.T.'s' or get sober enough to become restless; to prevent his going away, or to follow him if he did; and to bring him to the station in about a week's time. Mac. (rather more careless, brighter, and more energetic than his brother) was carrying out these instructions while pretending, with rather great success, to be himself on the spree at the shanty.

But one morning, early in the specified week, Job's uneasiness was suddenly greatly increased by certain symptoms, so he sent the black boy for the neighbour's wife and decided to ride to Come-by-Chance to hurry out Gerty's mother, and see, by the way, how Doc. Wild and Mac. were getting on. On the arrival of the neighbour's wife, who drove over in a spring-cart, Job mounted his horse (a freshly broken filly) and started.

'Don't be anxious, Job,' said Gerty, as he bent down to kiss her. 'We'll be all right. Wait! you'd better take the gun—you might see those dingoes again. I'll get it for you.'

The dingoes (native dogs) were very bad amongst the sheep; and Job and Gerty had started three together close to the track the last time they were out in company—without the gun, of course. Gerty took the loaded gun carefully down from its straps on the bedroom wall, carried it out, and handed it up to Job, who bent and kissed her again and then rode off.

It was a hot day—the beginning of a long drought, as Job found to his bitter cost. He followed the track for five or six miles through the thick, monotonous scrub, and then turned off to make a short cut to the main road across a big ring-barked flat. The tall gum-trees had been ring-barked (a ring of bark taken out round the butts), or rather 'sapped'—that is, a ring cut in through the sap—in order to kill them, so that the little strength in the 'poor' soil should not be drawn out by the living roots, and the natural grass (on which Australian stock depends) should have a better show. The hard, dead trees raised their barkless and whitened trunks and leafless branches for three or four miles, and the grey and brown grass stood tall between, dying in the first breaths of the coming drought. All was becoming grey and ashen here, the heat blazing and dancing across objects, and the pale brassy dome of the sky cloudless over all, the sun a glaring white disc with its edges almost melting into the sky. Job held his gun carelessly ready (it was a double-barrelled muzzle-loader, one barrel choke-bore for shot, and the other rifled), and he kept an eye out for dingoes. He was saving his horse for a long ride, jogging along in the careless Bush fashion, hitched a little to one side—and I'm not sure that he didn't have a leg thrown up and across in front of the pommel of the saddle—he was riding along in the careless Bush fashion, and thinking fatherly thoughts in advance, perhaps, when suddenly a great black, greasy-looking iguana scuttled off from the side of the track amongst the dry tufts of grass and shreds of dead bark, and started up a sapling. 'It was a whopper,' Job said afterwards; 'must have been over six feet, and a foot across the body. It scared me nearly as much as the filly.'

The filly shied off like a rocket. Job kept his seat instinctively, as was natural to him; but before he could more than grab at the rein—lying loosely on the pommel—the filly 'fetched up' against a dead box-tree, hard as cast-iron, and Job's left leg was jammed from stirrup to pocket. 'I felt the blood flare up,' he said, 'and I knowed that that'—(Job swore now and then in an easy-going way)—'I knowed that that blanky leg was broken alright. I threw the gun from me and freed my left foot from the stirrup with my hand, and managed to fall to the right, as the filly started off again.'

What follows comes from the statements of Doc. Wild and Mac. Falconer, and Job's own 'wanderings in his mind', as he called them. 'They took a blanky mean advantage of me,' he said, 'when they had me down and I couldn't talk sense.'

The filly circled off a bit, and then stood staring—as a mob of brumbies, when fired at, will sometimes stand watching the smoke. Job's leg was smashed badly, and the pain must have been terrible. But he thought then with a flash, as men do in a fix. No doubt the scene at the lonely Bush home of his boyhood started up before him: his father's horse appeared riderless, and he saw the look in his mother's eyes.

Now a Bushman's first, best, and quickest chance in a fix like this is that his horse go home riderless, the home be alarmed, and the horse's tracks followed back to him; otherwise he might lie there for days, for weeks—till the growing grass buries his mouldering bones. Job was on an old sheep-track across a flat where few might have occasion to come for months, but he did not consider this. He crawled to his gun, then to a log, dragging gun and smashed leg after him. How he did it he doesn't know. Half-lying on one side, he rested the barrel on the log, took aim at the filly, pulled both triggers, and then fell over and lay with his head against the log; and the gun-barrel, sliding down, rested on his neck. He had fainted. The crows were interested, and the ants would come by-and-by.

Now Doc. Wild had inspirations; anyway, he did things which seemed, after they were done, to have been suggested by inspiration and in no other possible way. He often turned up where and when he was wanted above all men, and at no other time. He had gipsy blood, they said; but, anyway, being the mystery he was, and having the face he had, and living the life he lived—and doing the things he did—it was quite probable that he was more nearly in touch than we with that awful invisible world all round and between us, of which we only see distorted faces and hear disjointed utterances when we are 'suffering a recovery'—or going mad.

On the morning of Job's accident, and after a long brooding silence, Doc. Wild suddenly said to Mac. Falconer—

'Git the hosses, Mac. We'll go to the station.'

Mac., used to the doctor's eccentricities, went to see about the horses.

And then who should drive up but Mrs Spencer—Job's mother-in-law—on her way from the town to the station. She stayed to have a cup of tea and give her horses a feed. She was square-faced, and considered a rather hard and practical woman, but she had plenty of solid flesh, good sympathetic common-sense, and deep-set humorous blue eyes. She lived in the town comfortably on the interest of some money which her husband left in the bank. She drove an American waggonette with a good width and length of 'tray' behind, and on this occasion she had a pole and two horses. In the trap were a new flock mattress and pillows, a generous pair of new white blankets, and boxes containing necessaries, delicacies, and luxuries. All round she was an excellent mother-in-law for a man to have on hand at a critical time.

And, speaking of mother-in-law, I would like to put in a word for her right here. She is universally considered a nuisance in times of peace and comfort; but when illness or serious trouble comes home! Then it's 'Write to Mother! Wire for Mother! Send some one to fetch Mother! I'll go and bring Mother!' and if she is not near: 'Oh, I wish Mother were here! If Mother were only near!' And when she is on the spot, the anxious son-in-law: 'Don't YOU go, Mother! You'll stay, won't you, Mother?—till we're all right? I'll get some one to look after your house, Mother, while you're here.' But Job Falconer was fond of his mother-in-law, all times.

Mac. had some trouble in finding and catching one of the horses. Mrs Spencer drove on, and Mac. and the doctor caught up to her about a mile before she reached the homestead track, which turned in through the scrubs at the corner of the big ring-barked flat.

Doc. Wild and Mac. followed the cart-road, and as they jogged along in the edge of the scrub the doctor glanced once or twice across the flat through the dead, naked branches. Mac. looked that way. The crows were hopping about the branches of a tree way out in the middle of the flat, flopping down from branch to branch to the grass, then rising hurriedly and circling.

'Dead beast there!' said Mac. out of his Bushcraft.

'No—dying,' said Doc. Wild, with less Bush experience but more intellect.

'There's some steers of Job's out there somewhere,' muttered Mac. Then suddenly, 'It ain't drought—it's the ploorer at last! or I'm blanked!'

Mac. feared the advent of that cattle-plague, pleuro-pneumonia, which was raging on some other stations, but had been hitherto kept clear of Job's run.

'We'll go and see, if you like,' suggested Doc. Wild.

They turned out across the flat, the horses picking their way amongst the dried tufts and fallen branches.

'Theer ain't no sign o' cattle theer,' said the doctor; 'more likely a ewe in trouble about her lamb.'

'Oh, the blanky dingoes at the sheep,' said Mac. 'I wish we had a gun—might get a shot at them.'

Doc. Wild hitched the skirt of a long China silk coat he wore, free of a hip-pocket. He always carried a revolver. 'In case I feel obliged to shoot a first person singular one of these hot days,' he explained once, whereat Bushmen scratched the backs of their heads and thought feebly, without result.

'We'd never git near enough for a shot,' said the doctor; then he commenced to hum fragments from a Bush song about the finding of a lost Bushman in the last stages of death by thirst,—

'"The crows kept flyin' up, boys!
The crows kept flyin' up!
The dog, he seen and whimpered, boys,
Though he was but a pup."'

'It must be something or other,' muttered Mac. 'Look at them blanky crows!'

'"The lost was found, we brought him round,
And took him from the place,
While the ants was swarmin' on the ground,
And the crows was sayin' grace!"'

'My God! what's that?' cried Mac., who was a little in advance and rode a tall horse.

It was Job's filly, lying saddled and bridled, with a rifle-bullet (as they found on subsequent examination) through shoulders and chest, and her head full of kangaroo-shot. She was feebly rocking her head against the ground, and marking the dust with her hoof, as if trying to write the reason of it there.

The doctor drew his revolver, took a cartridge from his waistcoat pocket, and put the filly out of her misery in a very scientific manner; then something—professional instinct or the something supernatural about the doctor—led him straight to the log, hidden in the grass, where Job lay as we left him, and about fifty yards from the dead filly, which must have staggered off some little way after being shot. Mac. followed the doctor, shaking violently.

'Oh, my God!' he cried, with the woman in his voice—and his face so pale that his freckles stood out like buttons, as Doc. Wild said—'oh, my God! he's shot himself!'

'No, he hasn't,' said the doctor, deftly turning Job into a healthier position with his head from under the log and his mouth to the air: then he ran his eyes and hands over him, and Job moaned. 'He's got a broken leg,' said the doctor. Even then he couldn't resist making a characteristic remark, half to himself: 'A man doesn't shoot himself when he's going to be made a lawful father for the first time, unless he can see a long way into the future.' Then he took out his whisky-flask and said briskly to Mac., 'Leave me your water-bag' (Mac. carried a canvas water-bag slung under his horse's neck), 'ride back to the track, stop Mrs Spencer, and bring the waggonette here. Tell her it's only a broken leg.'

Mac. mounted and rode off at a break-neck pace.

As he worked the doctor muttered: 'He shot his horse. That's what gits me. The fool might have lain there for a week. I'd never have suspected spite in that carcass, and I ought to know men.'

But as Job came round a little Doc. Wild was enlightened.

'Where's the filly?' cried Job suddenly between groans.

'She's all right,' said the doctor.

'Stop her!' cried Job, struggling to rise—'stop her!—oh God! my leg.'

'Keep quiet, you fool!'

'Stop her!' yelled Job.

'Why stop her?' asked the doctor. 'She won't go fur,' he added.

'She'll go home to Gerty,' shouted Job. 'For God's sake stop her!'

'O—h!' drawled the doctor to himself. 'I might have guessed that. And I ought to know men.'

'Don't take me home!' demanded Job in a semi-sensible interval. 'Take me to Poisonous Jimmy's and tell Gerty I'm on the spree.'

When Mac. and Mrs Spencer arrived with the waggonette Doc. Wild was in his shirt-sleeves, his Chinese silk coat having gone for bandages. The lower half of Job's trouser-leg and his 'lastic-side boot lay on the ground, neatly cut off, and his bandaged leg was sandwiched between two strips of bark, with grass stuffed in the hollows, and bound by saddle-straps.

'That's all I kin do for him for the present.'

Mrs Spencer was a strong woman mentally, but she arrived rather pale and a little shaky: nevertheless she called out, as soon as she got within earshot of the doctor—

'What's Job been doing now?' (Job, by the way, had never been remarkable for doing anything.)

'He's got his leg broke and shot his horse,' replied the doctor. 'But,' he added, 'whether he's been a hero or a fool I dunno. Anyway, it's a mess all round.'

They unrolled the bed, blankets, and pillows in the bottom of the trap, backed it against the log, to have a step, and got Job in. It was a ticklish job, but they had to manage it: Job, maddened by pain and heat, only kept from fainting by whisky, groaning and raving and yelling to them to stop his horse.

'Lucky we got him before the ants did,' muttered the doctor. Then he had an inspiration—

'You bring him on to the shepherd's hut this side the station. We must leave him there. Drive carefully, and pour brandy into him now and then; when the brandy's done pour whisky, then gin—keep the rum till the last' (the doctor had put a supply of spirits in the waggonette at Poisonous Jimmy's). 'I'll take Mac.'s horse and ride on and send Peter' (the station hand) 'back to the hut to meet you. I'll be back myself if I can. THIS BUSINESS WILL HURRY UP THINGS AT THE STATION.'

Which last was one of those apparently insane remarks of the doctor's which no sane nor sober man could fathom or see a reason for—except in Doc. Wild's madness.

He rode off at a gallop. The burden of Job's raving, all the way, rested on the dead filly—

'Stop her! She must not go home to Gerty!... God help me shoot!... Whoa!—whoa, there!... "Cope—cope—cope"—Steady, Jessie, old girl.... Aim straight—aim straight! Aim for me, God!—I've missed!... Stop her!' &c.

'I never met a character like that,' commented the doctor afterwards, 'inside a man that looked like Job on the outside. I've met men behind revolvers and big mustarshes in Califo'nia; but I've met a derned sight more men behind nothing but a good-natured grin, here in Australia. These lanky sawney Bushmen will do things in an easy-going way some day that'll make the old world sit up and think hard.'

He reached the station in time, and twenty minutes or half an hour later he left the case in the hands of the Lancashire woman—whom he saw reason to admire—and rode back to the hut to help Job, whom they soon fixed up as comfortably as possible.

They humbugged Mrs Falconer first with a yarn of Job's alleged phenomenal shyness, and gradually, as she grew stronger, and the truth less important, they told it to her. And so, instead of Job being pushed, scarlet-faced, into the bedroom to see his first-born, Gerty Falconer herself took the child down to the hut, and so presented Uncle Job with my first and favourite cousin and Bush chum.

Doc. Wild stayed round until he saw Job comfortably moved to the homestead, then he prepared to depart.

'I'm sorry,' said Job, who was still weak—'I'm sorry for that there filly. I was breaking her in to side-saddle for Gerty when she should get about. I wouldn't have lost her for twenty quid.'

'Never mind, Job,' said the doctor. 'I, too, once shot an animal I was fond of—and for the sake of a woman—but that animal walked on two legs and wore trousers. Good-bye, Job.'

And he left for Poisonous Jimmy's.

The Little World Left Behind

I lately revisited a western agricultural district in Australia after many years. The railway had reached it, but otherwise things were drearily, hopelessly, depressingly unchanged. There was the same old grant, comprising several thousands of acres of the richest land in the district, lying idle still, except for a few horses allowed to run there for a shilling a-head per week.

There were the same old selections—about as far off as ever from becoming freeholds—shoved back among the barren ridges; dusty little patches in the scrub, full of stones and stumps, and called farms, deserted every few years, and tackled again by some little dried-up family, or some old hatter, and then given best once more. There was the cluster of farms on the flat, and in the foot of the gully, owned by Australians of Irish or English descent, with the same number of stumps in the wheat-paddock, the same broken fences and tumble-down huts and yards, and the same weak, sleepy attempt made every season to scratch up the ground and raise a crop. And along the creek the German farmers—the only people there worthy of the name—toiling (men, women, and children) from daylight till dark, like slaves, just as they always had done; the elder sons stoop-shouldered old men at thirty.

The row about the boundary fence between the Sweeneys and the Joneses was unfinished still, and the old feud between the Dunderblitzens and the Blitzendunders was more deadly than ever—it started three generations ago over a stray bull. The O'Dunn was still fighting for his great object in life, which was not to be 'onneighborly', as he put it. 'I DON'T want to be onneighborly,' he said, 'but I'll be aven wid some of 'em yit. It's almost impossible for a dacent man to live in sich a neighborhood and not be onneighborly, thry how he will. But I'll be aven wid some of 'em yit, marruk my wurrud.'

Jones's red steer—it couldn't have been the same red steer—was continually breaking into Rooney's 'whate an' bringin' ivery head av the other cattle afther him, and ruinin' him intirely.' The Rooneys and M'Kenzies were at daggers drawn, even to the youngest child, over the impounding of a horse belonging to Pat Rooney's brother-in-law, by a distant relation of the M'Kenzies, which had happened nine years ago.

The same sun-burned, masculine women went past to market twice a-week in the same old carts and driving much the same quality of carrion. The string of overloaded spring-carts, buggies, and sweating horses went whirling into town, to 'service', through clouds of dust and broiling heat, on Sunday morning, and came driving cruelly out again at noon. The neighbours' sons rode over in the afternoon, as of old, and hung up their poor, ill-used little horses to bake in the sun, and sat on their heels about the verandah, and drawled drearily concerning crops, fruit, trees, and vines, and horses and cattle; the drought and 'smut' and 'rust' in wheat, and the 'ploorer' (pleuro-pneumonia) in cattle, and other cheerful things; that there colt or filly, or that there cattle-dog (pup or bitch) o' mine (or 'Jim's'). They always talked most of farming there, where no farming worthy of the name was possible—except by Germans and Chinamen. Towards evening the old local relic of the golden days dropped in and announced that he intended to 'put down a shaft' next week, in a spot where he'd been going to put it down twenty years ago—and every week since. It was nearly time that somebody sunk a hole and buried him there.

An old local body named Mrs Witherly still went into town twice a-week with her 'bit av prodjuce', as O'Dunn called it. She still drove a long, bony, blind horse in a long rickety dray, with a stout sapling for a whip, and about twenty yards of clothes-line reins. The floor of the dray covered part of an acre, and one wheel was always ahead of the other—or behind, according to which shaft was pulled. She wore, to all appearances, the same short frock, faded shawl, men's 'lastic sides, and white hood that she had on when the world was made. She still stopped just twenty minutes at old Mrs Leatherly's on the way in for a yarn and a cup of tea—as she had always done, on the same days and at the same time within the memory of the hoariest local liar. However, she had a new clothes-line bent on to the old horse's front end—and we fancy that was the reason she didn't recognise us at first. She had never looked younger than a hard hundred within the memory of man. Her shrivelled face was the colour of leather, and crossed and recrossed with lines till there wasn't room for any more. But her eyes were bright yet, and twinkled with humour at times.

She had been in the Bush for fifty years, and had fought fires, droughts, hunger and thirst, floods, cattle and crop diseases, and all the things that God curses Australian settlers with. She had had two husbands, and it could be said of neither that he had ever done an honest day's work, or any good for himself or any one else. She had reared something under fifteen children, her own and others; and there was scarcely one of them that had not given her trouble. Her sons had brought disgrace on her old head over and over again, but she held up that same old head through it all, and looked her narrow, ignorant world in the face—and 'lived it down'. She had worked like a slave for fifty years; yet she had more energy and endurance than many modern city women in her shrivelled old body. She was a daughter of English aristocrats.

And we who live our weak lives of fifty years or so in the cities—we grow maudlin over our sorrows (and beer), and ask whether life is worth living or not.

I sought in the farming town relief from the general and particular sameness of things, but there was none. The railway station was about the only new building in town. The old signs even were as badly in need of retouching as of old. I picked up a copy of the local 'Advertiser', which newspaper had been started in the early days by a brilliant drunkard, who drank himself to death just as the fathers of our nation were beginning to get educated up to his style. He might have made Australian journalism very different from what it is. There was nothing new in the 'Advertiser'—there had been nothing new since the last time the drunkard had been sober enough to hold a pen. There was the same old 'enjoyable trip' to Drybone (whereof the editor was the hero), and something about an on-the-whole very enjoyable evening in some place that was tastefully decorated, and where the visitors did justice to the good things provided, and the small hours, and dancing, and our host and hostess, and respected fellow-townsmen; also divers young ladies sang very nicely, and a young Mr Somebody favoured the company with a comic song.

There was the same trespassing on the valuable space by the old subscriber, who said that 'he had said before and would say again', and he proceeded to say the same things which he said in the same paper when we first heard our father reading it to our mother. Farther on the old subscriber proceeded to 'maintain', and recalled attention to the fact that it was just exactly as he had said. After which he made a few abstract, incoherent remarks about the 'surrounding district', and concluded by stating that he 'must now conclude', and thanking the editor for trespassing on the aforesaid valuable space.

There was the usual leader on the Government; and an agitation was still carried on, by means of horribly-constructed correspondence to both papers, for a bridge over Dry-Hole Creek at Dustbin—a place where no sane man ever had occasion to go.

I took up the 'unreliable contemporary', but found nothing there except a letter from 'Parent', another from 'Ratepayer', a leader on the Government, and 'A Trip to Limeburn', which latter I suppose was made in opposition to the trip to Drybone.

There was nothing new in the town. Even the almost inevitable gang of city spoilers hadn't arrived with the railway. They would have been a relief. There was the monotonous aldermanic row, and the worse than hopeless little herd of aldermen, the weird agricultural portion of whom came in on council days in white starched and ironed coats, as we had always remembered them. They were aggressively barren of ideas; but on this occasion they had risen above themselves, for one of them had remembered something his grandfather (old time English alderman) had told him, and they were stirring up all the old local quarrels and family spite of the district over a motion, or an amendment on a motion, that a letter—from another enlightened body and bearing on an equally important matter (which letter had been sent through the post sufficiently stamped, delivered to the secretary, handed to the chairman, read aloud in council, and passed round several times for private perusal)—over a motion that such letter be received.

There was a maintenance case coming on—to the usual well-ventilated disgust of the local religious crank, who was on the jury; but the case differed in no essential point from other cases which were always coming on and going off in my time. It was not at all romantic. The local youth was not even brilliant in adultery.

After I had been a week in that town the Governor decided to visit it, and preparations were made to welcome him and present him with an address. Then I thought that it was time to go, and slipped away unnoticed in the general lunacy.

By homestead, hut, and shearing-shed,
By railroad, coach, and track—
By lonely graves of our brave dead,
Up-Country and Out-Back:
To where 'neath glorious clustered stars
The dreamy plains expand—
My home lies wide a thousand miles
In the Never-Never Land.

It lies beyond the farming belt,
Wide wastes of scrub and plain,
A blazing desert in the drought,
A lake-land after rain;
To the sky-line sweeps the waving grass,
Or whirls the scorching sand—
A phantom land, a mystic land!
The Never-Never Land.

Where lone Mount Desolation lies,
Mounts Dreadful and Despair—
'Tis lost beneath the rainless skies
In hopeless deserts there;
It spreads nor'-west by No-Man's Land—
Where clouds are seldom seen—
To where the cattle-stations lie
Three hundred miles between.

The drovers of the Great Stock Routes
The strange Gulf country know—
Where, travelling from the southern droughts,
The big lean bullocks go;
And camped by night where plains lie wide,
Like some old ocean's bed,
The watchmen in the starlight ride
Round fifteen hundred head.

And west of named and numbered days
The shearers walk and ride—
Jack Cornstalk and the Ne'er-do-well,
And the grey-beard side by side;
They veil their eyes from moon and stars,
And slumber on the sand—
Sad memories sleep as years go round

In Never-Never Land.

By lonely huts north-west of Bourke,
Through years of flood and drought,
The best of English black-sheep work
Their own salvation out:
Wild fresh-faced boys grown gaunt and brown—
Stiff-lipped and haggard-eyed—
They live the Dead Past grimly down!
Where boundary-riders ride.

The College Wreck who sunk beneath,
Then rose above his shame,
Tramps West in mateship with the man
Who cannot write his name.
'Tis there where on the barren track
No last half-crust's begrudged—
Where saint and sinner, side by side,
Judge not, and are not judged.

Oh rebels to society!
The Outcasts of the West—
Oh hopeless eyes that smile for me,
And broken hearts that jest!
The pluck to face a thousand miles—
The grit to see it through!
The communism perfected!—
And—I am proud of you!

The Arab to true desert sand,
The Finn to fields of snow;
The Flax-stick turns to Maoriland,
Where the seasons come and go;
And this old fact comes home to me—
And will not let me rest—
However barren it may be,
Your own land is the best!

And, lest at ease I should forget
True mateship after all,
My water-bag and billy yet
Are hanging on the wall;
And if my fate should show the sign,
I'd tramp to sunsets grand
With gaunt and stern-eyed mates of mine
In Never-Never Land.

Henry Archibald Hertzberg Lawson was born on the 17th June 1867 in a town on the Grenfell goldfields of New South Wales, Australia.

His parents, father Niel, a Norwegian born miner and mother Louisa, a noted poet, publisher and feminist were married on 7th July 1866 when he was 32 and she 18. On Henry's birth, the family surname was Anglicised to Lawson. The couple were to have an unhappy marriage despite producing three children.

Lawson attended school at Eurunderee from October 1876 but an ear infection he contracted left him partially deaf. By fourteen he had lost his hearing completely.

Lawson later attended a Catholic school at Mudgee, New South Wales where he developed an interest in poetry and, on his mother's influence, immersed himself in books given that learning in the classroom, with his deafness, was a major hurdle.

In 1883, after working on construction jobs with his father in the Blue Mountains, Lawson joined his mother in Sydney where she was living with his siblings. Here, Lawson worked during the day and studied at night for his matriculation in the hopes of enrolling at university. However, he failed his exams.

His first published poem was 'A Song of the Republic' in The Bulletin on 1st October 1887. This was quickly followed by other published poems with one recognising him as "a youth whose poetic genius here speaks eloquently for itself."

In 1890 he began a relationship with Mary Gilmore but it broke down due to his frequent absences from Sydney.

Lawson received an offer to write for the Brisbane Boomerang in 1891, but financial troubles at the magazine made this a short stint of only a few months. Despite writing for other magazines in Brisbane it was a dead end.

He returned to Sydney and continued to write for the Bulletin which, in 1892, engaged him for an inland trip where he could write articles about the harsh realities of life in drought-stricken New South Wales. He also took some time to work as a roustabout (an unskilled or semi-skilled worker) in the woolshed at Toorale Station. This resulted in his contributions to the Bulletin Debate and became the experience he used for a number of his stories in subsequent years. For Lawson this was an eye-opening period. His grim view of the outback was far removed from the romantic idyll of bravery and beauty inked in the poetry of his contemporary Banjo Paterson.

In 1896, Lawson married Bertha Bredt, Jr., daughter of Bertha Bredt, the prominent socialist. The marriage ended very unhappily in June 1903. They had two children.

Despite this Lawson was finding his way in the literary world. His writing was achieving recognition. His most successful prose collection 'While the Billy Boils', was published in 1896. In it he virtually reinvented Australian realism.

His writing style of short, sharp sentences with honed and sparse descriptions created a personal writing style that defined Australians: dryly laconic, passionately egalitarian and deeply humane. Most of Lawson's work centres on the Australian bush, it's fabled outback, such as in the desolate 'Past Carin', and is considered by many to vividly portray the real Australian life at that time.

Like the majority of Australians, Lawson lived in a city, but had had plenty of experience in outback life, these two outlooks helped shape a very individual talent. Unfortunately, his life was also flawed with other issues.

In Sydney in 1898 he was a prominent member of the Dawn and Dusk Club, a bohemian club of writer friends who met for drinks and conversation.

Sadly, for Lawson despite his growing recognition and fame he became withdrawn and unable to take part in the usual routines of life. His struggles with alcohol and mental health issues continued to drain him. His once prolific literary output began to decline. At times he was destitute mainly due, despite good sales and an enthusiastic audience, to ruinous publishing deals he had entered into.

In 1903 he bought a room at Mrs Isabel Byers' Coffee Palace in North Sydney. This near 20-year friendship between Mrs Byers and Lawson was a bedrock for him. Despite his position as the most celebrated Australian writer of the time, Lawson was deeply depressed and perpetually poor. His ex-wife repeatedly reported him for non-payment of child maintenance, which resulted in numerous jail terms or periods in psychiatric institutions. He was incarcerated at Darlinghurst Gaol for drunkenness, wife desertion, child desertion, and non-payment of child support seven times between 1905 and 1909 and spent a total of 159 days in prison. He wrote about these experiences in the haunting poem 'One Hundred and Three'—his prison number—which was published in 1908.

Mrs Byers was a good poet herself and, although of modest education, had been writing vivid poetry since her teens in a somewhat similar style to Lawson's. Long separated from her husband and elderly, Mrs Byers was, at the time she met Lawson, a woman of independent means looking forward to a comfortable retirement. She regarded Lawson as Australia's greatest living poet, and hoped to sustain him well enough to keep him writing. She acted as his agent in negotiations with publishers, helped to arrange contact with his children, contacted friends and supporters to help him financially, as well as assisting and nursing him through his mental health issues and problems with alcohol. She wrote countless letters on his behalf and pursued any avenue that could provide Lawson with financial support or a publishing deal.

Regardless of all else Lawson was a vocal nationalist and republican and took pride that many of his works were helping to establish the Australian vernacular in fiction.

Henry Archibald Hertzberg Lawson died, of a cerebral hemorrhage, in Mrs Byer's home in Abbotsford, Sydney on 2nd September 1922.

Lawson became the first Australian writer to be granted a state funeral. It was attended by the Prime Minister Billy Hughes and the (later) Premier of New South Wales, Jack Lang (the husband of Lawson's sister-in-law Hilda Bredt), as well as thousands of citizens.

Henry Lawson – A Concise Bibliography

Short Stories in Prose and Verse (1894)
While the Billy Boils (1896)
In the Days When the World was Wide and Other Verses (1896)
Verses, Popular and Humorous (1900)
On the Track (1900)
Over the Sliprails (1900)
On the Track, and, Over the Sliprails (1900)
Popular Verses (1900)
Humorous Verses (1900)
The Country I Come From (1901)
Joe Wilson and His Mates (1901)
Children of the Bush (1902)
When I Was King and Other Verses (1905)
The Elder Son (1905)
When I Was King (1905)
The Romance of the Swag (1907)
Send Round the Hat (1907)
The Skyline Riders and Other Verses (1910)
The Rising of the Court and Other Sketches in Prose and Verse (1910)
For Australia and Other Poems (1913)
Triangles of Life and Other Stories (1913)
My Army, O, My Army! and Other Songs (1915)
Song of the Dardanelles and Other Verses (1916)
Selected Poems of Henry Lawson (1918)

www.ingramcontent.com/pod-product-compliance
Lightning Source LLC
Chambersburg PA
CBHW032019170626
46807CB00006B/2879